OFF THE RECORD

NASHVILLE FURY: BOOK 1

CHELLE SLOAN

Melinda,
 Love is always
worth the risk!

Chelle
Sloan ♡

Off the Record

Cover Design: Kari March Designs

Editing: Elaine York, Allusion Graphics

Line editing: Marla Selkow Esposito, Proofing with Style

Proofreading: Michele Ficht

❀ Created with Vellum

DEDICATION

To Mom and Dad

*Thanks for giving me the wings to let me chase each and every dream
I've had.*

Also, thanks for the free rent.

1

SADIE

ATTACH.

Save.

Send.

I drum my manicured fingertips along the top of my makeshift desk as I impatiently wait for my computer to give me the signal that the longest workday of my life is officially over.

Sent.

"Done!" I shout as I throw my arms in the air in celebration. I'm sure I even let out a high-pitched "woo hoo!" for good measure. I would never consider myself a "woo-hoo girl" by any means. That is how excited I am that this day, and this football season, is finally over.

I wait for a reaction from someone. Anyone. But I get nothing. Not a clap. Not a "thatta-girl." Not even a sarcastic "It's about damn time."

I look around the empty press box and realize that yet again I'm the last one left working. Oh well. I don't even care. All I care about is that after seventeen agonizing weeks, this horrific, historic-for-all-the-wrong-reasons season of the Nashville Fury is officially in the books.

God, that was painful.

Not the stories I wrote. Those, if I do say so myself, were some of the best I've ever written. There is never a shortage of topics to write about when you're trying to figure out why a team that has made the playoffs every year all of a sudden can't figure out how to win. Why can't the defense tackle? Why can't the offense score? Why hasn't anyone been fired?

This is why the fans turn to me. They need answers. I provide them. Even if it means I'm the one turning out the lights in the press box after every game.

"About time you're done. You make the rest of us look bad when you work that hard."

I jump at the sound of Tommy's voice, but my look of scorn quickly morphs into a smile. You can't be mad when Tommy Reese is giving you shit.

"Maybe you should get on my level, old man. Can't let the young girl beat you."

Tommy is the most veteran reporter in the group of ten of us who cover the Fury on a regular basis. He's the only reporter who has covered the team for every game of their twenty-year existence and has sources so deep in the organization that the team owner doesn't even know where he gets his intel. He also smokes more cigarettes than the Marlboro Man and hasn't had a drop of liquor in a decade. And despite working for the rival newspaper in town, he quickly became my unofficial protector when I got assigned to cover the Fury two years ago.

"You don't get to play the girl card and you know it," he says as I begin to pack up my laptop and notes. "I told you that shit wasn't going to work on me when you got the job, and it's not going to work now. Let's go. You deserve a drink. The rest of the guys are waiting."

And that's what I love about Tommy. He doesn't care that

I'm only twenty-seven. He doesn't care about my gender. I'm a reporter to him. Plain and simple.

It caused a lot of waves around town when I got this job. Not only was I a woman, but I was also the youngest by more than a decade. It was assumed because of my age that I didn't know anything. Add in that I have lady parts. Well, that obviously meant I had slept with someone to get here. At least, that was the chatter I heard when the rest of the reporters didn't think I was listening.

I did neither of those things. I worked my ass off and earned this spot fair and square. After two years of covering the Fury, that kind of talk has simmered. Mostly.

Occasionally, I'll get a fan who doesn't agree with me. Instead of just saying "I respectfully disagree," I'll get called a bitch who doesn't know a thing about football. Earlier this year I broke a story about a rookie getting a DUI, and I heard a reporter ask who I fucked to get the scoop.

Joke's on him. The only action of the sexual variety I'm seeing is from my good friend Ted.

He's my vibrator. He's great. Actually, he's more than great and he doesn't care if I haven't shaved in days.

"Gentlemen, the lady is finally gracing us with her presence!"

I laugh and take a little bow as my fellow reporters clap when I enter the media break room, which is down the hall from the press box. Now *this* is the reaction I was looking for ten minutes ago.

"Why, thank you, gentlemen. Your sarcasm doesn't go unnoticed," I say, putting down my oversized purse that carries my life inside it. Mary Poppins would be jealous of this thing. "Please tell me you left at least one beer for the lady."

"We left you two because you are such an overachiever," says Joe, one of the national writers. I take a seat next to him and twist open the ice-cold goodness. "What were you writing anyway? We were done an hour ago."

Joe has a fair point. Today's loss capped off a 2-14 season for the Fury, the worst, by far, in the team's history. The only thing to celebrate was that it was over, which is what I and the rest of the reporters are doing now. After the end of each season, the reporters traditionally hang around and have a celebratory, end-of-the-season beer, compliments of the team. After watching the horrible football that we were forced to endure this year, these beers were the least they could give us. They should have thrown in a pizza for good measure.

"I filed a story to have ready to go for when they fire Bancroft," I say, taking a pull from my beer bottle. "This way, when they do fire him, I don't have to rush to write a story."

I get a "what the fuck are you talking about" look from every man in the room. This isn't the first time I've been on the receiving end of this look. My guess is that it won't be the last.

"They aren't firing him. No way in hell," Joe says. "His contract is too big. And it was just one bad season. No one gets fired for one bad year."

I shrug my shoulders and sit back, not ready to fight with him or any other reporter about whether or not the offensive coordinator, Nick Bancroft, is about to be fired after the worst offensive season in Fury history.

"Plus," Joe continues, apparently not done with trying to flex his knowledge. "They are going to draft that hotshot quarterback from Clemson, and Bancroft will get his chance at redemption. None of us need to worry. We won't have to worry about football until the spring, and we can finally take the vacations our wives planned for us now. I, for one, am looking forward to ringing in the new year on a beach."

The conversation pivots to the trips they are taking, a few leaving as early as tomorrow. Many are on their way to family-friendly destinations such as Disney, or a beach house in the Carolinas. As for me? My annual singles' vacation isn't until

June, and it was picked by closing my eyes and pointing to a map.

The winner? San Francisco. The Golden Gate Bridge, Alcatraz, and anything else my heart desires. That's the joy of being single. I can do anything I want, and I don't have to answer to anyone.

And that is not at all depressing. That's at least what I keep telling myself. Most days I believe it.

Buzz. Buzz. Buzz.

The sound of my cell phone breaks me from my thoughts. And it's not just my phone going off with alerts. Every cell phone in the room is buzzing or chirping.

We all grab our phones, which are never too far out of reach, and check what just came through. An email. From the Fury.

Subject: Media release: Nashville Fury, Offensive Coordinator Nick Bancroft part ways

The synchronized mutters of "oh fuck" and "you have got to be shitting me" are heard from around the room. The guys scramble to turn their laptops back on, text their wives that they won't be home any time soon, and to cancel their vacation plans.

Me? I sit back, kick my feet up on the table, and smile as I finish my beer, knowing my June vacation plans are fully intact.

The story I just got made fun of for writing? It was for this reason. As my fellow reporters are frantically typing away, my story is already written and filed with my editor. As I pick up my phone and head to the website for *The Nashville Banner*, my story is already live with the esteemed honor of being the first to report.

I worked smart. I was first. And if I have anything to say about it, I will be breaking the story when the team makes the new hire, whoever he is.

Sadie: 1.

Rest of the reporters: 0.

2

HUNTER

"I'LL TAKE A MEDIUM COFFEE, two creams. To go. Thank you, darlin'."

The young girl behind the counter blushes and almost drops my change when she hands me back the bills that I promptly put in her tip jar. I give her one more smile before walking to the other side of the counter to wait for my drink—a smile that earns me another blush.

She's cute. A bit young, and I say that sincerely being only twenty-eight myself. I wonder if she's a regular worker here? Would I see her all the time if the Fury hire me?

I step away from the counter and take a look around the quaint sandwich and coffee shop that sits across the street from the Fury's training facility. I like it. There's country music playing in the background, but it's not blaring. There are some people having lunch together. Some have headphones on and are furiously typing on their laptops. I have a perfect view of my potential new office from the booth seating at the windows. I can picture it now, picking up a cup of coffee before heading to practice, or coming over here to grab lunch with the other coaches to strategize for the next game.

The best part? No one is staring at me. No one is whispering. No one knows who I am.

I can't lie, it's been a while since something like that happened.

I like it. A lot.

I don't remember a time in my life when I wasn't recognized. Growing up, I was the son of Bo McAvoy—the best quarterback to ever play collegiately at Alabama. When you grow up in Birmingham, that makes you sports royalty.

When I announced that I was carrying on the family tradition for the Crimson Tide, I couldn't go anywhere without a camera being in my face. The media created the narrative that I was going to be the second coming of my father.

However, I never lived up to that hype. My dad led his team to four championships, won two Heisman Trophies and was the top draft pick when he turned pro. He went on to have a ten-year pro career, retired in his prime and was inducted into the Hall of Fame on the first ballot.

Me? I was a good quarterback, but I wasn't great. What I lacked in my play-making ability, I made up for with my brains. I am what you call "football smart." I love strategizing Xs and Os. Designing plays. Outsmarting the guys across the sideline. It excites me more than throwing a touchdown ever did. So, after my last play at Alabama, which included lifting up my only national championship trophy, I transitioned my life from playing to coaching.

Much to my father's dismay.

I've been called a coaching prodigy. The talking heads on sports radio think that I'm the future of what a professional coach will look like. If I'm hired by the Fury, I will be the youngest offensive coordinator in league history.

All of that doesn't mean a thing to Bo McAvoy, though. I'm not a professional football player, therefore I am nothing.

I can't let his voice in my head today. Not when the biggest interview of my life is happening in an hour.

"Thanks. I don't think I tell you this enough, but you are the MVP of my life." The sound of a female voice grabs my attention. I look over to the counter and realize it is coming from a pretty brunette placing an order. "Oh! And good luck with your show tonight. I'm doing my best to make it."

I don't know why the sound of this conversation breaks me from my thoughts, but it does. I also don't know why I'm intrigued by a mundane conversation.

"You don't have to come. I know you're busy."

"Nonsense," the customer says, waving the comment away. "You keep me caffeinated every day. The least I can do is come and watch you perform."

I'm now officially eavesdropping. Yet, I can't seem to find it in myself to stop. If I'm being real, I couldn't care less about the conversation. What has me intrigued is that I can't stop staring at the profile of the brunette.

A brunette who is now looking at me.

I hurry and turn away, not wanting to come across as some sort of creep. Though, I can't help but sneak another look as she walks toward me to wait for her order. If she sees me looking again, she doesn't notice. And for that I'm grateful because I now have a direct view.

She's shorter than I am, which doesn't say much considering I'm six foot three. Her small frame is housing a set of curves I want to get lost in. I've never been a fan of women who resemble sticks, and this girl is anything but that.

She's not one of those overdone sorority girls I would see at Alabama. She looks… real. Her hair is on top of her head in one of those messy buns that I only know the name of because of my younger sister. Her black-rimmed glasses don't hide her hazel eyes. I don't think she has an ounce of makeup on her face either.

She is gorgeous. My physical type in every way. That's not even taking into account the smile I saw her give a few minutes ago. It's a smile that would make men spill war secrets. If I knew I was getting this job, I would be striking up a conversation with this woman immediately. Maybe even asking her out for dinner. Definitely getting her number. It has been years since I was in a relationship. When you're a coach who is still earning his stripes, you are told you won't be at the same place for very long, so don't get comfortable. I've never had an apartment lease longer than a year. I haven't had a girlfriend since college. What's the point in trying to date when you know you can't offer them anything long term? Plus, I've needed to focus on my career. I'm not going to climb the professional football coaching ladder by wasting time on relationships that will likely not go anywhere.

But if I'm hired in Nashville, all of that changes.

"Excuse me? Hunter?"

The sound of my name snaps me out of my trance. Apparently, a beautiful smile and an amazing ass render me stupid.

"Yes?" I say, hoping to cover up my obvious staring.

"Are you Hunter?"

I try not to, but I let out a disappointed sigh. I knew it was too good to be true that no one would recognize me. It might not be Alabama, or Houston, where I'm currently coaching, but I'm still Hunter McAvoy.

"I am. Are you a football fan?"

She lets out an almost evil laugh. "Not even a little bit."

It's my turn to give her a perplexed look. "Then how did you know my name?"

She glances at the counter, then back to me. "Because they are calling out an order for Hunter, and you are the only one here without a drink in his hand. Besides me. And I know my name isn't Hunter."

As soon as she's done putting me in my place, I hear the call, "Medium coffee for Hunter!"

I let out a nervous laugh. "Sorry. I don't know where my head went."

She gives me a side-eye, but luckily doesn't call me on my shit. "No worries. Though I'm afraid you are missing out on the greatness that is Sandwich City by only getting a coffee."

She's making conversation with me. I like it. I grab my coffee off the counter and turn my focus directly back to her. "It's my first time here. I wanted to play it safe. What should I have gotten? You know, since I'm missing out."

She thinks about it for a second, one eyebrow raising slightly over her glasses. "I know it's called Sandwich City, but I'm a sucker for their wraps. I pretty much live on them. I highly recommend the chicken Caesar. Though they do serve good coffee, so you didn't completely strike out."

The worker doesn't even call out her name when her order is ready. She tells him thanks, grabs her tray—a wrap and drink on it—and starts walking toward an open table.

I follow her like a lost puppy. I realize she hasn't invited me, but I'm not ready for this conversation to be over. Though I should leave. I should be taking this time to prepare for the interview that could change the course of my career. I should not be flirting with a woman whose name I don't even know, much less whose name I'll never learn if I don't get this job because I'll never see her again.

"What's so good about the chicken Caesar?" I say, taking a seat across from her.

"Make yourself comfortable," she says with a hint of teasing in her voice.

"I don't mind if I do."

We both stare at each other for a few seconds. I can tell she's trying to figure me out. Me? I'm wondering if her eyes have flecks of gold in them, or if I'm imagining things being blinded by her beauty.

"It's the dressing," she says, breaking the silence.

"The dressing?"

"Yes. You asked what was so good about the chicken Caesar." She shakes her head and laughs a little. Likely at the fact that I can't seem to remember what I'm saying around her. "It's the dressing. I don't know what they put in it, and they won't tell me. I've decided it's crack. It's delicious and I crave it daily."

I want to think of something witty to say. Something smooth. Something that will make her smile at me like she did the barista earlier. For the life of me, I can't think of anything. Instead, I just stare at her like a fucking idiot.

This isn't me. I'm charming. Or so I've been told. I was raised to be a southern gentleman. You wouldn't know it now with the way I'm acting around... Shit. I still don't know her name.

"I hope I'll be back to try it." My words come out shakier than I'd like, but hell, at least I'm speaking. "I'm sorry. I didn't catch your name?"

She gives me a knowing smile. "Because I didn't tell you."

Interesting. Is she playing hard to get? "That's not fair. You know mine."

"Who said I planned on playing fair?"

I laugh, loving how confident she is in her words. "You're right. Thank you for the wrap recommendation."

"In town on business?" she asks, fishing a laptop out of the biggest purse I have ever seen.

"An interview." Though, right now, her question makes me feel like the interview has already started.

"Interesting," she says, now booting up her laptop that is covered in stickers. "Well, if you end up getting the job, I highly recommend this place. I eat here almost every day."

"Do you live nearby?"

"Not really," she says, though she isn't looking at me. She's typing something furiously on her laptop. Message received. She is more interested in her laptop than a conversation with me. "My work is just nearby, which means I'm here a lot."

I want to ask her what she does for a living. I want to know her damn name. I want to know a lot of things about this beautiful woman who didn't kick me away from her table. But my Smartwatch vibrates, notifying me it's time for me to head over to the Fury's front offices.

"As much as I would love to stay and chat, and believe me, I would, I have to get going," I say, though I make no immediate attempt to stand up.

She finishes typing and looks up at me, giving me a smile that is a combination of devious and beautiful. Holy hell, am I getting mixed signals from this woman.

"Good luck on your interview. Maybe we'll see each other around again."

"Do I get to know your name?" I ask, finally standing up and grabbing my coffee.

"You'll know it soon enough." Her words are followed by that knowing smile before she focuses back on her laptop. I let my gaze hang on her for a few extra seconds before I turn to leave, wondering what her words mean.

As soon as I step out into the cool air of January in Nashville, I feel my phone vibrate in my pocket. I fish it out, wondering who is texting me. My family knows not to bother me today until I call them. Same with the few friends I've told about this.

I don't see a text alert. Rather, it's a notification that I get when a new story is written about me and is posted on the Internet.

Huh. That's weird.

I know for a fact that no one from Houston leaked that I was here. Nashville is also keeping a tight lid on candidates. Firing Bancroft was a gutsy move on their part. He has been bashing them to every media outlet that will listen to him. They know they have to get this hire right.

When I open my phone, I see the article clear as day:

"Hunter McAvoy in Nashville; interviewing for offensive coordinator job"

How in the hell did this get out?

I hurry and read the story, making sure what is written is at least accurate. On a quick glance, nothing seems out of place or completely erroneous.

I scroll back up to the top of the article, wondering who this reporter is. I'll have to keep my eye out for him if I get the job. He has to have some good sources if he was able to break this story when only a few people know I'm in town.

Except when I get back to the top and see the picture of the reporter, it's definitely not a him. I'm greeted by a photo of a beautiful, smiling brunette next to the name Sadie Benson. Her hair isn't up on top of her head in this photo, though, but a familiar pair of hazel eyes are looking at me.

As I look back inside the deli, that same set of eyes are now filled with mischief as Sadie gives me a little wave before closing her laptop.

3

SADIE

"GOOD REPORTING, Sadie! You kicked that story's ass."

I smile at Bill, one of the copy editors and a self-proclaimed Fury fanatic, as I walk into the newsroom of *The Banner*. "Thanks. I appreciate that. How've you been?"

"Not as good as you. Is there a story about Hunter McAvoy that you *haven't* broken? Huge scoops! What do you think about him? Is he the guy? Is it a good hire?"

What I want to say is that Hunter McAvoy is a brilliant offensive football mind and a great hire. I predict that under his coaching and guidance, the Fury will be back in the playoffs as soon as this year.

I also want to say that he's the hottest man I've ever seen in real life, and I don't know how I'm going to function at my job when I have to look at him all the time.

In preparation, I've already bought extra batteries for Ted.

My cheeks flush just thinking about his dark blond hair and his perfectly built frame. The man might not have played football for a few years, but you'd never know that based off of his physique. I know this because I interviewed him once in college. I doubt he remembers me. I was in a pool of a dozen other reporters, though I did ask one semi-memorable question. But you don't forget seeing a man like Hunter. No matter how many years have passed.

That was also the first time I noticed his smile. Back then it was a camera-ready one. One that every newspaper in the country wanted to put on the front page. The one I got at Sandwich City? It was the same, but different. More genuine. Still devastating.

For a few seconds when he sat down with me, I wondered what it would be like if I wasn't a reporter. I let myself pretend, just for a second, that I was a normal, twenty-something having an impromptu lunch with a good-looking guy. I might not be the most experienced when it comes to men and relationships, but I could tell Hunter was flirting with me.

Which is a whole other new feeling for me. Men don't flirt with me. I'm not what you'd call your classic beauty. I'm a reformed tomboy who has a few extra curves, and who tolerates the bare minimum of makeup. I'm not the girl guys like Hunter McAvoy have lunch with.

Though, I'd be a liar if I said I didn't like the idea of it.

It had been a very long time since a man flirted with me. Yes, guys with their keyboard courage hit on me on Twitter (not the best place to try to shoot your shot). In real life? Men who approach me are few and far between.

Sitting with Hunter, Pretend Me wanted to flirt back. She wanted to continue listening to his southern accent and let our impromptu lunch turn into an impromptu afternoon. Pretend Me might have even gone as far as to slyly offer him my phone number in hopes that he'd call me for another meal, only this time planned.

Then I remembered I was a reporter. And he was interviewing for a job for the team I cover. Just the thought of that was like an ice-cold bath to my thoughts and fantasies.

Not that they have completely gone away. Talking to Bill

right now? I'm the definition of cool, calm, and unaffected by Hunter McAvoy. To myself when I'm at home with Ted? Not so much.

"We'll see how he fits with the team," I say, remembering that Bill had asked me a question. And now that I've been thinking about Hunter for more than five seconds, I really want this conversation to be over before the coloring on my cheeks gives me away. "Have you seen John? I have a meeting with him."

"He's in the editors' meeting. Do you think they are going to draft that Clemson quarterback?"

I smile because Bill always has to sneak in one more Fury question. "They'd be stupid not to. I'll talk to you later."

I wave to a few other reporters as I head to my boss's office and take a seat at my usual spot on his raggedy couch. It has seen better days. There is a spring cutting into my back, and the cushions are down to their final threads. I don't care though. All of my best brainstorming has been done sitting here while John sits at his desk. Why mess with things now when I've been on the best professional roll of my career?

I might have downplayed my excitement to Bill, but I have been kicking ass on all things related to the hiring of Hunter McAvoy.

Seeing him at Sandwich City was sheer luck. The fact that he told me he was in town for an interview was the gift I didn't ask for, but I wasn't about to turn it down. Should I have told him who I was? Maybe. Do I regret writing the story? Not one bit.

A week after his interview, he was hired. Again, I was first on the story thanks to my source inside the Fury front office.

I've really been kicking ass and taking names lately.

"There's our girl!" John says as he comes into his office. "I just left a meeting where every editor praised you up and down for the work you've been doing. You're impressing a lot of people, Benson."

I shrug off the compliment. I've never been good at taking

them. Especially from John. "Thanks. It was my first coaching search, so I wanted to do a good job."

John sits down at his desk, propping his feet up on the corner like he always does. "Good job? You've been doing a great job. You're a good reporter, Sadie. I've always known that about you. But since you started working the Fury beat? You've excelled. I'm proud of you."

I smile and say thanks, almost embarrassed by the praise. John is the only boss I've ever known. He gave me a shot at a sports internship during my sophomore year of college. I worked for him each summer, and when I graduated from Tennessee, he hired me to cover high school sports. I did that for three years before I was promoted to cover the Fury. He gave me my first real chance in the big leagues. I don't want to let him down.

"So, what story do you want next?" I ask, getting my notebook ready to jot down the story ideas.

"I want you to get the one-on-one with him."

I look up from my notebook and give John a questioning look. Which I hope covers the blush that is trying to creep through as he mentions the thought of me and Hunter one-on-one.

And now, thinking about not blushing is making me blush. Because oh, the things I'd love for Hunter McAvoy to do to me one-on-one.

Shit. Bad thoughts, Sadie. Bad, dirty thoughts!

Quick. Think of unsexy things.

Dentures.

Burps.

Opossums.

Phew. That was a close one.

"The one-on-one?" My voice comes out still a little too high-pitched, but John doesn't seem to notice. "Don't they always give that interview to Tommy?"

The Fury is famous, at least famous among the reporters, for giving only one exclusive interview to a reporter of their choosing when a new coach or executive is hired. And "of their choosing" always means Tommy.

"Yes, they have in the past. But I don't want you to give up on it." John moves his feet off his desk to assume his serious pose. Which for him is his hands clasped together, elbows on his desk. "You have been doing good work, Sadie. Actually, it's great work. If you continue doing what you're doing, you could be getting a call from the Mothership."

If I gave John a questioning look before when he brought up the one-on-one, I am straight-up looking at him like he's an alien now. The Mothership is what we call our national news outlet, *US Daily*. It's the largest newspaper in the country. If you get a job there, you've made it.

"*US Daily?* What are you talking about? You know they only hire reporters who have covered teams for at least ten years. Plus, they already have a woman on staff. You know sports departments can't have too much estrogen walking around freely or they crumble."

He laughs, knowing that even though I'm joking, I'm mostly right. "It's just whispers right now, but there could be an opening. I know the national editors have been impressed with your work. Landing the one-on-one with McAvoy would be a big win for you."

John and I finish up our meeting, strategize for the next month of coverage, and he makes me promise on his coveted stack of classic *Sports Illustrated* magazines that I will not only take my vacation to San Francisco in June, but that I will not fight him on taking a week off after the Super Bowl, which is in two weeks.

His reasoning? I work too much and taking time off between the Super Bowl and the draft won't kill me.

I try to process everything as I take my short walk back to

my apartment from *The Banner.* Is John right? Could a national job be on the horizon for me? Can I afford to take time off if I could seriously be hired at *US Daily?*

Being a national football writer is something I've dreamed of since I started reading *US Daily* as a kid. My dad used to save the sports page for me every Sunday, and we would talk about every story. We would dissect every word. That's what I get for being the daughter of a high school English teacher who is also a sports freak. It was what we did together.

It's why being a sports reporter is the only thing I've ever wanted to be. I dreamed of the day that my name would grace the pages of *US Daily.* I knew it wouldn't be easy. It's not. It's a demanding job. I'm always on call. There's no room for a personal life. There's barely time to cook a meal, let alone schedule one with someone else. I don't care, though. I love it. It's who I am. I can't imagine doing anything else with my life.

It's why my apartment is small and barely decorated. It's why I haven't had a real relationship since college. It's why I can't cook more than a pot of spaghetti.

None of that matters when my goals are within reach.

And they are. I just need to keep my eye on the prize.

No complications.

No distractions.

Especially ones that come in the form of a sexy and charming coach.

4

HUNTER

"ARE YOU READY, MR. MCAVOY?"

The question comes from an intern, and I resist the urge to tell him to not call me Mr. McAvoy. Mr. McAvoy is my father—who couldn't be bothered to come to Nashville for my introductory press conference, which is set to start at any minute.

"Ready as I'll ever be."

My tone is more confident than what I'm feeling inside, which doesn't make any sense. It's not because I'm nervous to face a group of reporters. I couldn't give a shit about them.

Well, that's mostly true.

I don't remember a time when I wasn't being followed by a reporter or a camera. The first time I was interviewed was when I was eight. He wanted to know where I planned to play college football. At the college football national championship game, I was flooded with no less than one hundred cameras during a three-hour media day. One time a reporter followed me around a grocery store.

The headline read: **"What does Hunter McAvoy eat for breakfast? You won't believe his cereal choice."**

It was Cheerios. Not even the flavored kind, the plain ol' original. That must have been a very slow news day.

So, when I say I don't care about the media, I really don't. They have been the annoying rock in the bottom of my shoe for most of my life. From my experience, they are all about getting the story by any means possible. If they have to elaborate, they will. If they have to twist your words for a good headline, they will do it without thinking twice.

Then there are the reporters who just have to flash you a pretty smile, and you unknowingly become the unnamed source in your own story.

I really should have been more upset after Sadie wrote the article spilling the secret that I was in town for my interview. The Fury freaked out that my name leaked, and Houston wasn't all too happy about the news getting out, either.

As much as I wanted to hate it, and her, I had to admit she did nothing wrong. The article was accurate. In fact, everything I have read of hers since I was hired has been good. I generally don't read much of what is written about me—I found over the years it was mostly half-truths or straight-up lies—but I couldn't help but read what the girl who has been on my mind since I first saw her had to say.

She's smart. She writes well. She knows her football. I haven't met many good reporters, but she seems to fit that bill.

And it has nothing to do with the fact that I can still hear her laugh. Or that her ass has been the subject of my dreams since our first encounter.

The sound of a door opening breaks me from my thoughts as Paul, the head of media relations, waves me into the interview room. I don't even get the chance to smooth my tie one more time before the flashes of cameras start going off from every direction. Somehow, I find my focus and make my way to the table where I'll be seated next to Jimbo Gordon, the Fury's veteran head coach.

If my dad is a legend as a player, the same can be said for Jimbo Gordon as a head coach. He won three championship rings before coming to Nashville, and up until this year, he led the Fury to the playoffs every season. He's also in his late seventies, and he says to anyone who will listen that the only way he's retiring from coaching is if he's taken off the field in a body bag. Now *that* would be a headline.

I reach my hand out to shake Coach Gordan's, pausing and turning to give the photographers what they want: a grip-and-grin photo of the elder statesman head coach, and his bright, shiny, young offensive coordinator.

As I stand posed with a smile plastered on my face, I can't help but look around the room. I tell myself it's to familiarize myself with the setup of reporters, but I know deep down there is only one reporter I'm looking for. In the back are the video guys, pointing their cameras at me. There are the photographers in front on the floor, trying to get different angles of a standard handshake. Sitting in the middle of the room are a flock of reporters, all a bunch of middle-aged white men who look like they have never missed a meal.

My eyes make their way to the front row of seats... and there she is. Sadie is furiously typing away on a familiar-looking laptop. I don't normally notice things like laptops, but then again, not many women have a sticker on theirs that says, "Not Today, Satan." I also can't help but notice that her hair is exactly how it was when we first met.

I wonder what it looks like down over her shoulders? Or what it would look like fanned out across my pillow?

Coach Gordon gives my hand a final squeeze, signaling for me to take a seat and, even if he doesn't know it, to drag my mind out of the gutter.

Paul prepared me for how this would go, and now, twenty minutes in, everything has gone to script. Coach Gordon began the press conference with a statement about me and why I'm a good fit for the Fury. After that, it was my turn to recite the speech that I rehearsed so much over the past two days, I could say it in my sleep.

The second I was done talking, hands from the reporters flew into the air, which is exactly what Paul said would happen. Each question thrown at me was a little more asinine than the last.

"How does it feel knowing you are the youngest offensive coordinator in league history?"

"What's it like being Bo McAvoy's son?"

"What did your dad say about you getting this job?"

"Does it bother you that half of your players are older than you?"

"Talk about why you think you're experienced enough to have this job."

I hate when reporters say, "talk about." It's not a question. It's a demand.

As the press conference rolls along, I answer every question, each one more remedial than the last. Finally, there are no more hands in the air.

"Any last questions?" Paul asks, and I secretly hope no one says anything. That is, until I see a hand from the front row go up.

"Hunter. Sadie Benson from *The Banner*. Having not been a coordinator before, you have no prior track record of what kind of offensive scheme you plan on running. Do you have an offensive plan in mind that will be implemented no matter what? Or will you wait and tailor your offense around whoever the team drafts to be the next quarterback?"

I have to blink a few times as the question settles in my brain. That wasn't an easy question. That wasn't a standard press conference question. That was a thought-through, intelligent, football-minded question. And it came from the mouth of a woman who has done nothing but surprise me since the moment she told me my coffee was ready.

"Great question, Sadie. You're right. There isn't film on how I've run offenses in the past. Having been a quarterback, though, I understand that offenses run better when your signal caller is comfortable. Whoever our next quarterback will be, this offense will play to his strengths. No matter who is under center, I will look at the personnel at my disposal and put together the best offense I can around the pieces I have."

As soon as my answer is complete, Paul closes the press conference, reminding reporters that he'll be in touch with them when draft prep begins.

As the reporters file out, I take a sip of my water, trying to calm myself down. I don't know what it says about me that just the sound of a beautiful woman asking me football questions turns me on so much that I need an extra minute before I stand up.

My reaction to Sadie is inappropriate on so many levels, especially in public and when cameras are present.

For starters, I'm a coach. She's the media. There are clear lines that have been drawn between coaches and reporters for years. It's defined and respected. The two don't intermingle. They aren't friends. They for sure don't date.

Plus, I might have told myself the day I met Sadie that I could see myself asking her out, but at the end of the day, I'm focused on my career. I'm not here for a relationship. I'm here to make my mark on the coaching world. I'm here to show that I might be young, but I am going to be damn good at this job. I'm going to lead the Fury back to the playoffs, and if I have my say so, to a championship.

I'm here to show everyone that I'm not just Bo McAvoy's son. That I am my own man.

None of that will happen if I let myself be distracted. Especially by the likes of Sadie Benson.

"Sadie. Can you come back here? Hunter. Do you have another minute?"

Paul's request takes me by surprise, and from the look on Sadie's face as she turns back toward us, the same can be said for her. Hell, I didn't even know he was right beside me. "I don't know if you two have officially met. Hunter, this is Sadie Benson. She covers the team for *The Nashville Banner.*"

I don't know how she wants to play this, and I sure as hell don't want to give away that my dick has just now calmed down from her question during the press conference, so I choose the nonchalant route. "Nice to officially meet you."

"Likewise," she says, giving me a cordial smile, clearly picking up on tone and choice of words. "Congratulations on the position."

She extends her hand to shake mine, which I gladly accept. I'm not going to think about how smooth her skin feels against mine, or that I have to fight the urge not to run my thumb across the top of her knuckles.

"Hunter, I wanted to introduce Sadie to you because she will be spending one day with you, one-on-one, for an exclusive interview. Sadie, congratulations, the one-on-one is yours."

I drop Sadie's hand like it's on fire from Paul's words. Paul has unloaded a lot of information on me since it was formally announced that I was hired, but I'm sure I would have remembered the possibility of Sadie getting a one-on-one interview with me. And as I take a glance at Sadie, the look on her face is just as shocked as mine. Though I doubt it's for the same reason—unless she's also trying to figure out how to navigate an entire day with her without getting hard.

"Sadie, do you have any ideas of where you'd like this?" Paul continues, clearly not realizing the inadvertent bomb he dropped on me. "The setting can be of your choosing, as long as Hunter is comfortable."

Comfortable? Paul is worried about my comfort? Does he not realize that if this woman is talking football to me for hours on end that I will not be able to walk for a week? That sure as shit is not comfortable.

Fuck. I need to get these thoughts under control. She's a reporter. I'm a coach. Yes, she's attractive. Yes, a woman talking football to me is apparently my sexual kryptonite. But this isn't the first, or last, time I will be interviewed by her. I can't let my attraction get the best of me every time we are in the same room. If I do, then this will be a very long season.

With a lot of cold showers.

"I'd like to interview him with his family in Birmingham."

The words "family" and "Birmingham" snap me out of my thoughts. That cold shower I was contemplating not even a minute ago? She might as well have dumped an entire ice bath over my head.

Of course, she would want to interview my dad. Figures. This proves that despite my attraction toward her, she's just like every other reporter I've encountered. It's not about me as my own man. It's about how my dad has influenced my life. Or how he molded me into the coach I am today.

The answer? He didn't.

But I can't say that. No one knows that the relationship between me and my father is cordial on a good day. So I do what I've done my entire life when a reporter has wanted to interview me and the great Bo McAvoy.

I suck it up.

"Sounds great. Pick a day next week and we can head to Birmingham."

5

SADIE

"DID you pack extra batteries for your recorder?"

"Yes, Dad."

"And your laptop charger? You know you tend to forget that."

"Already double-checked for it."

"And the pepper spray? You still carry that, right?"

"Yes, I still carry it. Though I doubt I will need it."

He's silent for a moment, and even though this is a normal phone conversation, I can feel him giving me his dad stare through his wire-rimmed glasses. It's the stare that screams, "I don't care how many times I've asked you, I'm going to always ask you, so deal with it."

"You will be alone in a car with a man you barely know," he says, breaking the silence. "A lot can happen on a three-hour drive."

"It's two hours and forty-five minutes."

My attempt at a joke falls short on my father. I can hear the exasperated breath he lets out. I'm quite familiar with the sound. If I had to put money on it, he has his head tilted back, asking for some sort of celestial guidance in regard to my sarcastic humor.

"Don't get sassy with me, young lady. You know Helen and I worry about you. And you wouldn't have to hear all of my dad warnings if you didn't require these packing phone calls."

I smile at my dad's words as I toss my notebook and pen into my purse. I don't know if the word "require" is the best word to use, but our phone calls while I'm packing have become a tradition for us. It started when I was in college. I was so nervous before my first out-of-town assignment that I was sure I was going to forget something. So, I called my dad and stepmom to start naming off things I might need. Had I not called them, I would have forgotten important things like my hairbrush, my computer charger, and toothpaste.

Since then, I have called my dad to help me pack before every out-of-town assignment. Yes, this is only a short drive to Birmingham—we'll go down and come back in the same day— but it felt weird to not call my dad as I prepared for Hunter to pick me up. It's tradition, after all. And you don't break tradition.

That's at least what I tell myself as I toss my extra phone charger into my purse. I refuse to admit that I need my dad as a buffer to keep my thoughts away from the fact that I'll be alone in a car for two hours and forty-five minutes with Hunter McAvoy.

I can do this. I can be strong. I won't even need my random gross things to keep my mind out of the gutter.

The day is straightforward. Hunter insisted on driving to Birmingham, and during the car ride, he agreed to allow me to ask him some initial interview questions. That will make the drive go by in a snap. We'll then arrive at his parents' house, where I'll interview his mom and dad about their son's accomplishments. Readers love good family anecdotes. The photographer we hired out of Birmingham will take some photos to accompany the article, and before I know it, we'll be heading back toward Music City.

Easy, right? What could go wrong?

Nothing. Nothing will go wrong. That is, as long as Hunter doesn't look at me like he did the first day we met. And as long as he doesn't smile. And as long as I don't feel a spark like I did when we shook hands at the press conference.

As long as none of those things happen, or anything else that makes me think about him naked, then everything will go off without a hitch.

BeepBeep! Beep! Beep! BeepBeep! Beeeeeeeeeep!

"When do you plan to change that alarm sound?" My dad asks as the alert on my watch goes off, telling me it's time to go downstairs and meet Hunter. "That is, without a doubt, the most annoying sound in the world."

"Never. I've never missed a reminder because of it. I have a system. You remind me of everything I need, and the alarm tells me it's time to go. It's fool-proof."

"Whatever you need to tell yourself, slugger."

I smile at the old nickname my dad gave me when I was six. Who knew me wanting to play baseball would lead to a nickname carried on years later? "I have to go downstairs and meet Hunter. I'll text you when I'm back in town tonight."

"Be safe, Sadie. I love you."

"Love you, too, Dad."

I hang up the phone and grab my oversized purse before locking up my apartment and heading down to the street level. My apartment might be convenient to both the stadium and the newspaper, but street parking is horrible for guests, which is why I told Hunter I'd meet him out front at nine a.m.

As soon as I exit my building, I notice a newer-model, sleek, red pickup truck parked against the curb. Even though the windows are slightly tinted, I can see Hunter clear as day. I'm immediately drawn to his profile, the strong cut of his jawline, and even though I can only see a little bit of him, he definitely is something nice to look at in the morning.

Stop it, Sadie! Right the fuck now!

Pimples.

Body odor.

Toenail clippings.

I've got a combined five-and-a-half hours of being alone with him. Maybe I didn't think this thing completely through. I take one long breath before opening up the truck door, doing my best to level my voice so I don't come across sounding like a teenage girl who is being picked up by the most popular boy in school. "Hi. Thanks for picking me up."

"You ready?"

The shortness in his tone takes me off guard. That, and he didn't even look my way or acknowledge me when I got in the truck. Not a glance. Not even a side-eye. I'm not saying that he had to look at me like he did when we first met, I'd actually prefer it if he didn't, but a glance or a nod of the head would have been nice.

I wonder what crawled up his ass this morning?

"Sure," I say, a bit defeated at how this trip is beginning. "Let's go."

The car ride is deathly silent as we make our way out of Nashville. The radio isn't even on. It's an uncomfortable silence that I was not mentally prepared for.

"Do you mind if I ask you a few of the questions I had planned?" I say, getting my recorder and notebook out of my purse.

"Fine."

Well, if that isn't a welcoming invitation for a personal and forthright interview, I don't know what is.

"Do you remember the first time you thought to yourself, 'I want to be a coach'?"

"Not really."

I blink a few times. Really? That's his answer? If the temperature in the cab of his truck was icy before, it's downright frigid now.

I attempt to rephrase the question. "You don't? Not even an old play you drew up on a notebook in elementary school?"

My attempt at being more conversational falls on deaf ears. He doesn't answer. He keeps his focus strictly on the road.

I try to ask a few more questions. They run from the basic "What is your favorite part of coaching?" to the complex "What do you think is the best offense to run in this age of football?" All of my questions come with one- to three-word answers, and a pissy tone thrown in for good measure.

I should be happy about this. Well, not the interview. His quotes that are barely sentences won't do shit for my article. But him being cold to me is exactly what I need to keep my mind out of the gutter and focused on the article. This is what today is about. Today is not about how his demeanor makes me sad and confused. It's about the story, only the story.

This is what I keep telling myself as we cross the Tennessee border into Alabama. I keep telling myself that all the way to Birmingham.

And when we pull into his parents' driveway, I almost believe it.

6

HUNTER

I REMEMBER the first time I realized that as long as my last name was McAvoy, I'd always be Bo's son, first and foremost. That no matter what I did, my accomplishments would always be tied back to him.

I was seven years old.

I had just thrown my first touchdown in Pop Warner football. I was so excited. I saw my receiver wide open, and before I knew it, he was running into the end zone.

It was one of the best moments of my life.

That was until my coach said words that I'll never forget: *"It was just like your daddy threw that ball."*

I remember being confused. I was pretty sure it was a compliment. At least, in my coach's eyes, it was. But my dad didn't throw the touchdown. I did. It was at that moment I realized that every touchdown I threw for the rest of my life... every decision that involved a football... would all be somehow tied back to Bo.

Later, I figured out that everything I did was never good enough for him. If I threw for 150 yards in a game, he would tell me why it should have been 160. When I was the number two quarterback recruit in the country in high school, all I heard for months was what I did wrong to not be number one.

That is why I became a perfectionist. Maybe if I got it perfect, it would be good enough for my dad.

Little did I know that was a losing battle.

"Did Hunter always want to play football? Was he born with a football in his hand?"

Sadie's question brings me back to the present. We've been in Birmingham for a few hours, and she's been interviewing my parents for half of that time—though I've barely been paying attention. I tried to listen to a couple of her questions, but every time I did, it was some sort of question revolving around football and my childhood. I've been around one too many interviews to know that she's trying to see where the earliest Bo McAvoy comparisons can be found.

And here I thought she was different. I should have known better. I let a beautiful smile and a great ass cloud my judgment.

"In Alabama, every little boy is born with a football in his hand," my mom, Francine, says, a smile on her face from ear to ear. She never gets tired of saying that I was a 'Bama boy since day one. "When a boy is born in this state, the hospital asks you if you're an Alabama or an Auburn fan so they can dress him accordingly. It's the most precious thing. I bet I have pictures somewhere I can show you."

"I'll hold you to that," Sadie says, giving my mom the smile I'm all too familiar with. It's the one that sucked me in that first day I met her. "Was there ever a chance he wouldn't play college for Alabama?"

"He thought he could go somewhere else," my father says gruffly from his chair. "Then he came to his senses."

Dad's curt tone sucks the air out of the room almost instantly. I can see my mom's shoulders grow tense. My blood turns cold as I stand next to the fireplace in my childhood living room, remembering the one time I asked if we could visit another campus that wasn't in Tuscaloosa. That wasn't one of the best memories of my teenage years, but it's definitely one of the ones that's most memorable, and not in a good way. It was the worst argument we ever had.

I didn't win.

I give Sadie credit, though, she doesn't flinch. She simply turns the page of her notebook and continues to ask more questions about my childhood and early football career, my mother all too happy to answer everything she wants to know about her first born's football successes.

This is the first time I've really allowed myself to look at her today. I was purposely a dick to her this morning. I was hoping that if I kept answering her questions with barely there answers, she'd just be quiet. She held out much longer than I thought she would.

From the second she suggested coming here, all I could think about was that she was like every other reporter. She might be asking some easy questions now, but I am just waiting for the "so, does your dad help you draw up plays?" question. Because it happens all the damn time.

The answer: hell no. And he never will. The man might be in the Hall of Fame, but he couldn't design an offensive game plan if a gun was held to his head.

Now that I'm allowing myself to look at her, I realize everything I missed today. She's wearing a loose blouse and a fitted pair of pants. I bet if I would have let myself look at her this morning, the ass that has been haunting my dreams would have been showcased in the best way. Her hair is on top of her head in what I've now come to know as the signature Sadie look. Her face has more makeup on it than I've seen her wear before, but it's not overdone.

It's perfect. She's perfect. Well, she would be if she wasn't a reporter. Figures, the one woman who has made me think about anything other than football in years is the one person I can't have.

"This question is for each of you," I hear Sadie ask my parents. "What was your proudest moment of Hunter during his football career? Playing or coaching."

Oh, this ought to be good...

"I have so many," my mom begins as I walk over and take a seat next to her. "There are so many of his playing days that I'll always cherish. I couldn't name just one. As a parent, though, I think my proudest moment was when he told us that he knew what he wanted to do with his future. His eyes lit up when he talked about becoming a coach. He was so excited about it. And as a parent, that's what you want. That something, or someone, that will make our child's eyes light up, and we know then and there that they are ready to be set free. He was becoming his own man, and I'm very proud of the man he is today."

I might have dated the head cheerleader in high school, but without a doubt, my number-one fan, always and forever, will be my mother. Want to talk about the stereotypical football mom? Francine McAvoy is it, hands down. She never missed a game when I was a player. Since I turned to coaching, she has called me after every game to tell me good job, or to give me a pep talk if we lost. And don't get me started on her wardrobe. If you want to know where I'm coaching, all you have to do is look at what colors my mom is wearing on any given day and go from there. Today? She's decked out in red and black with gold jewelry. She's a combination of a southern belle and a Fury superfan.

My dad, on the other hand? He might have been there physically when I played, but he was never there emotionally. While my mother was cheering her loudest, he was silently judging me. Hell, he still is. Only now he doesn't make his critiques silent.

"That's great," Sadie says, bringing me back to the present

conversation. "How about you, Mr. McAvoy? What was a proud papa moment for you?"

I appreciate Sadie trying to use some humor to ease the tension. Too bad for her it won't work.

"Easy. His National Championship win at Alabama."

Sadie waits for him to elaborate, but he doesn't, so she continues. "Why that moment?"

"I knew by then he wasn't heading for the league. He had already made his choice to go into coaching. Which is a fine profession. You know, for those who can't hack it as a player. Helps that he's a McAvoy. And I'm proud of him for getting hired in Nashville. But there's nothing like being the guy on the field holding up the trophy. That moment was the only time he was going to get to do that."

The answer shouldn't surprise or anger me, but it does. Hearing his words, spoken to a reporter no less, makes my blood both boil and turn cold at the same time. I don't know if I want to storm out of the room, or stare at him in shock that he would say that out loud.

"He could lead the Fury, or one day his own team, to a championship," Sadie says, making direct eye contact with my father. "I'm fairly certain those coaches get to hoist up a trophy. Or did I misinterpret pictures that I have seen after every championship game?"

"It's not the same," my dad fires back.

"It's not?" she asks, now leaning forward in her chair. Is she about to go toe to toe with Bo McAvoy? By the defiant look in her eyes, she absolutely is. She's staring right at him, daring him to look away. Begging him to tell her she's wrong.

Holy hell.

"Well, I think it is," Sadie continues. "Not like I'll ever have the chance to do it. Us reporters don't know much, I guess. Except I do know that if Hunter led the Fury to the championship this year, he would be the youngest coordinator in league history to win a championship. And if he did, hypothetically speaking, lift that trophy, it would be one hell of an accomplishment. One that a father might be proud of. But I digress. I'd like to now ask you about what you think of Hunter's play-calling, Mr. McAvoy? Could you run his offense, or is it too advanced from when you played all those years ago?"

Sadie's words stun me. I'd have to check, but I think my jaw is on the ground.

That. Was. Amazing.

She defended me. No reporter has ever gone after my dad like that. And asking him if he could run my offense? Fuck. I know for a damn fact that is the first time anyone has asked him that. Usually, they are all about kissing his ass.

But not Sadie. Not by a longshot.

I now replay every question I heard her ask today. They were all about me. Not about what my dad might have taught me. Not about how his career influenced mine.

She wanted to know about *me*. As a person and a coach. How my younger days shaped who I am today. How they think I will do in Nashville. Trying to see if my mom kept any early plays that I might have drawn up as a kid.

I feel like an absolute asshole. I assumed Sadie's motives for this interview weren't pure. I treated her like shit because I couldn't fathom any other reason for why she would want to come to Birmingham to interview my family. Everyone has always used me for a story. I thought she was the same.

Yet I should have known that she would be different.

She's been different from the first time I laid eyes on her.

7

SADIE

"I OWE YOU AN APOLOGY."

The only thing keeping me from jumping out of my seat at Hunter's words is the seatbelt across my shoulders and the computer on my lap.

We've been on the road for nearly an hour, and just like the ride down to Birmingham, he has been silent since we left his parents' house.

Until now. And I don't know how to respond to him.

I want to be mad at him. I want to slam my computer shut and ask what the hell I did that warranted the silent treatment all day.

I also want to hug him, because I have a feeling his mood has everything to do with his father, and this whole day is my fault, as it was my suggestion to go to Birmingham.

I also want to jump his bones, because even with him being all grouchy and angry, he still gives me butterflies in the best and worst ways every time I look at him.

Basically, I want to scream in frustration because I'm feeling a lot of things right now that I most definitely shouldn't be feeling when it comes to Hunter McAvoy.

"Are you apologizing for giving me the silent treatment for most of the day? Or are you apologizing to me and hoping I pass it on to the photographer after you bit his head off for suggesting you play catch with your dad?"

"When you put it like that, I guess both," Hunter says apologetically, though he still hasn't looked at me.

"I'll pass your words of overwhelming sympathy on to the photographer."

My words are laced in sarcasm. I don't care. Mad is the emotion that wants to win right now, but it's really hard when I let my eyes wander over to the driver's seat. As he lets out another sigh, this one I'm guessing of frustration, he switches his hands around that he's driving with, putting his right hand on top of the wheel.

This shouldn't be sexy. Driving a truck should not be sexy. Yet, Hunter makes it sexy. Even when I'm pissed at him for the way he acted today, I can't help but have ridiculously dirty thoughts about this man.

Dentist appointments.

Boogers.

Granny panties.

It's not just the dirty thoughts that are making my head a confusing place to be right now. Behind his anger and prickliness, I saw a side of Hunter I didn't expect to see today, a vulnerable one. He probably doesn't think I noticed. When his dad was passive-aggressively talking shit about his profession, I caught a glimpse of Hunter sitting next to his mom. He looked defeated. Sad. Angry.

My heart broke for him.

How long has he been dealing with this? My guess would be way before I showed up on their doorstep. Seeing that exposed side to Hunter added another layer to my conflicting feelings. Now he just wasn't an attractive man driving a sexy truck who gives me butterflies when he smiles at me. He is a man who is trying to use every weapon in his arsenal to prove to his doubters—aka his father—that he was capable. That he could be the best at his craft, that he would excel, no matter what.

I know that feeling all too well.

"I'm truly sorry, Sadie. I've been acting like an ass all day, and you've been taking the brunt of it."

I turn slightly to face him, and for the first time today, Hunter takes his eyes off the road to catch a glimpse of me. "Can I ask why you were Captain Grouchypants today?"

"Captain Grouchypants?" he asks as the smallest hint of a smile breaks through.

"I said what I said."

He lets out a soft laugh. "Off the record?"

If there is such a thing as a "safe word" for journalists, it's "off the record." When a reporter hears that, all things stop. Notebooks get put down. Recorders are turned off. Cameras stop rolling. In my case right now? I power down my laptop and promptly put it and my phone in my purse.

"Off the record," I say, reassuring him I'm not recording this.

"Sorry. It's not that I don't trust you—"

Hunter's words come out shaky. It's almost as if he's nervous, which is the first time that has happened since we've met. He has always been so calm and collected. Well, when he wasn't being an asshole. I have a feeling I'm right, though. He has been fidgety since he broke the silence. My point is proven when he shifts his driving arm again, putting the left arm back on top of the steering wheel, leaving his right arm resting against the center console.

"Hunter," I say, gently putting my hand on his forearm. I don't know why I'm doing this. It's completely inappropriate. But I want him to know that right now I'm a safe space. "You have no reason to trust me. I'm a reporter you met less than a month ago who wasn't exactly forthcoming on my identity when we met. I get it. No offense taken. But you can talk to me. Off the record."

He nods before taking a deep breath. If he feels my hand on his arm, he doesn't acknowledge it. I also don't let go.

"If you couldn't tell, my dad and I don't have the best relationship."

"I noticed."

I feel him tense underneath my touch. "You did?"

"I interview and read people for a living," I begin, giving his arm a reassuring yet gentle squeeze, hoping to calm his nerves. "Choice of words is key into figuring out what people really mean. They might say the right things, but *how* they say them mean just as much. Or sometimes it's what they don't say that speaks the loudest."

"You picked up on some things?" he asks, his voice again shaky.

I could tell from the first question I asked that Bo McAvoy's relationship with his son was strained, at best. While his mom couldn't wait to show me the endless amount of photo albums of young Hunter, his dad only watched from afar. And the way he answered questions about Hunter's coaching career? You would have thought he invented football, and the only reason his son was a coach was because of his last name.

That was the moment I knew, at least partly, why Hunter was on edge all day. I honestly don't blame him.

"Many," I say, regret in my voice for having seen behind the curtain that is the McAvoy family.

"Are you going to write about them?"

Hunter's question is laced with concern. I let out a frustrated sigh, because I honestly don't know the answer. "What we are talking about now? No. I gave you my word that this was off the record. Now, what he said at the house? I don't know yet. I have to use a few things. But I promise, whatever I write, I won't show the world what I saw today."

Hunter nods, I hope he understands the situation I'm in. I shouldn't have even promised him that. If I wrote a story that Bo McAvoy didn't approve of his son's career, and that he was a jackass to his flesh and blood, it would make national headlines. The job at *US Daily* would be in the bag.

I'm breaking about ten different, unwritten reporter rules by telling him I wouldn't write about how Bo treated him. I should care, but I don't. Their relationship is a private matter. I'm not about to be the one who airs that dirty laundry to the world.

Even though it would make my career. If I would have known that an interview in Birmingham would reveal all of this, I wouldn't have asked for it.

"When you said that you wanted to come to Birmingham for the interview, I assumed you were like every other reporter. That you were only using me to get an interview with my dad."

And there it is. The final piece of the grouchy Hunter puzzle. And while I should be offended that he thought I was using him to get an interview with the great Bo McAvoy, I'm not. I don't blame him. He barely knows me. When every reporter has only ever used him to get to his dad, why would he think I was different?

Little does he know, I am different. At least, I strive to be. Every article by every other reporter written about Hunter in some way, shape, or form circles back to his dad. I knew this going in. However, I wanted to know about young Hunter. What drove him? What made him want to be a coach? Who better to ask that to than the people who raised him?

Or so I thought. Here I was just trying to be different, and I released a can of worms that I didn't realize was about to bust open.

"That's why you didn't speak to me this morning?" I ask cautiously, even though I think I know my answer.

He nods. "I'm sorry to have assumed that about you."

"I'm sorry you've been interviewed by shitty reporters your whole life."

This makes him laugh. "I should have known you would be different."

"And what makes you say that?"

He gives another glance my way, and his eyebrow goes up a little. "Isn't it obvious?"

I let out an exasperated sigh and fall back into my seat, my hand finally moving from his arm. "Are you really playing the girl card right now? I thought you were better than that, McAvoy."

"Now look who's doing the assuming," he says with a small smile. And dammit. The butterflies are back. "You are different because you are a different kind of reporter. I read the things you wrote about me when I was first hired. You're talented. You ask different questions. You take different angles to stories. It makes you stand out. You are damn good at your job, Sadie Benson. I'm sorry I assumed you were using me. It won't happen again."

Some girls get giddy when a boy tells them they are beautiful. Some get excited when a guy will send a "good morning" text.

Me? Compliment my writing or my job, and I will be putty in your hands.

Hunter saying that I am damn good at my job? Holy fuckballs, Ted better be ready for tonight.

It takes all the strength I possess in my five-foot-five frame to not squeal like a schoolgirl. I'm also doing my best not to clench my legs together because... yeah. All those feelings from earlier? They are now manifesting into one main one.

A crush. I am officially crushing on Hunter McAvoy.

"Thank you." It's all I trust myself to say. Luckily, I say it without my voice going into a high-range octave.

"You're welcome."

He smiles, and this time our silence is of the comfortable variety. Before I know it, he is pulling up to my apartment complex. This started as the longest car ride in the history of ever. Now I don't want it to end.

I don't have a reason to stay in his truck, though. I can't ask him upstairs for a drink. Hell, I can't even pretend that I have too much to carry and I need a second set of hands.

This is where our day ends. Even as rocky as it was, I'm not ready for it to be over.

Snapping me out of that thought is the cool Nashville air. I didn't even realize Hunter got out of the truck, let alone that he walked around to open the door for me.

"Well, aren't you the gentleman?" I say, gathering my purse and stepping down from my seat.

"My mom would have smacked me today if she knew how I treated you this morning," he says, a hint of embarrassment in his words. "Figured I could at least make up for it now."

I smile as I step onto the sidewalk. "Thank you for today."

He gives me a confused look. "Really? Even after this morning? And... well, most of the day?"

My hand reaches out again for his forearm. I don't know why I keep doing this. It's like my fingers have a mind of their own, and all they want to do is reassure him through my touch. I should pull away. I don't. Even after our eyes make contact, my fingers stay connected to his skin. As I look at him, all I see is a mixture of confusion, want, and something that I can't identify passing through his eyes.

I'm sure mine are the same.

"Even after all of that," I continue. "You really have a lot to be proud of, Hunter. Don't let his words bring you down. You are an incredible man. It's too bad he chooses not to see it."

My words hang in the air, and Hunter doesn't reply. Instead, he takes his free hand and places it on top of mine, giving my fingers a gentle squeeze that sends a wave of sensation through my entire body.

When Hunter broke the silence earlier, it legitimately shocked me. But this? This is downright terrifying.

Because I've never felt anything like this in my entire life.

"Thank you, Sadie. That means a lot."

His voice is so sincere I don't know how to respond. All I know is that I'm standing in the middle of a Nashville sidewalk, all but holding hands with Hunter.

This is bad. This is very, very bad.

"I should probably go upstairs," I say, my voice weak.

He gives my hand one more squeeze before he releases it. I immediately let go of his arm. "I guess I'll see you around."

I nod and dig my keys out of my purse, my eyes focused on finding the damn things. They are definitely avoiding Hunter's gaze. It's too much. Too intense.

All of this is too intense.

I eventually find them and give him a small wave as I make my way to my door, though I feel his eyes on me the entire time. I don't dare turn around. I don't trust myself or what I would do if I did. All I want to do is go upstairs, drop my purse, kick off my shoes, take a cold shower, or find Ted, whichever is closer.

However, Hunter doesn't make that possible. At least, not yet.

"Hey, Sadie."

I hesitantly look back over my shoulder. He's standing right where I left him. The look in his eyes is still too much for me to handle.

"Yeah?"

"You thanked me for today, but I didn't get a chance to thank you."

Does he not remember what happened today? "And what do you need to thank me for?"

I have noticed a lot of smiles on Hunter in the short time I've known him. There is the camera smile he used at his press conference. There was the fake one he used today around his dad. There was even the flirty one he gave me when we first met.

But this one? This smile, the small one that goes a little higher on the right, might be the most genuine one I have ever seen.

"For being you. Because you are pretty amazing."

And with that, Hunter gets in his truck and leaves me standing outside my door, my jaw slacked and my emotions all over the place.

Screw the shower. I need to find Ted.

8

SADIE

THERE ARE a lot of things I'm good at. Hell, I'd even venture to say I'm borderline great at them.

I'm a hard worker. I'm organized. I'm a good friend, though I choose to keep my circle small. I call my dad at least three times a week and visit him and my stepmom every Monday night for dinner.

The things I'm not good at? Well, those are easy to spot. And I don't deny them.

I'm a horrible cook. I'm even worse when it comes to decorating my living space. I can't sing to save my life. And I'm really, really bad at taking days off.

Like extraordinarily bad.

It stems back to early in my career. I took a day off, turned off my phone and said that I was unplugging for the day. When I turned it back on six hours later, I realized that I missed a story on a high school coach getting fired for inappropriate relations with a student.

I never turned my phone off again. Not even now as I head west on I-40 toward Memphis for a boss-mandated week of relaxation.

The Super Bowl has come and gone. I've reported on everything I can about Hunter being hired. To call the story about him and his family a success would be an understatement. According to John, it was the most clicked-on sports story in *Banner* history. And that's without me writing about how his dad is a passive-aggressive jackass.

With nothing pressing left to write about, I packed my bags —with my father's over-the-phone guidance, of course—and picked up an abundance of road snacks before hitting the road to Memphis. My plans are to take in the atmosphere of Beale Street, visit the National Civil Rights Museum, and eat my weight in barbeque.

And not think about Hunter.

That's my mini-vacation to-do list. Maybe this won't be so bad after all.

My stepmom was adamant that this was not a real vacation. Her justification? I wasn't leaving the state. She couldn't wrap her head around the fact that I have a week off and I'm only going two-hundred-miles west.

She's also never had Memphis barbeque, so I didn't argue with her. I assured her that I was taking my annual solo trip in June to San Francisco still, and this was just a small getaway to recharge my batteries. I left out the part where John all but forced me to get out of town for a bit.

She seemed to like that answer. My dad, on the other hand, completely understood my motives and put in a to-go order from our favorite barbeque restaurant.

He gets me. Helen, though she has made a lot of strides over the years, has never been able to figure me out. Which is fine. I'm not mad. I'm a tomboy, book nerd who loved sports for the games and not the boys who played them. She and my stepsister Bethany are the definition of girly-girls with their fashionable clothes, perfect makeup, and never a hair out of place.

Having a tomboy for a stepdaughter was not what she signed

up for when she and my dad got married my sophomore year of high school. But over the years, we seem to have found a comfortable balance. One year, she asked me to teach her the basics of football so she could watch it with my dad. Which he loved. In return, she showed me how great regular manicures can be. Especially for someone who has to look at her fingers every day while typing.

I take a quick look down at my fresh manicure—I went with a deep blue color this time—before checking the GPS to make sure I'm still on the quickest route. This was another reason I chose to come to Memphis. It was a quick and easy drive, but it was far enough away that I could separate myself for a few minutes from real life.

Or, more specifically? From all thoughts involving Hunter McAvoy.

I haven't seen the man in two weeks, and I can still feel the weight of his gaze on me as he dropped me off at my apartment building. I can still see his smile. I can still feel his skin under mine as I tried to give him comfort. I can still hear the sincerity in his voice when he told me "thank you."

It's been a good thing that I haven't had to see him again after our trip to Birmingham. I needed that time to pull myself together on all things related to that man.

If it was just a physical attraction, that would be one thing. I could handle being sexually attracted to a man I couldn't have. But it wasn't. Now at night, rather than just fantasizing about his body, I'm thinking about how he made me feel that first day we met at the shop. I'm thinking about how much I admire his determination to prove his father wrong. I'm thinking about how when we were standing outside my apartment building, it was like we were the only two people in Nashville.

This is bad. It's so very, very bad.

If I'm reacting this way now, how am I going to handle the season? With him being the offensive coordinator, I don't have to interview him every day. But it will be a lot. And if my heart and my body can't get on the same page as my brain that this man is off-limits, then I need to figure out a lot more grotesque things to think about.

Or buy stock in batteries.

Why did he have to be literally everything I want in a man? He's gorgeous. He's funny. He's charming. He loves football. He loves his family. Yes, even despite his issues with his dad, there is love there. And the way he looked at his mom when she praised him? You can't fake that.

The man is perfect. And he is so off-limits, it isn't even funny. Figures. The first man who has made me want to date in years is a man whom I can't even pretend to consider.

I laugh to myself as signs for Memphis tell me I'm about forty miles away. Even if we could date—and that's going under the assumption that he also wants to date me—what would that even be like?

For weeks I've not allowed myself to go down this mental road. I knew it wouldn't do any good, so why even entertain the idea? But now? With nothing to do and a half hour left in my drive, I let myself fantasize.

Some girls might picture the perfect date as a fancy dinner. In Nashville, a popular date-night activity is catching a live band or getting drinks at the latest up-and-coming restaurant. Or so I've been told by some of the other female news reporters I occasionally grab drinks with. But for me? The perfect date is a night spent at home.

That's where I imagine Hunter. Relaxing on my couch after we enjoy our dinner. I'm cleaning up the take-out boxes, because obviously I didn't cook. I ask him if he wants a drink, which he takes me up on, and when I go to take it to him, he grabs my wrist and pulls me down on the couch so I'm sitting across his lap. The drink spills a little, but neither of us care. How can I when my body is touching his? He takes the drink from my hand, puts it down on the table, and guides me so I'm now straddling him. Our eyes lock, and there is no denying the fire that we are holding for each other. In my fantasy, he wants me just as much as I want him. His fingertips are slowly grazing up and down my sides, and even though this is only in my head, just the thought of it sends goose bumps down my spine.

My hands are wrapped around his neck, softly playing with the spot where his hair meets his nape, and I can't help myself. I lean in for the kiss. He doesn't stop me. In my mind, this isn't our first kiss. This kiss is familiar. Hot and sweet. Slow but intense. Promising of more later.

Knock-knock-knock.

The sound of a tap against my car window brings me back to the present. Actually, it scares the shit out of me. Somehow, someway, I managed to steer my car to my hotel in downtown Memphis while fantasizing about me and Hunter making out on my couch.

Nose hair.

Road kill.

Skunks.

I roll down my window, hopeful that my three gross images have calmed me down enough to be able to think straight.

"Hi. Sorry about that."

"No problem, ma'am," the valet says. "Are you checking in?"

I nod and retrieve my bags from my car and hand my keys off to the very nice young man who did not call me out for sitting in my car like a loon for God knows how long reveling in my dirty thoughts. If just those thoughts of Hunter can make me forget reality, then I absolutely, without a doubt, need to push these feelings to the far, far recesses of my mind.

With a little shake of my head, clearing away any last thoughts of kissing on my couch, I make my way into the Memphis hotel. I've stayed here plenty of times before. To the left is a seating area. The center is open for comers and goers.

To the right is the check-in desk, which is where I make my way.

I take two steps before I nearly fall on my face.

No. It can't be. What are the odds?

I shake my head again, hoping that my mind is playing a dirty, dirty trick on me. Because that's the only logical explanation I can think of as to why Hunter McAvoy is standing at the check-in counter at the same hotel I'm staying at in Memphis.

Mucus.

Dirty diapers.

Chia pets.

9

HUNTER

"GIVE US ONE SECOND, Mr. McAvoy, and we'll get you into a room."

I bite back a snarky response to the "one second" part of the front desk clerk's statement. Nothing about this check-in process has been one second. Instead, I paste a smile on my face and wait not so patiently for my key card.

I'd like to think that I'm an even-keeled guy. I generally don't get bothered when things inconvenience me. But right now? When I'm running on fumes and have been in five states in seven days while scouting more than twenty players? Yeah... right now I'm bothered.

All I want is a hot shower and a bed.

The draft is in two months, and from now until then, it's my job, along with the other coaches, to make sure we have scouted every player we could possibly draft. Especially because we have the number-one pick.

That pick won't define our draft. It's who we take in the later rounds that will help build our future. And for the past week, I've been touring colleges from Florida to California and everywhere in between trying to find those hidden gems.

I thought I was done scouting for the week. I was set to fly home to Nashville from Missouri when I got a call from a former teammate who coaches at Memphis. He told me he had a guy I *had* to see. That he was a game changer. As much as I wanted to be back in Nashville, and to finally get some use out of the king-size bed that I have barely used, I figured there wasn't any harm in one more stop.

I'll see him tomorrow. Today I need sleep. And a shower. And eventually food.

Except right now, none of those things are happening because "one second" has actually turned into "twenty minutes."

"I'm sorry, Mr. McAvoy, this is taking longer than expected," the front desk clerk says with a smile that screams "I hope he doesn't bite my head off." "We're trying to get a room ready for you, it will just be another minute."

"Take your time." I mean for the words to come out pleasant, but I can hear the bite to my tone. And by her reaction, I did, in fact, snap at her. I feel bad for my behavior. She's just doing her job. I'm the one who walked in without a reservation demanding a room. Apparently, when I don't get sleep, I'm a bit crabby. And by a bit, I mean a lot.

I turn away from the desk—mostly so I don't accidentally give this poor girl a death glare—and I'm struck stupid by a sight that I did not expect to see outside of the Nashville city limits.

My mood instantly lightens.

And by the look on Sadie's face, seeing me is just as much of a surprise. That and the fact that she nearly tripped over her feet when our eyes made contact.

The reaction makes me laugh. I haven't seen Sadie since I dropped her off after our trip to Birmingham. That doesn't mean I haven't thought about her, though.

I have. A lot. More than I'm willing to admit out loud. And most of the ways I have thought about her are not appropriate for polite conversation. Not that I can actually share my feelings about Sadie to anyone. She's my forbidden fruit. The apple I want to taste but I know I can't have.

"Hunter?" she says, now standing behind me at the front desk. "What are you doing in Memphis?"

"I could ask you the same thing," I say, my tone much more pleasant than it was just a few minutes ago.

"I know deflection when I hear it," she says, her words teasing. "I know you've been out scouting all week."

"Stalking me now?"

"Ha! You wish," she says, all but rolling her eyes as she steps up to the counter to hand her credit card and license to another hotel staff member. "It's my job to know what the team I'm covering is up to at all times. That includes coaches."

"And what is it I'm doing?"

She doesn't answer for a second, instead keeping me waiting as she goes through her check-in process. I don't mind, though. It gives me the chance to take in her profile. Her rounded nose is the perfect size for her face. Her cheeks are the slightest shade of pink, but I don't think it's from makeup. The spot where her neck meets her shoulders is begging for my lips to be on them. And then there is the ass that I haven't been able to stop thinking about since I first laid eyes on her. The whole, gorgeous package.

"You've been out scouting all week," she says, breaking me from my trance. "If I heard right, you started in Florida, ended up in Texas and California, before making stops in Colorado and Missouri, before landing back here. This stop wasn't planned, but if I'd have to guess, I'd put money on the fact that you're here to check out the Memphis running back I've been hearing buzz about."

I shouldn't be shocked anymore by Sadie and the things she knows. I should also know by now that whenever she talks football to me, I'm a fucking goner. Yet, hearing her recite exactly everything I've done over the past week sends an unexpected wave of excitement through my body.

It also makes me say things I shouldn't—or normally wouldn't—to a reporter.

"Have dinner with me tonight."

My request, which comes off more like a demand, catches her off guard. I don't blame her. Hell, I said it and I'm still not sure where it came from.

"Have dinner with you?"

I can do two things right now. I can wave it off and make it seem like a joke. Or I can own it. I can ask her again and ignore every red flag that is popping up in my brain right now telling me why having dinner with Sadie Benson is a horrible idea.

Fuck the red flags.

"Yes. Have dinner with me." I ignore her silence and take a step closer to her. I'm not close enough that I can touch her, but I can smell the faintest scent of something floral coming from her body. All that does is make me want this to happen even more. I want to be closer to her. I want to wake up tomorrow smelling that on my skin. "Unless you have plans?"

I see her swallow heavily, clearly not knowing how to respond. In the time that I've spent thinking about her, most of that has been wondering if she felt what I did. Did she have even an inkling of the attraction that I had toward her? When we met at Sandwich City, I knew it was one-sided. During our drive to Birmingham, I thought there might be times when she was feeling what I felt.

Then, she put her hand on my arm. And I was confident there was a chance.

Right now? Watching how my invite has made her cheeks flush? How she has been looking at everyone and everything but me since I mentioned dinner? Now I know.

She's feeling this too.

"Sadie? Do you have plans tonight?"

She finally meets my gaze before shaking her head. "No. No plans."

"Then have dinner with me."

She doesn't say anything again, but this time she doesn't stop looking at me. Which is good. I can see her weighing every part of this in her eyes.

"Just dinner?"

I nod and give her a reassuring smile. "Just dinner."

"On or off the record?"

And there it is. The million-dollar question. Or, if I'm reading this code right, she's asking without uttering the words, "Is this, or is this not, a date?"

"Off the record." I take another step forward, wanting to make sure I'm as clear as I can be. "Tonight, I don't want to talk about football. I don't want to talk about our jobs. I just want to have dinner with a beautiful woman whom I haven't been able to stop thinking about since the moment I laid eyes on her. I want to explore the streets of Memphis with her. I want to get lost in a conversation where we both wonder where the night went. What do you say?"

"Sir! Your room is ready! Mr. McAvoy! Your room is ready!"

I hear the woman calling for me. I don't care. Minutes ago I was fuming, wondering what took her so long. Now I wish she would have taken a few minutes longer. I'm not leaving Sadie's space until I have my answer. Luckily, she doesn't make me wait much longer.

"Yes. I'll have dinner with you. Off the record."

Her words come out in almost a whisper, but I hear them clear as day. Even more, I hear the meaning behind them.

Tonight isn't Coach McAvoy and Reporter Benson.

Tonight is Hunter and Sadie.

And I really, really like that play.

10

SADIE

I'VE FANTASIZED about a lot of things when it comes to Hunter. And yes, most of them have been of the sexual variety.

Sue me. The man is a football coach who could simultaneously pose for a *GQ* cover. *Cosmo* named him one of their most eligible bachelors. He is *that* good looking.

There was the obvious daydream in my car today that left me so discombobulated I autopiloted my way to Memphis.

There have also been the times when I'm alone in my apartment with Ted an arm's reach away. Those fantasies consist of me wondering what it would feel like for his weight to be on top of me. And what it would be like to wake up in his arms. They were blissful thoughts until I realized that Ted could only do so much.

After Birmingham my fantasies became less sexual and more... intimate. They morphed into thoughts of us holding hands, cuddling on the couch or watching football together. And somehow, those thoughts seemed more scandalous than any sexual scenario I could dream up. I pushed aside thoughts that I was probably not his type or that I was imagining the way he looked at me. These were my fantasies. And I was going to bask in them.

Yet somehow, in all the times I thought about me and Hunter together, I never thought about what a first date would look like. In all the seconds and minutes and hours that Hunter has overtaken my thoughts, I never gave any thought to what I'd wear to make his jaw drop a little. I never debated where we would go. I never thought about the gazillion butterflies that were bound to be in my stomach at just the thought of him coming to pick me up for a night out.

I might have never thought about where we'd go, but even if I were to be given a hundred guesses, I never would have chosen this. A casual Memphis barbeque restaurant sharing a plate of pork nachos while we laugh about the most embarrassing moments of our childhood.

The conversation is easy. The company is wonderful.

The butterflies in my stomach are setting up permanent residence.

They started as soon as I heard the knock on the hotel room door. Oh hell, who am I kidding? They started the second we walked away from each other at the check-in desk after he asked me to dinner. They slowly increased as I looked through every piece of clothing I packed to find something to wear tonight before I settled on leggings and an off-the-shoulder, light blue sweater. They multiplied by a trillion when I opened my door to see him standing in front of me in dark jeans and a navy sweater over a white, button-down shirt.

The count of butterflies hovered somewhere around fifty gazillion when he put his hand on the small of my back as we entered the elevator to head to the lobby. They haven't lessened since we sat down at our table. At this point, I don't think they will.

Especially if he keeps looking at me like he is right now—like he's trying to see through to my soul.

If I wasn't so enamored by this man, it would be unnerving. "Favorite television show?"

I laugh at his question. Only because before this he asked me my favorite movie and what kind of music I liked to listen to. "Are you the reporter now?"

He shrugs before taking a sip of his beer, a small smile gracing his face. "You're always the one asking the questions. I figured it was my turn."

"I have never once asked you what your favorite television show is," I say, hoping my tone comes off flirty. That's what I'm going for, at least. It's been a while since I've actively tried to flirt with a man on a date.

Even though I know I shouldn't be.

"No. But you should have. No reporter has ever asked me about my favorite television shows," he says, reaching across the table to take my hand in his. One at a time, he laces our fingers together. A slow but deliberate process that I can't help but stare at.

And there go the butterflies again.

"I thought we weren't talking about work tonight?" My voice coming out a bit rough. I can't help it. The man is messing with every one of my senses right now. Because yes, I can smell the woodsy scent of his cologne across the table.

He slowly brings my hand to his mouth. I'm sure I'm staring, but I can't make myself look away as he places the softest kiss on my hand before putting my hand back on the table.

"You're right. No work talk," he says, a devilish grin passing over his face. "Unless you are dying to know what my favorite television show is. You *would* be the first reporter to ever ask that."

It's like he knows that even out on a date, I can't resist the chance for a scoop. Even if it's not a real interview.

"Fine," I say with a half-defeated sigh. "What is your favorite television show, Hunter?"

He flashes me a smile that screams nothing but mischief. "I think you should guess."

"That's not how an interview works, Coach McAvoy."

My words have the desired effect. His eyes get a little fire in them as he leans closer to me. "Maybe I like throwing you off of your game."

Oh, holy hell. The butterflies now are compounded by the pulsing in my lady parts. He has now taken my hand back in his and it's... It's too much. I can't think. I can barely breathe. That's the only reason I can fathom why I say the first television show that pops into my head.

"*SportsCenter.*"

He drops my hand and clutches his hand over his heart, mocking that I've somehow stabbed him with my words. "Wow. That hurts. You think that there is nothing more to me than football or sports?"

I shake my head, partly to shake off the embarrassment, and the other part to try and get my wits back. "*SportsCenter* is a perfectly fine guess."

"For a frat boy."

"Weren't you in a fraternity at Alabama?"

"That's beside the point," he says, taking my hand back in his. And just like that, my brain is getting scrambled again. "I'll have you know that I'm a very cultured man. My television choices are of high quality and have been applauded as some of the greatest television shows in history."

Now it's my turn to give him the questioning eyebrow. "Oh, really? Then tell me, oh cultured and sophisticated one, what is your favorite show that is among the best in history?"

He doesn't answer for a second. It's not an uncomfortable silence. It's more like a buildup. An anticipation.

I'm here for it.

"*Friday Night Lights.*"

It's another second again before both of us start laughing uncontrollably.

"You did all of that buildup just to tell me your favorite television show is about a high school football team?"

He shrugs, but gives me a smile in return. It's that sly smile. It's the one where it signals that he's telling me a secret. The smile that says this is a part of him that only a few people get to know.

It's my favorite.

"It was too much fun not to."

Before I can respond, our main dishes are brought out to us. Not knowing what we wanted, we decided to split a big plate of meats and sides. It looks like we're feeding the entire Fury team.

We keep our word to avoid interview questions for the rest of dinner. We share stories of our childhood and families. Well, I did. I tell him about how my mom died when I was five, and how for a while it was just me and my dad until he married Helen. He doesn't dive deep into the family well, and I don't blame him. He does tell me a story about one Halloween when he dressed up as a cheerleader and his sister, Whitley, was the football player.

Now that's the photo I wish his mom would have shown me in Birmingham.

The conversation is easy and flowing. Before I know it, he has paid our bill and we are walking hand in hand toward Beale Street, still talking about everything and anything. It's a bit chilly for Memphis in February, but I don't mind. I'm not ready for this night to be over.

"I can't believe I'm out with a Tennessee graduate," he says, giving a shiver as if he said something that tasted horrible on his tongue. "Please tell me you don't own twenty pieces of orange checkerboard clothing."

"I do not, but even if I did, it's better than that houndstooth your school insists on claiming for itself," I say, giving his shoulder a nudge. "You think I like being seen in public with a 'Bama man? I have a reputation to uphold, ya know."

"Your reputation?" he asks, pulling me around so I'm now standing in front of him, our bodies just inches away from each other. "I'm one of the most famous men to ever graduate from my school. How would it look if someone saw me out with *you?*"

I know we are teasing each other about our schools being rivals, but his words are laced in a double meaning that we are both deeply aware of. I'm now looking up at him, my hand still in his. I feel like I'm short of breath, but it's not because of the chilly air or the walk. It's because being this close to Hunter is physically taking my breath away.

"Are you okay?" he asks, but instead of taking a step back, he takes a half a step closer.

I look down because his gaze is too much for me to handle. "What are we doing?"

My words come out as a whisper, and for a second, I wonder if I actually said them out loud. Especially because Hunter doesn't answer right away. When I've convinced myself I only said those words in my head, he takes my chin in his free hand, tilting my head up to look into his eyes.

"I don't know, Sadie. All I know is that I can't *not* touch you. I need to hold your hand. I needed to know what it would be like walking next to you like you were mine to have."

"We shouldn't be doing this."

My breathy words are the truth, but they taste like a lie as they pass through my lips. The sensation of my hand in Hunter's feels right. The way he is looking at me right now? Like I'm the most beautiful thing he has ever seen? No other man has ever looked at me like that. No man has made me feel as feminine and as wanted as I do right now.

How can something that feels so right and natural be so wrong?

"Sadie?" Hunter's words are soft, and even though we are on a busy street in the middle of Memphis, I can hear them like it's the only sound around us.

"Yes?"

"I know we shouldn't be doing this. But if I don't kiss you right now, it will be the biggest regret of my life."

Then he does. Before I can object, before I can utter again why this is a horrible idea, Hunter leans down and presses his lips against mine. In the middle of Beale Street, with strangers walking past us, with jazz music filling the air, Hunter gives me the best first kiss of my life.

And it is better than any fantasy I have ever had.

11

HUNTER

IF SOMEONE WERE HOLDING a gun to my head right now and demanded to know what Sadie's lips tasted like, I would not be able to tell them.

What I do know is that whatever flavor they are, it's my new favorite. I also know that at this moment, there is nothing better in the world than kissing Sadie. Feeling her so close to me is making me feel more than I ever have in my entire life. And that includes winning a National Championship.

I also know that at this moment, Sadie Benson absolutely owns every part of me.

Our kiss started soft. When our lips first met, they were hesitant. That lasted all of three seconds before my mouth opened, and hers followed soon after. We are still kissing, and I'm sure it's bordering on indecent for a public audience, but I don't care. I can't make myself stop.

I never want to stop kissing her.

Unfortunately, I don't have that luxury as a body slams into me from behind, nearly knocking me over and taking Sadie down in the process.

"Get a fucking room, you two!" the man yells at us, stumbling away.

"Watch it, asshole!" I scream.

I'm about ready to chase this guy down when I feel Sadie's hand on my chest. I look down, and all I see are the most mesmerizing pair of hazel eyes looking up at me. "He's not worth it. Plus, I don't think making out on Beale Street is really the best idea."

I study her face, worried I'll see regret. I'm thankful when I don't. Instead, I see Sadie smiling up at me, her eyes sparkling. Her lips are plump from our kiss, and her cheeks are flushed. Her hair is a bit wild, and I can't stop staring at it. It's the first time I've seen it down, and it just adds to her beauty.

She's never looked more radiant.

"I think making out on Beale Street is a great idea," I say, wrapping my hands around her waist to bring her flush to me. "In fact, I think we should do it again."

I lean in for the kiss, but this time she stops me, putting two fingers on my lips. But it's not a rejection. The smile on her face is a dead giveaway.

"I have a better idea."

I gently kiss her fingers before taking her hand in mine. "And what do you suggest?"

"We dance."

"Dance?"

She nods. "What? Does Hunter McAvoy not dance?"

I don't. I hate dancing. One of the reasons I wasn't a great quarterback is because of my lead feet. But for Sadie? Who is looking at me right now with hope and want in her eyes? I'll do the fucking Macarena to keep that look on her face.

I lean down and kiss her forehead. "Don't hold it against me if I step on your feet."

She laughs, looping her arms around my neck. "I promise. Just listen to the music and sway with me."

The music she's referring to is coming from a saxophone player about five feet from where we are standing. I can't pinpoint the song he's playing, but I know I've heard it before. And I know now every time I hear it, I will remember this moment. The moment that a girl who bewitched me from the second I met her made me dance with her on the streets in Memphis.

My hands instinctively go to the small of her back, and I bring her close to me. Our chests are touching as she places her head right over my heart. It's beating out of control and I know she can feel it. The only reason I'm not embarrassed is because I can feel her heart as well, and it's matching pace with mine.

I don't know how long we dance. I don't know if people have been walking around us. Hell, for all I know, we have thirty cell phones pointing at us right now. There could be a hundred and I wouldn't care. I'm oblivious to my surroundings. With Sadie in my arms, I feel invincible. Alive. Like nothing can be better than this moment, right here, right now.

Sadie says something, but I can't hear it. Between the music and the fact that her face is buried in my shirt, her mouth is covered.

I lean down so she can hear me. "What was that, gorgeous?"

She lifts her head off my chest. And then I see it. A small tear sliding down her cheek. "This isn't fair."

I take my thumb and gently wipe the tear away. "What isn't fair?"

She takes a breath. Our swaying nearly comes to a standstill. "This. Us. Hunter... this has been the best night of my life. You... me... I think... I think there is something here between us. I don't know if it's just me who feels it but—"

"No," I say, cutting her off, squeezing her to me a little tighter. "I feel it too, Sadie. I feel it in my bones. I can't stop thinking about you. I haven't been able to stop thinking about you since the coffee shop."

"I can't either. But you know we can't, right? This... tonight... it can't happen again."

I hear the words she's saying. I know she's trying to protect our careers. Careers we have both worked fucking hard to get. Our professions—coaches and reporters—aren't supposed to be friends, let alone lovers.

But she's right. And I fucking hate it.

For the first time in my life, I hate my job. I hate this situation. I hate fucking everything.

"You're probably right," I say, resigned and despising the words as they come out of my mouth.

"I know I am," she says, the sadness clear in her voice.

Despite our words, neither of us let go. We embrace each other a little tighter, swaying some more to the sounds of Memphis.

And then the song stops.

We take it as our cue to leave. We link our fingers together and walk slowly back to the hotel. Neither of us say a word. We don't need to. We are soaking in this moment and this night, knowing it can't happen again.

I want to hesitate when we approach the front of the hotel. I want something to delay us so I get just a few more minutes with her. I don't want to take her to her room. I know the second we stand in front of that door that it's the end. It will be over before we even had a chance to start.

I don't get my way, though. We make our way onto the elevator and it goes directly to her floor. We both slowly step out of the car, our hands still locked.

"I meant what I said," Sadie says, looking up at me with sad eyes as we approach her door. "Tonight was the best night of my life."

"Mine too," I say, brushing my fingers along the side of her face. She leans into my touch, and I soak up every second that I can feel her skin against mine.

"Can I ask you for one thing?"

Her words are soft, but I hear them clear as day. "Anything." And I mean it. I'll give her literally anything she asks for right now.

"I'm probably stupid for asking this. It will probably make it worse. But can I have one more—"

I don't give her a chance to finish the sentence. My lips are on hers in an instant, and I kiss her with everything I have. There is so much that needs to be said through this kiss, and I know this is the only moment I have to say it.

It's a kiss that screams what we could have been. It's a kiss to let her know how much tonight has meant to me. It's a kiss I want her to know I will never forget, and I hope she doesn't either.

When our lips part, I see the tears forming again, and I know now what I have to do. The hardest thing I've ever had to do in my life.

I have to let her go.

"Good night, gorgeous," I say, placing one last kiss on her forehead.

"Good night, Hunter."

I stand and watch as she fishes her key card out of her purse. With sad eyes that look back at me one more time, she unlocks her door and walks inside her room.

I watch as she shuts the door, and I stand there for an extra moment. I know she's not going to open it up. But I can't leave just yet.

Yet, I know I have to walk away.

12

SADIE

THE MONTH of March can suck a big fat one.

Work is tedious and slow. It's more than a month away from the draft. I write stories every day on players the Fury will likely choose—including the obvious, first-overall pick, quarterback Bryce Donald. Those stories don't take me long to write though, so most of my days are spent realizing how little I have to look forward to in my life.

I realize this every year when my work life is slow. For some reason, this year it's hitting a little harder.

I'm not admitting to myself why that is.

I go to the gym occasionally. I've met up with a few friends from the paper for dinner and drinks. And like clockwork, every Monday night, I'm at my dad's house for my weekly dinner with him, Helen, and Bethany, which is where I'm at tonight.

Want to know what also happens like clockwork? Every day I wake up and miss Hunter.

I know it's ridiculous. And silly. And totally not like me. I can't help it. The man got under my skin that night in Memphis more than any man ever has.

Before Memphis, I could safely say I had a crush on Hunter. After Memphis, I can safely say that if circumstances were different, I'd be trying not to fall too hard, too fast.

I'm officially, and regretfully, smitten.

How can I not be? He's hot as hell, funny, loves football, loves his mom, makes me smile like I've never smiled before and laugh until my stomach hurts. Add to it that he didn't make me feel self-conscious when I suggested ordering our weight in barbecue. In fact, he added more to the order to make sure we could try them all.

Then he kissed me. Then, he held me in his arms as we danced in the middle of Beale Street. And then he soothed me when my emotions became too much for me to handle. I hated crying in front of him. I'm not a crier. I didn't want to, but I couldn't help it. The man makes me feel things I didn't know I could.

I got a taste of what being with Hunter is like. And I can't let myself have another bite.

"Only one thing can make someone look like that, and that's a man," Bethany says as she catches me staring off into space as I help prep Monday-night dinner. "Spill it, sis."

I want to laugh at her calling me sis, but I don't. Yes, we are stepsisters. But our relationship has never been a close one, let alone close enough to think of each other as real sisters.

We went to the same high school, so we knew of each other when our parents started dating when we were freshmen. We weren't friends, though. Our interests and friends were polar opposite. I was a tomboy and worked for the school newspaper. She was a cheerleader whose afterschool activity was boys. I didn't own a piece of makeup, and she loved all things glitter. My tomboy ways may have slightly faded over the years, but her love of all things pink and pretty has not.

And she still loves the boys.

To this day we have very little in common. She hates sports.

She loves fashion and makeup, and is a successful cosmetologist at a hip Nashville salon. She's blond where I'm brunette. She's tiny where I have plenty of curves. We couldn't be more different if we tried.

The only thing we have ever had in common is our bad luck in the dating department. Mine I have always blamed on my job and lack of time to try to date. Hers is because, well, she has absolutely horrible taste in men.

"There's nothing to spill," I say as I move the chopped cucumbers to the salad bowl.

"I call bullshit on that," she says, mixing the salad for me as I add the last of the vegetables. "It actually surprises me. I've never seen you with that look on your face. Now me? I see that face in the mirror monthly."

"Is it really only monthly?"

She lets out a sigh of defeat. "Maybe more like weekly, but that's not the point. Come on. *Please!* You can tell me. Plus, it will make me feel better that I'm not the only one depressed and single."

I let out a chuckle because I am depressed and single. And until Hunter came along, I was never that person. My job was my only focus. I figured that if I met someone and he fit in with my life and job, then great. But otherwise, I was fine living the solo life.

Funny how your mentality changes in such a short amount of time.

Though I'm not about to tell Bethany that.

"I'm not depressed."

She tilts her head and gives me a look that screams that she's not buying it. "Really? You're not? There's no man who is keeping you up at night? No man who is driving you wild and you don't know why?"

"Nope," I say, a little too much emphasis on the *ope*. "I have no clue what you're talking about."

I hurry and move around the kitchen island, trying to find something, anything, else to chop or prep. Anything to get me out of this conversation.

"I think you do," Bethany says as she takes a seat at the island, watching me act like a lunatic. "I don't know why you won't tell me. It's not like I'll even know who you're talking about."

Now that is true. She doesn't even know what the Fury is, let alone who Hunter is. She wouldn't know a professional football coach if he was standing in front of her. I don't even know if she realizes there is a football team in Nashville.

I have wanted to talk to someone, anyone, about this. I thought if maybe I talked about Hunter, it might help dull the ache in my chest that has been there every day since I woke up in that hotel in Memphis the morning after our date. But all of my friends are in the newspaper business. I don't want them to look at me differently when I say that I committed the female sports reporter cardinal sin—falling for a coach.

But Bethany wouldn't look at me differently. Actually, my stepsister might be just the person I need right now.

"Fine," I begin, letting out a defeated breath. "Yes, I met someone. Yes, I like him. But nothing can happen between us because he's off-limits. End of story."

I find a green pepper to cut and start furiously chopping, hoping that now that I've said it out loud, I'll suddenly feel better.

I don't.

"What do you mean, he's off-limits? Is he married?"

That's her first guess? Who does she take me for?

"No, he's not married."

"Seeing someone?"

"No."

"Gay?"

I laugh. "If he is, then he has a funny way of showing it."

Her lips raise in a smile. "Is that because things have happened between the two of you that confirms the fact that he does not play for the other team?"

I can't help but laugh at Bethany, who is being very animated now describing what she assumes happened. "Yes. Something happened. And before you ask, no, we did not sleep together."

"But you want to."

Do I want to? *DO I WANT TO?* Fuck yes, I want to. I wanted to that night. I wanted to invite him into my hotel room and have a night so amazing that Memphis would have become my favorite city on the planet. I wanted to wake up in his arms and do it all over again. I wanted him to stay with me for the week and have the best vacation of my life.

Instead, I woke up alone with puffy eyes from crying all night. I then spent the next three days trying to enjoy the sights of Memphis, only to find myself missing him a little more each minute. I ended up cutting my stay short and hiding in my apartment for the rest of the week.

"Yes, I wanted to."

"So why is this man off-limits?"

"Because..." I take a breath, fortifying myself to say the words I need to. "Because he's a coach. For the team I cover. It's the definition of 'frowned upon.'"

"So?" Bethany says, giving me a confused look. "You are both adults. If he likes you and you like him, I don't see what the big deal is? It's not like you work for the same company."

How can I make her understand this?

"The big deal is that when you're a female who covers football for your job, many people assume that you don't know what you're talking about. That the only way you could possibly know about football, or get the scoop on a story, is that you are fucking someone to get it. So, imagine if people, namely my employer, found out that I was sleeping with a coach. That I was sharing a bed with a man whose employer tells him that reporters are not your friends, that in fact, they are the enemy, and that they will do anything to get a story. That is why we can't be together."

I see the moment it all clicks for Bethany, and before I know it, she's standing behind me at the island, her arms wrapped around my shoulders. And I don't know why, maybe it's the combination of her gesture and my admission, but I can't hold it in anymore.

My tears are slow as they fall down my face, and neither of us say anything for a long minute. We just stand there, letting my admission hang in the air.

"I'm sorry, Sadie. That fucking sucks."

I let out a laugh between the tears. Because she nailed it. Right on the nose.

"Yeah, it does. But what is there to do?"

The question is rhetorical. She and I both know it. What can I do? Neither of us are about to give up our careers. We're not about to let some feelings, compounded by one amazing night, get in the way of those.

Bethany gives me one more squeeze. "Sadie, I have known you for a long time. In all the years I have known you, I've never seen this look on your face. I know the situation feels impossible. And it might be, I don't know. But I do know that you shouldn't give up on it yet. Because if there was a man who put that look on my face? I'd hold on to him and never let go."

And with that Bethany takes the salad off the counter and leaves me standing in the kitchen, wondering what the hell I've got myself into.

13

HUNTER

"ARE YOU GOING TO ORDER? The menu isn't that complicated. Pick a damn sandwich and let's go."

I hear the words coming from Davis, my wide receivers' coach, but his nagging isn't making me order any faster. The only thing I can see on the Sandwich City menu is "chicken Caesar wrap." Which makes me think of Sadie.

At least today I made it until noon before she took over my thoughts. Usually it happens the second I wake up.

"I'll have the chicken Caesar wrap with fries. And a sweet tea."

"Fucking finally," he mumbles. I choose to ignore the comment as I hand my credit card to the cashier before we make our way to the other side of the counter to wait for our to-go order.

Out of habit, I can't help but look around the café, hoping I'll see a brunette with hair on top of her head staring into a computer. I do this every time I come here. And every time, I'm disappointed.

Even more so today.

This isn't the first time I've been to Sandwich City since we first met, but it is the first time since our night in Memphis. And as soon as I looked up at the chalkboard menu over the cash register, the first thing that caught my eye is that damn wrap.

I can't even get lunch without thinking about her.

"Seriously, I didn't realize lunch was such a big decision," Davis says as he turns around to face the café. From his vantage point, he can see every table. Not that I know this from experience.

"Am I not allowed to weigh my options?" I ask, wondering why the delay in my lunch order is such a big deal.

Davis turns back toward me, giving a shrug to my words. "I'm just saying, if it took you ten minutes to figure out lunch, what the hell is going to happen on draft night?"

I ball up the wrapper of my straw and throw it at him, which he easily ducks away from. I know he's saying it in jest, but the dig hits the mark.

Draft night is a pressure-cooker. The team only has a few minutes to make each selection. Luckily, I'm not the one who will be making the Fury's picks on draft night. That job is for Coach Gordon and Neil, our general manager. It is my job to present to them the best offensive players to consider. That's a big responsibility. One I don't take lightly.

Which is why I've been working Davis and the rest of my offensive coaches to the bone over the last few weeks. We've been pulling long hours at the facility scouting players and coming up with draft scenarios. It's what we need to do to make sure we have the best draft class possible.

It also helps that working long hours means less time I have to let my mind wander back to that night in Memphis, or how Sadie's lips felt against mine.

It has been three weeks since that night. Three. Long. Fucking. Weeks. I would have thought by now I wouldn't feel like this anymore. I wouldn't feel like a part of me is missing because we made the smart decision not to be together. Instead, it just gets a little worse every day.

"Oh shit," Davis says as he slaps my shoulder. "Isn't that the reporter chick from the paper? Fuck, she is fine as hell."

My head snaps to the door as soon as the words leave Davis's mouth.

Fuck, I have missed her. I know that sounds ridiculous, but I have. I realize our relationship stopped before it even had a chance to start. It's not like I went from talking to her every day to nothing. We never had a texting stage. We never even had a dating stage. But I recognize possibility when it's in front of me. And the possibilities with Sadie were endless. They made me hopeful.

Now all they do is make me wonder what I did in my twenty-eight years to have my perfect woman put in front of me, only for me not to be able to have her.

"I keep wondering when it will be my turn for an interview," Davis says, his words pulling me back to the present. "Maybe I should go to talk to her. Ask her if she wants a little one-on-one time."

"Shut the fuck up," I snap, my harsh reply taking him off guard. "You will not speak to her. Especially not like a horny fucking teenager."

Davis holds his hands up in surrender, realizing that I'm not kidding. "Damn, man. Sorry. Didn't realize you called dibs."

Is that how this is coming off? That I'm calling dibs? Fuck, that can't happen.

"I'm not calling dibs," I say, trying to get my tone under control. "I would just like it if you, as a member of my staff, would act like an adult and not a pubescent boy looking at his first *Playboy*. She's a reporter trying to do her job. She doesn't need assholes like you treating her like a piece of meat."

My words get through to Davis, who mutters an apology.

Luckily, Sadie was likely too far away to have heard what he said. Thank God.

How do I know that? Because since Davis announced her arrival, I haven't taken my eyes off of her for more than a second.

And she hasn't looked at me once.

She's dressed more casually than the last time I saw her. Her hair is back up on the top of her head, and her glasses are perched on her nose. She looks almost exactly how she did the first time I saw her in this very place.

She took my breath away then, and she's doing it again now.

What is it about this woman that makes me absolutely insane?

"Order for Hunter!"

The sound of my name gets Sadie's attention, and before I can look away, her eyes find mine. At first, there's shock. I don't blame her for that one. I might have looked around the café to find her when we got here, but I still would have been surprised if she was, in fact, here.

When the shock went away, the next emotion that passed through her eyes about broke my fucking heart. It was sadness. It was only there for a second before she looked away. But I saw it. I recognized it. I see it in my eyes every fucking day.

She's hurting just as much as I am.

I know I've been an intolerable bastard since I came back from Memphis. If that look she gave me is a glimpse of what she's feeling, then I'd bet she's equally as miserable as I have been.

Why does it have to be like this? How in the world is this fair to either of us? Why in the world do we have to suffer because of some unwritten rule that our professions have latched on to? We are responsible adults. We can keep our professional and personal lives separate.

Well, that I'm not sure about. But I know for Sadie I'd be

willing to try. Hell, I'd do about anything right now just to have a chance to see where this goes.

And just like that, a plan forms in my head.

This could completely blow up in my face.

This could be the worst decision I've made in a very, very long time.

But it's worth the risk.

"Order for Hunter! Going once! Going twice!"

I grab the to-go bags and hand them to Davis. "You go. I'll meet you back there."

He takes the bags awkwardly, not expecting me to pass them to him. "Why?"

Shit. Why am I?

"I'm going to talk to Sadie and make sure your voice didn't carry." That explanation was the first thing I could think of, even though it's a loose excuse. "Last thing I need is to have to tell HR to expect a phone call from a reporter about inappropriate comments being said about her."

His face goes white, and shit, I almost feel bad about that. But I don't because I need him out of here. And fast.

"Okay. Sorry if I caused any trouble."

I watch him leave the café and cross the street before I make my way over to Sadie. If she sees me coming, she doesn't show it. She is already typing at rapid speed, her eyes not leaving the computer.

"Is this seat taken?"

She doesn't move at the sound of my voice. In fact, she doesn't react at all.

"Fancy seeing you here."

Again, nothing. Though, this time I take her silence as a green light and sit across from her.

"What are you working on? Trying to write another story about me without me knowing?"

My questions don't get a verbal response, but at least this time I see the corner of her lip rise slightly.

And there it is. My opening.

"How about I give you a scoop?"

Her eyes snap up to mine. It was like dangling a piece of meat in front of a tiger.

"What kind of scoop?"

I curl my finger at her, asking her to come closer so I can whisper. "We're trading our first pick to Denver for a sack of potatoes, some bubble gum, and a player to be named later."

Before the joke is even out of my mouth, she balls up a napkin and throws it at me.

"You play dirty, McAvoy. You know I hear the word scoop and I forget all my senses."

I laugh, because that was way too easy. "I don't play as dirty as you do. You have to give me credit. You're talking to me, at least."

This makes her laugh and a smile adorns her face. In this moment, all the depression I have felt over the last three weeks fades away.

"Fine," she says with a playful huff. "I'm talking to you. Hello, Hunter. How are you today?"

"Much better now that you're here."

I flash her a flirtatious smile which earns me an exaggerated eye roll. "Really? That's what you're going with? You're not much of a player, ya know. You can do better than that, McAvoy."

She makes the motion to go back to her writing, but before she can, I grab her wrist. Not hard, but enough to send a shock through my body. And by the look in her eye, she felt it too.

It's the same shock that passes through us every time we touch. That can't be a coincidence, right?

"You play dirty, McAvoy," she says quietly, her eyes glancing quickly around to see if anyone is looking at us. She might have repeated her words from earlier, but this time I can hear the different meaning in them. Just with this one touch, we are both transported back to that night on Beale Street. Just one touch is reminding us both of how good we feel when we are together.

"Not as dirty as you, Benson," I say, still not letting go of her wrist.

"And how is that?"

I decide to slightly change the course of this conversation. "The first day we met, you said that you weren't a football fan. You tricked me."

She shrugs away from my hold and leans forward on her elbows, the smile on her face nothing but mischievous as my goal of lightening the mood works. "I didn't lie. I'm not a fan. I have to be unbiased as a reporter. You just assumed what the meaning of my words meant."

I also lean forward, matching her position. "Touché. Still, I feel as if you owe me."

Her eyebrow quirks up. "I owe you? If anything, you owe me. You were quite the grump that day in Birmingham. And frankly, I don't think I'm over it."

I hear the humor in her voice, even though I know I was a complete asshole to her that day. "You're right. The least I can do is cook you dinner to make up for it."

"Dinner? Hunter... we—"

I look around, making sure that no one here knows us. Or, at least, me. I know this might be my only chance to say this, and I don't want to mess this up.

"Sadie, I have been a miserable bastard since Memphis," I say, taking her hands in mine. "That night... I can't stop thinking about it. I can't stop thinking about you."

I know now that I was right earlier about the look in her eyes. It was sadness. It's the same look she's giving me now.

"I can't stop thinking about you either."

"Then why are we doing this to ourselves?" I ask, my voice rising just a bit out of the frustration of the situation.

"You know why, Hunter. The Fury would freak out on you. And me? Might as well throw the Scarlet A on me now if word got out that I was dating a coach."

"Who says it has to get out?"

My words shock her. Her eyes go wide and her jaw drops a little. Honestly? They shock me a bit, too. I don't want to hide this. I want to be free to go to lunch with my girlfriend and hold her hand and sneak a kiss across the table. But if hiding us is what I need to do to see her again, then I'm willing to do it.

"Are you saying what I think you're saying?"

I take a breath, giving her hands another squeeze. "Come over for dinner. We'll talk. We'll figure this out. Just don't make me go another night wondering what could have been."

I don't know how long we sit in silence. It's probably only a few seconds, but I swear it could have been a few hours. I know what I'm asking for is risky. Both of us could lose our jobs over this.

I also know she's worth the risk.

I start to wonder if I was smart in asking her to take this chance. That is, until I hear four amazing words from her beautiful lips.

"Send me your address."

14

SADIE

WHAT THE FUCK am I doing?

What the fuck am I doing?

What in the actual ever-loving fuck am I doing?

Dinner? With Hunter? That he made himself with his own hands? Hands that I know feel amazing when they touch me?

I can't have dinner with Hunter. At his home. Alone. Unsupervised.

Nope. This is such a bad idea. Like the worst idea in the history of bad ideas.

I'll jump him. I will see him in his home looking sexy as hell, and I will want to climb him like a fucking tree. A girl only has so much willpower, and I know I used every ounce of it that night in Memphis.

Sadie: Tell me again why I'm here?

I had this same freak out while I was getting ready, so I called Bethany for a pep talk. Her words were enough to get me out of my apartment, but apparently not strong enough to get me out of my car. Hence my needing a few more words of encouragement.

Bethany: Because as much as you want to talk yourself out of this, you know you want to go. You like him. And that's OK. Get out of your head. Enjoy the night. Text me tomorrow with all the naughty deets!

I toss my phone into my purse and take another deep breath.

I can't do this. What made me think I could do this? What spell did he have me under today when I agreed to this?

That's it. He must be some sort of wizard or something. That's the only logical explanation I can think of as to why I'm now sitting in my parked car outside his condo for a date. And not any kind of date. A date where he's cooking me dinner while likely looking all handsome and stuff. And since we're at his home, he's probably going to be casual and comfortable and all sorts of tempting.

Which means I'll want to have sex with him. More than once.

And that is such a bad idea. A really tempting, horribly bad, idea.

Maybe I'll be able to resist him. Maybe when I walk inside, I will see behind the veil that is handsome, charming, funny, sweet Hunter. Maybe he's really an asshole. Maybe his cooking will suck, and I'll have to leave on account of food poisoning. Maybe his condo will look like he lives in a frat house. Maybe there will be no furniture except for a lawn chair in the living room and a television propped up by a milk crate with a gaming system loaded with every Madden game ever made. Hell, maybe he doesn't even have a bed frame.

Guys without bed frames are douches.

As I continue to wage a war inside my brain, a knock against my car window scares the daylights out of me. So much so I almost hit my head on the top of my car from the shock.

I look to my left and see Hunter, who is laughing hysterically at me.

"Not funny," I say in mock anger as I partly open my door.

"I beg to differ. My only regret is not videoing your reaction."

I let out a huff and turn to grab my purse and the six-pack I bought that is sitting in my passenger seat. "Why did you feel the need to come out and scare the bejesus out of me?"

With a gorgeous smile and his southern manners, he opens the door for me the rest of the way as I slide out of my car. Before I know it, he's guiding me toward his condo with his hand on the small of my back, his thumb gently rubbing up and down on the outside of my blouse.

Morning breath.

Vomit.

The word moist.

"At first it was cute watching you have an internal debate with yourself about whether or not you should come in," he says as we step inside. "But the longer you sat there, the more I was worried you were going to start your car back up and go home. And I couldn't let that happen, so I decided to come out and make sure you didn't run away. The scaring you part was just an added comedic bonus."

"Well, it wasn't very nice."

He takes the beer from my hand and puts it on a small table in his foyer. I really want to keep pretending to be mad at him. But I know I can't keep it up. And by the look on his face when he turns back to me, he knows it too.

He takes my chin in his fingers, gently tilting my face up to look at him. He uses his other hand to thread our fingers together.

I didn't realize how much I missed his touch until right now.

Well, that's a lie.

"I'm sorry," he says, gently rubbing his thumb over the top of my hand. "I didn't mean to scare you."

"Well, you did." My words come out breathy, though I don't mean for them to. I can't seem to control my voice, or my body, when I'm around this man. Especially when he is looking at me like he is right now, his eyes full of desire and want.

"How can I make it up to you?"

"I'm sure you can think of something."

"Let's see if this does the trick."

His lips meet mine in the softest of kisses. But he doesn't go in for another one, or one more intense. Rather, he lets his lips trail to the corner of my mouth. To my cheek. To my jaw. To my neck.

"That… that's working."

He chuckles before working his way back up to my lips, giving them one last kiss. This one longer than the first before he backs away.

"All better?" he asks softly.

I nod because right now, I can't find my words.

"Are you still thinking about leaving?"

"I was never going to leave," I admit, my voice still low as I try to regain my composure. Even though I know this is a bad idea, and I can think of a million reasons why I should leave, I'm not.

I can't. I don't want to. Tonight I want to just be a woman who has dinner with a man who makes her feel beautiful on the inside and out. I want a Memphis Part Two.

Fuck our jobs. Fuck the stereotypes. Fuck it all.

Tonight I'm choosing me.

Tonight I'm choosing Hunter.

———

"WAIT! THAT REPORTER WAS YOU?"

I laugh before taking a sip of the beer I brought over. "One and the same."

"Why didn't you say anything before? You were a legend in our locker room for months!"

I set my beer down on the patio table. The one strategically placed between me and Hunter. "And when would it have been a good time to slip it into conversation? It's not like I can just randomly say, 'Hey, do you remember the reporter who asked your college coach an innocent question about his thoughts on paying college athletes? And do you remember the rant he went on that went viral? Guess what. That was me.'"

We fall into laughter as we enjoy the beautiful night on his patio. It is an unusually warm March night, so we decided to take advantage of it after we ate dinner.

Which was delicious. It was simple, grilled chicken with a honey mustard glaze, roasted vegetables, and baked potatoes, but the fact that he went to the trouble to cook it made it that much more special.

Which is another reason why I need a table between us. All of those possibilities that I concocted in my head about being able to resist him? He has tossed a flamethrower to every single one.

His cooking was delicious. His house is decorated perfectly to fit his style. A lot of black, white, and grays, with pops of blue scattered. He showed off his office, which was decorated with football memorabilia in every available space. His bathroom is immaculately clean.

And I might have even snuck into his bedroom to check for a bed frame. He has one. Because, of course, he does.

Then there is him. The man is more beautiful on the inside than the out. Which says a lot. I know how he made me feel in Memphis. And part of me wondered if I built that up in my head because of some magical night where the stars aligned and I danced with a prince on Beale Street.

I didn't build it up. In fact, he's more than I remembered. We haven't had a lag in conversation all night. Even now, as we tiptoe around conversations about our jobs, it still doesn't feel wrong. I know it should. But it doesn't.

I. Am. So. Screwed.

"Well, you should have said something," Hunter says, pulling me back to the present. "It would have broken up some of those asinine questions I got at my opening press conference."

I give him a sideways glance. "You better not be talking about my question."

"Of course not," Hunter says, getting up to move to the seat next to me. Shit. No more table between us. That point is emphasized as I get a hint of his woodsy cologne. "Yours was the only question that actually made me think. I like it when I have to think of an answer."

"Oh, really," I say, sitting up as I tilt my body toward his. I don't know why I do this. It's like I have this pull to him when he's near me. "I'll have to remember that the next time we're at a press conference."

We fall into a comfortable silence—the first of the night—as he reaches for my hands. Hands that I willingly let him hold.

"See, we can do this," Hunter says.

"Hunter..."

"Just listen," he says, bringing his lips to my knuckles for a kiss. Damn, that was a dirty move. "I think there are certain things we can agree on."

"And that would be?"

"Why, I'm glad you asked. I have a plan." The smile on his face right now is mischievous. All I want to do is lean over and kiss that look off of him. "I am attracted to you. And, for the sake of speeding this conversation along, I'm going on the assumption that you find me attractive as well."

"Sure. We'll go with that," I tease.

"We'll deal with that comment later," he says, picking up on my flirty tone. "We are two consenting adults who are attracted to each other. Bonus, we both enjoy spending time together. Would I be right on those two points?"

I nod. No sake in arguing with the obvious.

"Knowing those factors, and knowing that we are two determined individuals who have never let a little roadblock get in their way, it would be silly for us to not continue to do something that brings both of us happiness."

"What about—"

His finger is on my lips before I can get the next sentence out. "Our jobs. Yes, that is the elephant in the room. The Fury would be less than happy to find out that I'm spending my free time with someone who shouldn't know all the team's dirty secrets."

"And my job would rather not have to question me about whether or not I got information in a non-ethical way from my boyfriend."

"Boyfriend, huh? I like the sound of that," he says teasingly.

I give his arm a playful slap. "Let's get back to the point."

"Fine, but you can't take that word back. I like it and I'm keeping it." He gives my hand one more kiss before he continues. "I don't like this idea, but I can't think of anything else, so I'm just going to say it. What if we start seeing each other and see where this goes, but keep it between us? We owe it to ourselves to find out if this is just attraction, or if what we're feeling could be for real. But while we do that, we don't tell anyone. No one needs to know."

I let his words marinate as I replay them in my head. I know he's right. Our jobs, at least right now, cannot find out if we were to pursue this. But lying to everyone? Our families? Friends? That part doesn't sit well with me. At all.

"I hate being a dirty little secret."

"No, gorgeous," he says, scooping me so I'm now sitting on his lap. I hate that immediately I feel more at ease being in his arms. I don't want to feel this way. But apparently my body already knows what my head isn't ready to admit. "You aren't my dirty secret. God, I wish I could shout from the rooftops right now that I had dinner tonight with a woman who has had me in knots since the moment I laid eyes on her. I want to call my mom and tell her that you're my girl and I'm bringing you to dinner this Sunday. I don't like the situation. At all. But if we can do this, say for six months, and show both the Fury and *The Banner* that we can have this relationship, and keep our professional lives separate, then they have nothing to worry about."

Can we do that? Six months? Six months would be for a good portion of the upcoming season. If we can make it a season with me doing my job, Hunter doing his, and nothing happening, then neither one of our jobs could object. Well, they could. But at least now we'd have proof we can keep personal and professional lines drawn.

I have never been so torn about a decision. Everything he said is right. Can we do it? Can we keep something this big to ourselves for that long?

The alternative of not trying this is not having him in my life at all, save for the occasional interview. I then think about leaving here tonight. I think about never getting to kiss him again. I think about one day him finding a woman he wants to date, and I'll have to come to terms with the fact that she gets to feel his lips against hers.

The thought terrifies me.

"Six months," I repeat, knowing that we need to make this a clear ground rule.

"Six months. It will be no time at all. What do you say? Take a chance on us?"

He circles his arms around my waist, pulling me even closer to him before kissing my hair. I knew I was saying yes before this gesture. But right now, at this moment, somehow I know for a fact that even though there are a million reasons not to do this, I would be an idiot to walk away from Hunter.

"Let's do it."

The smile on his face is instant and infectious. "Really?"

I nod, a smile slowly forming across my face. "Really."

He doesn't say another word. Instead, he does the most perfect thing.

He kisses me like I've never been kissed before.

15

HUNTER

MINE.

That's the only word that I can think of as my lips find Sadie's. After months of wanting and wishing, of almost having then having to let her go, I can finally say that Sadie is mine.

Well, I can't say it out loud. I know we have to keep this quiet.

That doesn't change the fact that this woman is officially mine.

Kissing her on my patio might not be the best idea right now. I do have neighbors who I'm sure aren't counting on a show. But I can't seem to move from this spot. Her body feels too right as she molds herself to me. Her lips feel too good. And honestly? I'm afraid if I stop kissing her she'll decide that she doesn't want to be in a relationship where she has to hide. Or she realizes that dating me is too big of a risk.

If I keep kissing her, she can't change her mind. I'll just have to never stop kissing her.

No arguments here.

"Hunter," she says breathlessly.

"Less talking." My mouth travels from her lips to her neck.

God, it tastes so sweet. The floral scent she wears is taking over my senses. "More kissing."

She giggles. "We should move this inside."

I unbutton the top two buttons of her blouse, giving me more skin to explore. "I'm not done kissing you yet."

She brings her head back upright, cutting off my access to her neck. I dislike that immediately.

"I wasn't done kissing there."

My pout is immediately erased when I see the seductive smile come across her face. She moves closer to my ear, and just when I think she's about to start doing some exploring of her own, she does one better.

"If we go inside right now, I'll let you kiss me wherever you want."

I don't even let her walk. As soon as the words leave her mouth I have her scooped up in my arms and I'm carrying her inside.

"Hunter!" she shrieks, the happiness in her tone unmistakable. "At least turn off the lights."

I groan and turn around, but I don't put her down. Nope. I quite like carrying Sadie through my condo.

I hurry up and flip off the patio and kitchen lights. Anything else I'll deal with later. I have much more important things to attend to right now.

Like getting Sadie into my bedroom.

Then getting naked.

In that order.

"You know I could have walked," she says between giggles as I place her down on my king-size bed.

"I know you could have. Consider it my first act as your boyfriend," I say as I look down at her while I kick off my shoes and socks.

There have been many nights where I've imagined what Sadie would look like in my bed. Never in my wildest dreams did she look as breathtaking as she does right now. Her hair is fanned across my pillows, the light blue of the comforter contrasts with the dark brown of her hair. Her eyes are filled with desire and passion. She's still dressed, but I can see the curves of her body. I'm nearly salivating at the thought of having her naked underneath me.

I lower myself next to her and immediately my lips are on hers. It's like she's a magnet. Whenever I'm in proximity of her, I have to touch her in some way.

I know that's not good for the fact that we have to keep this a secret. But for right now... for tonight... I'm taking full advantage that I can kiss and touch her wherever I like.

Because she's mine.

"I thought I said we'd circle back to the boyfriend label," she says a bit breathlessly, her hips writhing as my mouth continues to explore her skin.

"I'll make you a deal," I say after kissing her one more time. "If I can make you come with just my mouth, right now, then I'm officially your boyfriend."

Her eyes shine with excitement. "And if you don't?"

"I'll just have to keep trying until I do."

I begin my exploration down her body, my lips finding a new place to kiss with each inch. I finish unbuttoning her shirt as I place kisses on the tops of her breasts.

Note to self, come back and explore more here later.

When her shirt is off, I leave a trail of kisses across her stomach. Her skin is smooth, and now that her shirt is fanned open, I can see every one of her luscious curves.

Another note to self, worship her curves at a later time.

I continue kissing her stomach as I work her pants down, taking the lace that I feel underneath them down as well. I take one second to look back up at her, and when our gazes meet... fuck... the heat that I'm seeing in her hazel eyes only propels me on.

"Lie back, gorgeous. I have to taste you."

I place a kiss on her thighs, and the smell of her sex is making me insane with want. I leave soft kisses on either side, working my way toward the center, and when I get there, I can see that she's already wet for me. I have been hard for her since we were on the patio. The sight of this? My cock is now solid steel.

"Wet for me already?" I ask, my tongue slowly beginning to work her center.

She doesn't answer. She just grinds her hips into my face, and fuck, that only makes me harder.

I'm done talking. I work my tongue over her clit, rotating between sucking, licking, and flicking, which is driving her mad by the way her body is moving on my bed, her hands clutching the comforter like she needs to ground herself.

Just driving her insane isn't my goal. My goal is to make my girl see stars. To make her know that after tonight, there will be no other man who will ever make her feel the way I can.

"Hunter... please... I'm so close."

Her words light a fire in me. I insert two fingers, which sends her hips off the bed. I place a hand over her stomach, grounding her to me. I don't know where she thinks she's going, but I'm not done yet.

I work my fingers as my tongue continues to feast on the sweetest treat it has ever tasted. And then, with one crook of my finger, I feel her still. And then I hear the hottest sound I have ever heard.

"Hunter!"

Sadie explodes on my fingers, and I'm pretty sure on my deathbed I will remember this experience. I slowly bring her down, her legs shaking as her orgasm releases.

I place one more kiss on her pussy before I get up to fetch a warm washcloth to clean her up. When I get back to my room,

Sadie is in the same position as I left her, looking spent and satisfied.

"Are you okay?" I ask, taking the washcloth to her center.

"I am more than okay... boyfriend."

I look up to find Sadie smiling back at me. I wish I had a camera right now to capture this moment. She's sitting up on her elbows, her blouse open, a white lace bra the only thing covering her. Her hair is a mess, her lips are swollen from our kisses, and she looks sated and satisfied.

In short? She's the most beautiful thing I have ever seen.

And she's not going anywhere because she's all mine.

16

SADIE

"GOOD MORNING, GORGEOUS."

Hunter's words are soft and right next to my ear, and the feel of his breath against my skin makes me squirm. I swear I don't mean to rub my ass on his dick. His very hard, very alert dick that is currently giving me the best wake-up call in the history of wake-up calls.

"Good morning, yourself," I say, rolling over on my back. Hunter is propped up on one elbow, and from this angle, half of his body is over mine. It doesn't take long for him to lean down and kiss me. A kiss I willingly accept.

If this is how I'm now woken up each morning, I could quickly get used to this.

Just the thought of that brings everything from last night back into focus.

Admitting that we both feel something for the other.

Agreeing to give this a shot.

Hunter making me come with his mouth. Holy shit, that was the best orgasm of my life.

I expected that to lead to sex. In my limited experience with men, that's how things went. Either the guy or the girl did a little foreplay, and then the sex happened. Orgasms were *to be determined* for the woman. Orgasms were always a must for the man.

But not last night. Instead of Hunter wanting his, all he did was hold me. We didn't talk about all the "what ifs." I fell asleep in his arms, the rhythmic rise and fall of his chest lulling me to sleep. At least for one night, we had a bubble around us. A bubble where we didn't have to think about the repercussions that could happen with our relationship. A bubble where we didn't have to hide our feelings for each other.

Last night was just about being together.

And it was incredible.

As soon as his lips release mine, I feel the bubble burst. And by the look in his eyes, he does too.

"We need to figure this out," I say, my voice low and a bit sad.

"I know," he says, giving me one more kiss at the corner of my mouth. "But can we at least do it with coffee?"

"If we don't do it over coffee, there will be no relationship to have. I need caffeine, boyfriend."

This makes him smile. "I'd hate to upset my girlfriend one day in. Let's go."

I stay in bed as Hunter puts on joggers and a T-shirt. I let him leave the room before I get out of bed and find one of his T-shirts to slip on. It hangs down to my mid-thigh and is in no way sexy. At least, I don't think so.

When I walk into Hunter's kitchen his eyes turn to fire. The look he is giving me right now, one of appreciation and desire, is thrilling. The smile on his face is downright dirty.

I wonder what his thoughts on kitchen sex are?

"What are you smiling at?" I say, taking a seat on one of the barstools around his island.

"Well, a few things," he says, placing a cup of coffee in front of me. "First, I really, really, like you wearing my T-shirts, and I think that should be your standard-issue clothing when you are over here. But before that, I remembered something from last night."

"I remember a lot of things from last night," I say, smiling over my cup as I take a sip.

"You better," he says, taking a seat across the island from me. "What I was remembering was when we went upstairs to my bedroom. My door was open. I didn't realize it last night because, well, let's just say I was focused on very specific things. But for some reason this morning, I remembered that I thought I had shut my door before you came over. Do you have any idea how that happened?"

Fuck. I am so busted.

"I don't know what you speak of," I say, though I'm looking everywhere but at him. I could tell in his tone he's not mad. In fact, I know he's teasing me. But if I admit this, then I admit a level of crazy I'm not sure I'm ready for him to know about.

"I think you do."

I finally make eye contact, and the smile on his face, the small one that says he knows my secret, melts me on the spot.

Dammit. This man is going to have me eating out of the palm of his hand with just one look.

"Fine," I say, taking a breath before admitting this. "I might have snuck a peek to see if you were hiding anything."

Hunter laughs, which is good. At least right now my act of crazy is still amusing. "Like a dead body or something?"

"No. I wanted to see if you had a bed frame."

His look turns to confusion. "A bed frame?"

I let out a sigh. Here it goes.

"You are perfect. In every way. You probably even work at soup kitchens in the offseason. I was trying to find one way you weren't. So, before dinner, when I went to use the bathroom, I might have taken a quick look inside your room. I was *really* hoping you didn't have a bed frame to prove that there is *SOMETHING* wrong with you."

His laugh is instant and takes over his body. And I must admit, now that I said it out loud, it is funny. Crazy. But funny.

"Well," he says, getting up from his stool to walk around the island so we are now on the same side. "There is something wrong with me."

I turn to watch him walk toward me, which is exactly what he wanted. His hands are now on both sides of me, clutching on to the island, caging me in between him.

"And what is that?" I say as I look up at him.

"I haven't kissed you in way too long."

"Well." My voice is breathless as I loop my hands around his neck. "We better remedy that."

———

"WE REALLY NEED TO TALK."

This is the first time I've had a chance to voice that thought. Hunter has been otherwise keeping my lips occupied for most of the morning. Our kissing went from the kitchen to the living room. And though we frustratingly stayed clothed, I can think of a lot worse ways of starting my day than by making out with Hunter McAvoy.

"Do we really need to?"

At least, that's what I think he says. It came out mumbled as his head was buried between my boobs.

"Yes," I say, lifting his head up. His mouth is in a pout and... damn, this man is freaking adorable. "If we're going to do this, we can't just wing it."

"Fine," he says, sitting up to face me on his couch. "I think our first rule is that you spend the night as much as possible."

"And how do you see that working?" I don't hate the idea, I'm just curious.

"Well, it would be a lot like last night. You come here. We eat dinner. You sleep here. At some point we get naked. You wake up naked with me. Done and done. What's next on the list?"

I laugh, loving the simplicity of his answer, even if I have much bigger things on my mind. "Hunter, be serious."

He takes my hand in his, and already his touch calms my nerves. "You tell me what you're concerned about, and we'll figure out how we handle it."

I take in a breath, which gives me a second to decide what I want to talk about first. "Well, actually, the first thing did have to do with... seeing each other. My apartment is within walking distance of *The Banner*. And the parking sucks. There is a very good chance someone could see you if you came to my apartment."

"Fine. You'll come here, then."

"Is it safe?"

He nods. "As far as I know, no one from the team lives around here. Most of the players live downtown, and the rest of the coaches are in the suburbs. See. I figured out our first problem and you didn't even know it."

This makes me laugh. "Okay. Next problem, Mr. I Have It All Figured Out. You know we can't go out on dates like a normal couple. We can't go downtown just to catch some music. We can't chance being seen. Are you okay with that?"

"That does suck," he says, giving the tops of my knuckle a brush with his thumb. "That just means I'll have to get creative on date nights. And it also means a lot more being naked."

All I can do is laugh because this man has an answer for everything. We agreed that we needed to try to keep our distance from each other when we were both at the Fury facility, at least for now, as to not accidentally give off any weird vibes. We agreed that in the times we do have to see each other at work, we need to be as casual as possible. And, just in case we left our phones anywhere or in plain sight, our numbers are now saved as "boyfriend" and "girlfriend."

His choice. He's very excited about this title, obviously.

We even set ground rules for the nights that I might have to bring work home with me. Simply, he can't comment on anything I'm working on. To make things fair, he said he would make sure to keep game plans under lock and key, so I didn't get an inside look at what the Fury might be planning for their next opponent.

"See! This is simple," Hunter says, moving closer as he wraps his arm around my shoulder. "We should write the handbook on having a secret relationship."

"Don't get too excited there. We haven't dealt with one major topic."

"And that is?"

"Our families."

And with that one word, I can tell that I have let the wind out of Hunter's sails. So, I move a little closer to him, hoping that I can soothe his worries as he's done for me so much already.

"I don't want to lie to my family," I say, my fingers playing with the fabric of his T-shirt. "I've never held back anything from my dad. I'm a little nervous to tell him, but I don't want to lie either."

He kisses my hair, and in some way, I think it comforts him as much as it does me. "I don't want you to lie to them. You do whatever makes you feel comfortable."

"I also don't want to make you uncomfortable. We're in this together."

He lifts my chin so we're now looking at each other. "I know my family dynamic is completely different than yours. If you can trust your family and you feel it's safe, then tell them. Hell, I'll come over for dinner. I'll meet your dad and win him over. I just don't want you to think that if I don't tell my family, it's because I'm ashamed of you. And if it were just my mom and Whitley, then I'd be calling them now and telling them all about you. But Bo... I don't know how he'll react. He'll probably tell me that dating a reporter is just one more dumb move that I've made in my life. And I don't... I can't... he doesn't get to tell me anything about this."

I place a kiss on his chest, hating that he has to deal with that.

"Is there anything else?" Hunter asks.

"Yes, there's one more thing."

"What is it?"

I lift my head up, then promptly straddle him on his couch. "It's been a long time since you've kissed me."

17

SADIE

I KNEW at some point by dating Hunter that there would be a time when we would be at one another's houses, both of us doing work.

More specifically, both of us doing work while trying not to look at what the other one is doing.

I just didn't think it would happen so soon. Yet, this is how we have been every night for the past week.

We are three days away from the draft, which means both of us have been fairly busy. Well, Hunter more so than me. I've been writing two to three stories a day about guys they could possibly pick. I've also written every story I possibly could on Bryce Donald, the quarterback whom they would be idiots to not pick first overall. Not that I know this from Hunter. We have been keeping our word and not talking about what we are working on.

I sit on the sectional and work diligently on my laptop. He has created his space on his dining room table. That's his zone. He has been poring over draft videos and scouting reports, even after he and the coaches leave the facility for the night. It's like he's making it his personal mission to know the life story of every player in the draft.

Want to know what he doesn't know? What it's like to have sex with me.

We have been together for one month. One month since we said that we'd give it a try.

In that one month, we've learned a lot about each other. He has learned that I can't cook a thing. He's made it his mission to teach me how to make grilled cheese. I burned the first two attempts, so it's not looking good. We figured out that we like the same pizza toppings, which is quite convenient on the nights that I ruin dinner. I've learned that he has never seen an episode of *Game of Thrones*. We're now in a serious binge of that.

However, he doesn't know if I like to be on the top or the bottom. I don't know if he's a rough or gentle lover.

Why haven't we had sex yet? I have my theories, though I haven't asked him. Because... well, how do you ask your boyfriend why he doesn't want to have sex with you *without* seeming desperate?

So, I wait. And wonder. And continue to write my stories on his couch while he talks to himself about draft scenarios at his dining table.

"You okay over there?" I ask, his grumbles getting louder.

"I'm just trying to go through different scenarios for the second round."

I could have guessed that. That's all he's been doing for the past two days.

ALL he's been doing.

I'm usually never this horny. Hell, it's been years since I've even had sex. But just a few orgasms from Hunter now have me all sorts of hot and bothered.

"You should take a break," I say, my eyes still focused on my story. "You've been working all day. You're not solving the draft puzzle tonight."

I hear him let out a sigh, and he comes over to the sectional where he promptly moves my computer to the coffee table and puts his head on my lap.

"Maybe I wasn't done writing?" I say teasingly, my fingers beginning to play with his hair.

This must be having a good effect on him because he nuzzles deeper into my leg. It's like he's a cat. "You were."

"How do you know that?"

"Because when you're writing on a deadline, you always bite your bottom lip because you're concentrating. When you are trying to work ahead, you are much more relaxed."

I smile and lean down to place a kiss on his head.

"I didn't realize you were paying that much attention to me." What man notices those little things? Especially one who I thought was so in his zone that he barely realized I was even here?

He gives my leg a small kiss. "I notice everything about you."

Well, not everything. Or else he'd realize that I'm going out of my mind for him.

"You think very loudly," he comments, though he's still not looking up at me. "What's going through that brain of yours?"

"I'm sorry. Was my thinking getting in the way of your draft strategizing? Or was I slacking on the head rub."

"Ha ha. You've got jokes," he says, rolling over so now he's looking up at me. "What's on your mind, gorgeous?"

Can I just tell him? Is it that easy? He was honest with me when he said we should give this a try. The least I can do is give him the same courtesy.

"Just say it, Sadie."

I take in a deep breath. Here goes nothing. "Are you not attracted to me?"

This makes him sit straight up. "Are you out of your mind? Why would you think that? I'm borderline obsessed with you."

"Because…" I let my words trail, because damn, this is hard to say. "Why haven't you tried to have sex with me?"

I don't know what response I was expecting from such an intimate and vulnerable question. What I wasn't expecting, laughter.

But that's what he does. The asshole laughs.

"This isn't funny."

This only makes him laugh some more. "Oh, baby. If you only knew."

Now I'm just pissed. "Care to enlighten me since I'm *clearly* not in on the joke?"

Hunter moves toward me and somehow scoops me up off the couch and sets me so I am sitting across his lap.

"First off, if you don't know this by now, I think you are perfect in every way. Which makes me hate this all that much more that I can't give you a normal relationship," he begins, his fingers softly stroking the side of my face. "We don't get to date. We are cocooned in this bubble. So I didn't want to rush the sex. I wanted to give us time to get to know each other and get a handle on our normal, because nothing that we do will be conventional. I thought if we waited, at least that was something normal I could give you. Looking back, I should have told you my grand plan. I'm still getting used to this boyfriend thing. I'm sorry."

"Well, I guess that makes sense," I say, my voice just above a whisper.

"Sadie," he says, his lips now just a few inches from mine. "I want you every second of every day. There is not a minute that goes by that I don't wish I knew how it felt to be inside you. I just want to make sure we don't rush into anything."

I close the distance between us, fusing our lips together. As soon as I open my mouth, he slips his tongue inside. We have mastered this. If there were awards to win for kissing, we'd take first place every time.

But I want more. And now I know, so does he.

"Take me to bed, Hunter."

He doesn't waste a second. Much like he did that first night, Hunter carries me up to his room. Only this time I don't object.

My mouth is on his neck as he takes the steps two at a time. They only leave his skin when he places me down on his comforter. He immediately joins me in bed. Our lips find their way back to each other as our hands are frantically trying to unbutton and remove every piece of clothing we have on.

"I am so sorry I kept us waiting," he says as his lips travel down to my breasts.

"No. Don't apologize." I mean it. His admission made my heart melt a little more for this man. "But don't make me wait anymore."

And he doesn't. He rolls to the side of the bed and takes a condom out of his bedside table. He doesn't take long to cover himself and find his way back to me.

"I'll never make you wait again."

Then he enters me.

And it was absolutely worth the wait.

18

HUNTER

AND WITH THE first pick of the 2020 draft, the Nashville Fury select... Bryce Donald, quarterback, Clemson.

As the words leave the commissioner's mouth, our draft room goes absolutely insane. Grown men jump out of their chairs and start hugging the first person near them. Manly, back-slapping hugs, of course. We're a professional football team, after all.

Though, we've known Bryce was our top pick from the moment I stepped foot into the Fury facility four months ago, hearing it being said out loud, in front of thousands of fans and millions of people watching at home, makes it official.

This is the player who's going to turn the franchise around. And as the offensive coordinator, it's my job to make sure that happens.

"We got our guy," Coach Gordon says to me, adding in a backslap for good measure.

"Hell yeah, we did," I say, excitement pouring out of me. "Now we need to nail the next six rounds."

"From your mouth to God's ears, son."

The only round that happens tonight is the first—the league and the television broadcast determine that. Since we had the first pick and we don't plan on making any trades, our night is technically over. Yes, we have some assistants keeping an eye on things to make sure nothing gets crazy and to see which players are selected, but for the most part, the heavy lifting is done for the night.

"When do you have to go in for interviews?" I ask Coach Gordon. I'm genuinely curious. It has nothing to do with me wondering when he's going to see my secret girlfriend.

A secret girlfriend who gave me a good luck blow job before I had to leave for the facility today.

She's the fucking best.

"In a few minutes. Which is why I came over here. Do you mind coming in with me?"

My body goes still at his request. "Me? You want me to come with you? For the interviews?"

I'm shocked. Reporters rarely want to talk to coordinators, which was another reason why Sadie and I have been hopeful this can work. We figured we could make it through a few interviews during the season and keep our cool.

Apparently, we are testing that theory earlier than we both thought.

"Is there another Hunter McAvoy? Yes you. The Mob thinks it's a story that a new offensive coordinator gets a bright new shiny quarterback to play with in his first season. Or some shit like that."

The Mob is the nickname that Coach Gordon has for the reporter pool. He's not a fan of the media. At all. And that's actually putting it lightly. One time he said that they were a waste of space on Earth and didn't deserve to share the same air as the rest of humanity. I don't even want to imagine what his reaction would be if he found out about me and Sadie.

"Well, we'd hate to have an angry mob on our hands. Just let me know when it's time."

This is fine. Everything is fine. I'll run to the bathroom, splash a little bit of cold water on my face and get my head right. It's just a few questions. About a player I've been scouting and talking to every day for the past two months.

Questions asked by your secret girlfriend.

Yup. Everything is fine.

Coach Gordon gives me a slap on the back, which might be just as effective as the cold splash of water. "No time like the present. Let's go and get this over with."

"Now? As in, right now?" I almost choke on my words. Can't the man give me five minutes?

Coach Gordon gives me a questioning look. "You have somewhere else to be?"

I give my head a shake because he's going to realize something is up.

Get your fucking shit together, Hunter.

"No, sir. Let's do this."

We head to the interview room where we held my introductory press conference. Paul is there to meet us, and when he opens the door, the sight in front of me is much different than what I remember from January.

There aren't as many reporters this time. Now it's just the local group. The television cameras are still in the back. A few photographers are on the floor in the front. The group of middle-aged men are again congregated in the middle of the seating area.

And then I look to the front row and there she is. My girl. Typing away like her life depends on it.

I can't help but smile. She's in her element. Yes, she's sexy and kind and funny and makes me feel like I can conquer the world. But she's also independent and determined and motivated and that's just as sexy as anything else.

Except for the time she wore my old college football jersey to bed. That shit was fucking hot.

"Drafting Bryce Donald put that smile on your face?"

The comment comes from one of the male reporters, and I'm immediately reminded that I'm here to do my job, not to drool over my girlfriend.

Game face on, McAvoy. Don't fuck this up.

"For sure," I say, plastering on my camera-ready smile. "You draft one of the highest-rated quarterback prospects in years and see what kind of smile is on your face."

My banter works, and the middle-aged men laugh at my response. Sadie, though, doesn't look up from her computer. Even though we don't make eye contact, I see a slight smile break through as she shakes her head like I told the worst dad joke she's ever heard.

Before I can make eye contact with her, Coach Gordon and I take our seats, and the questions start coming at us like rapid fire. Most are about Bryce. Some are about what we plan to do over the next two days of the draft. Most are basic questions that anyone who has been interviewed can see coming a mile away. And yet again, Sadie hasn't asked anything.

"Last question."

Sadie raises her hand and Paul calls on her. I wonder what she has up her sleeve?

"Coach Gordon, you have never had a rookie quarterback start on any team you've coached during your career. Are you confident that Bryce could be the first, or are you looking to pick up a veteran in free agency to allow him a year to learn?"

And I'm hard.

I could be on my deathbed, knowing all the knowledge I'll ever know on this Earth, and I will still not know the answer as to why when Sadie Benson talks football, I get hornier than a virgin on prom night.

I have no clue how Coach Gordon answers Sadie's question.

As soon as the words left her mouth, all I heard was Charlie Brown's teacher from all the *Peanuts* specials talking. Somehow, by the grace of God, I do hear her question to me.

"Coach McAvoy, what do you think? Could he start in the opener? Do you think Bryce is the future of this franchise?"

Coach McAvoy.

Holy hell, why does that turn me on so much?

Focus, Hunter. Focus!

"We wouldn't have drafted him if we didn't think he was the future of our franchise," I say, my eyes meeting hers. I give her credit, she's keeping her game face on better than I am. Or so I'd guess. "Bryce is a more than capable quarterback and if he does the right things and works hard, the job could be his this season."

Sadie nods her head, signaling that she has the answer she was looking for, but I'm not done.

"The future doesn't have to wait. The future can start right now. Tonight is the beginning of a new era of Fury football."

Her eyes are now locked on mine in a questioning look. If I had to guess what she was trying to convey to me, it would be something along the lines of, "you've answered my question, now shut the hell up."

But I don't. I need to say the next words. I need to tell her this. "Will it take work? Yes. Will it have some highs and lows? Yes. But tonight we made a choice, and every choice we make this weekend will affect our future. We will stand by those choices because they are what we think is best for our team and for our future. We can't wait to see what comes next."

I don't know where that speech came from. It's like looking at her in this room made me see everything that I have in front of me. My job. Our relationship. The future. For the first time in my life, I have everything I have ever wanted, as well as a few things I didn't know I needed.

I stand up from the table and steal one more glance at her

before Paul escorts me out. She's not looking at me, so I can stare at her an extra second. And I don't know what she's saying, but I swear I see her talking to herself.

Did she just mouth the word diarrhea?

19

SADIE

DIARRHEA.

Socks with sandals.

Bleu cheese.

Those things aren't even disgusting enough for me to shake away the butterflies that Hunter's speech just gave me.

And I fucking hate bleu cheese.

Never in a million years when I asked him that question did I expect a monologue that not only had to do with the Fury, but also our relationship. At first, I thought I might be reading too much into it. No way, during the first time that we had to be in the same room together around people whom we have to hide our relationship from, would he do that.

Oh, but he did. When our eyes met, I knew I wasn't imagining it. His gaze was locked on me. It's like there wasn't another person in the room.

And as much as it freaked me out, it also sent a feeling through my body that I hope never goes away when it comes to Hunter.

When he was done, I couldn't look at him. I had to avert my eyes because I didn't trust myself. I had to whisper to myself three massively grotesque things, or else I was likely to follow Hunter back to his office and jump him.

As soon as it was appropriate, I bolted out of my seat and made a beeline for the reporter's work room at the Fury's facility. I hurry and get to my chair at my workstation and take three deep breaths as I sit down.

Holy hell, that was intense.

I allow myself a minute to gather my thoughts before I start writing. I have to. It's the only way I'll be able to concentrate.

I take those minutes to look around the other workstations in the pressroom. The Fury added a workspace for the reporters a few years ago when they did a remodel. We all have our own areas that they insisted we decorate to make us feel more comfortable. Which is nice of them. I'm here more than I'm ever at my desk at *The Banner*.

The decorations are what I'd assume to be typical for a group of sports writers. Some have pictures of their wives and kids displayed. Others have bobbleheads or an assortment of sports memorabilia. Me? There's a picture of me and Dad at a UT game. There's one of me, Dad, Helen, and Bethany at Christmas. There's no picture of a significant other. Not that I ever had one to hang up.

And even now that I do, I can't.

With that sobering thought, I open my phone, meaning to go to the voice recording app that I use to record press conferences. I do this with every intention of beginning to transcribe the interviews. Instead, my finger clicks to my photos.

Staring back at me is the last photo I took.

One of me and Hunter from last night.

The draft is a very long, very tiresome, grind for the both of us. All either of us wanted to do was relax before the insanity of the draft began. For us, that meant Chinese delivery and a few episodes of *Game of Thrones*. At some point, we found ourselves lying on the couch, his arms wrapped around me with my back to his front. I love that position. Every time he holds me like that, I feel… cherished. Safe. Dare I say loved.

So, I grabbed my phone and snapped a picture of us. Us cuddling, me feeling cherished.

I could stare at this picture all day. We look so content. Like we don't have a care in the world. Like we aren't keeping a secret that could ruin both of us.

I swipe to the next photo. We are in the same position, but this time Hunter is kissing my cheek as I laugh. What the picture doesn't show is that he started tickling me after he realized I took the first picture.

I look back up at my empty desk area and let out a sad sigh. I would love nothing more than to print these out and hang them at my workstation. That's what people in relationships do, right? I know I can't, though. I know it's foolish to even fantasize about it. It can't happen, so why waste time and energy even thinking about it? We still have at least five months before we can even think about telling people about us.

That doesn't stop me from wanting it.

"Earth to Sadie! Yoo-hoo! You there?"

I almost drop my phone at the sound of Tommy shouting in front of me. I scramble to lock my phone and quickly put it face down next to my computer.

"Jesus Christ, you scared me," I say as my hand covers my heart.

He laughs. "You were staring at your phone like it was hypnotizing you. Do we need to have a talk about screen time?"

"Ha ha, old man," I say, quickly rebooting my laptop back to life, hoping that avoids any suspicion of what I was doing. "You can talk to me about screen time when you finally figure out how to download an app by yourself."

Tommy waves off my comeback, and we both turn to get to work.

Phew. That was close.

"I wonder who they are picking tomorrow?" someone says out loud as I begin working on my next story. "Larry, you get any inside information?"

"Well, it could go a few ways," Larry begins, a smugness to his voice. It makes my skin crawl. "I think they will try to draft that receiver from Oregon. And you know, when I was talking to the coaching staff last week, they all but told me that if Cole Campbell wasn't drafted, that he was their guy."

A snort comes out of my mouth before I can hold it back. I *really* didn't want to be in this conversation—I just wanted to get my work done and go home, but apparently my lack of self-control is making that impossible.

"Why are you laughing, Benson?" Larry says in a challenging way. "You don't think they'll try to get Campbell? They would be stupid not to. You *do* know who Cole Campbell is, right? Or do you need me to fill you in?"

Larry has never been a fan of mine. In fairness, it's not me, specifically. It's my gender. He's one of those old-school, *women belong in the kitchen and not the locker room* kind of guys. One of his favorite things to do is to try to call me out on something I don't know.

He has never succeeded.

And tonight is not the night he does.

Not today, Satan.

"Yes, I know who Cole Campbell is," I say, turning to face him and the rest of the reporters who are now staring at us like this is a duel straight out of the Wild West. "I don't think anyone in here needs me to read his bio, but in case anyone forgot, he's a six-foot-eight offensive lineman who has played with, and protected Bryce Donald since they played Pop Warner football together in Ohio. They have been on the same team since they were six years old. The only reason he did not go in the first round is because he had an off-season knee surgery that pushed him back to a second-day pick. So, therefore, it would absolutely be idiotic to *not* draft the player who knows your new franchise quarterback better than any person on the planet. And I knew *all* of that information, and I didn't have a meeting with the coaches last week. It must feel *really good* being in the know like that, Larry. Really, it was a good scoop on your part. I one day hope to be as good of a reporter as you."

Larry's face turns beet red, and I hear snickers from the other guys as I put my earbuds in and get to work.

Another day, another idiot I had to prove myself to.

Maybe one day it won't be like this. Today is not that day.

I'm just about to get in a groove on this story when I feel my cell phone vibrate next to me. I flip it over and quickly look around to make sure no one is peeking over my shoulder when I read this.

Boyfriend: *You are so fucking hot.*

I can't help but laugh at his out-of-the-blue text. I mean, I'll never get tired of Hunter saying that to me, but why now? The press conference has been over for almost an hour now. If he was going to text me, I figured it would be right after.

Girlfriend: *And what do I owe this text message to?*

Boyfriend: *I had to walk past the workroom, and I heard you dropping the hammer on Larry. I fucking love it when you talk football. Instead of sexting, you should just talk football to me, bonus points if there's a boob picture that accompanies the text.*

I let out a laugh, but quickly catch myself. As I take a look around, it seems that everyone has headphones in and is busy typing away. Thank God.

Girlfriend: *I'll keep that in mind next time I need to seduce you.*

Boyfriend: *I doubt you'll ever need to try and seduce me. Your beauty does it every time I see you.*

Was that cheesy? Yes. Does it give me the butterflies in my

stomach that I've now coined it the Hunter McAvoy Feeling? Also, yes.

Girlfriend: You need to stop texting me. I'm smiling so big someone might notice.

Boyfriend: Who knew me making you smile was a bad thing? I like making you smile. It's a great honor as the boyfriend to make you smile.

Girlfriend: It's not. It's just... never mind. Don't you have players to draft or something?

Boyfriend: You know not until tomorrow. But fine. I get it. You have to work, and me texting you makes you think of inappropriate things. I'll stop texting you. =)

Girlfriend: Thank you. Talk to you later. <3

I'm just about to put my phone down when another message comes through.

Boyfriend: Wait! I need to tell you something first.

I have no idea what I'm waiting on. I thought he was going to send another reply right away, but he doesn't. It's almost a full minute before I get his next one.

Boyfriend: I hate that you had to defend yourself to that asshole, but I've never been prouder of you. Keep kicking ass, gorgeous. <3

My smile is so big now that I'm sure someone is bound to notice. But I don't care.

That Hunter McAvoy Feeling is too big to suppress.

20

HUNTER

"IS THAT IT?"

I regret the question as soon as it leaves my mouth. I think we're done. But the way I worded the question leaves room for Coach Gordon to say, "no, there's more to do."

I'm sure there is more to do. I just hope it can wait until tomorrow. My body and brain are drained. I feel like I haven't left the Fury facility in days.

The draft started Thursday and ended Saturday. It's now Sunday, and the entire day has been spent making offers to undrafted players we want to invite to training camp. That's almost as grueling as the draft process.

The last four days have been a blur of adrenaline and exhaustion. It was all worth it, though, because we fucking nailed it. Every analyst on all the major television networks are saying we knocked the draft out of the park, highlighted by drafting Bryce Donald and Cole Campbell. Our team is better today than it was earlier in the week. We are already being predicted to go back to the playoffs.

This week was a rush like I'd never experienced. But now it's over and my body is crashing. All I want is to go home, order a pizza, and curl up on the couch with my girl.

"Nah. Get out of here, McAvoy," Coach Gordon says, waving me off. "You've done good work this week, son. A lot of what we did this week was because of you."

His praise hits me square in the gut. I shouldn't react like this. It was just a few words from a superior to an employee. But when you grow up and never hear words like that, they take on a whole new meaning when you hear them.

"Thanks, Coach. Just doing my job," I say, hoping to sound nonchalant at his praise as I gather up my tablet and notebooks. "I'll see you tomorrow."

If he says anything else, I don't hear it. Before I'm even out the door, I have my cell phone out, hitting dial on Sadie's number.

"Yeah."

Sadie's greeting takes me off guard. I didn't expect her to gush over the sound of my voice, but a little more than a mumbled syllable would have been nice.

"Nice to talk to you too."

I hear her let out a sigh as I open the door to my truck.

"I'm sorry. That probably sounded bitchy."

"Not very. Just a little. I'm sure I can find ways for you to make it up to me."

Usually my playful banter makes her laugh, but this time, nothing.

Oh shit. Did I do something wrong? If I did, I'd like to know what. I've barely talked to her since the draft started. We've exchanged a few texts, but that was it. We were both going to be so busy we decided to not spend the night with each other so we didn't have to coordinate our schedules.

"Is everything okay?" I ask.

"Yeah," she says, sounding defeated. "The website crashed at the paper. I had two stories I had saved in the system that are now gone. The one time I don't back them up to my computer, this happens."

"I'm sorry," I say, backing my truck out of the Fury's parking lot. "What can I do?"

"Nothing, unfortunately." I hear her fingers typing away between her words. "It also means I probably won't make it over tonight. I have at least another hour of work left, and I'm too exhausted to even think about going anywhere after that."

I check the time on my dashboard. It's just past seven o'clock.

"When was the last time you ate?" I ask her, developing a plan as I drive away.

"What time is it?"

"Seven."

"I had a bagel sometime before noon."

Well, that's unacceptable. So is the thought of not seeing Sadie tonight.

"All right, here is the plan. Text me your building code. I'll be over in an hour."

"Hunter, someone might—"

"No. Don't finish that sentence. Just do what you're told. Keep writing and I'm going to make everything better."

I don't know how, but I know she's smiling now. "You are a bossy boyfriend."

"I am. And I don't like it when my girlfriend is grumpy. Get your work done. I'll see you soon."

———

"GET IN HERE, YOU BEAUTIFUL MAN."

Now that's the greeting I was looking for when I called earlier. I lean down to kiss her, but I'm not fast enough. She has already stolen the pizza box from my hands, leaving me standing alone with my lips puckered at her doorway.

"It's good to see you too."

She puts the pizza box down and quickly makes her way back toward me, jumping into my arms. My hands immediately cup her ass as I hold her close as we kiss each other like we haven't seen each other in years, rather than just a few days.

God, I've missed her.

I know we haven't been dating long, but I am already used to her sleeping next to me. The last three nights just felt... off. I reached over the first night to bring her back into my arms and she wasn't there. My bed felt empty.

It wasn't just the lack of sex or sleeping arrangements. I missed talking to her. I missed the way she does a little dance each morning when she's brushing her teeth. I miss how she always tucks her head into my shoulder when we get into bed, but always rolls away after five minutes to get into her sleep position.

Fuck... I've got it bad.

"That's much better," I say, giving her one more kiss as she slides down my body.

"I'm sorry. I'm moody when I'm hangry."

"Noted," I say, closing the door behind me. "Did you get all your work done?"

She grabs plates out of the cupboard as I join her in the kitchen, my arms instinctively going around her waist. "I just hit send on my last one. Thank you for coming over here. I know my apartment isn't the best... but—"

I lean down and place a kiss on her cheek. "It's fine. I know your apartment is close to your work and someone could see me, but it's Sunday night. I doubt anyone saw me come in. Plus, I have been curious about where you live."

"It's not much," she says, wiggling out of my hold to grab us each a beer before escorting me to her living room. "It's small, but it's just me. And I'm barely here. Doesn't make sense to spend money on a big place for it to go to waste."

She's not wrong, though I won't say that out loud. Her space is small. I'm fairly certain her entire apartment is the first floor of my condo. But it's not the size of the space that has me curious. It's the fact that I'm the one who just moved to Nashville, but she's the one who looks like she just moved in.

There are barely any photos. A few on her refrigerator. One on her TV stand. The furniture is nice, but sparse. There are no decorations or anything that gives her apartment life.

Hell, even I have accent pillows. I mean, my sister, Whitley, made me get them, but still.

"Go ahead. Ask it," she says as we take a seat on her couch.

"What?"

Was I that transparent?

"I can see the wheels in your brain turning. If I had to guess, you're probably saying to yourself, 'Damn. She was checking to see if I had a bed frame and she doesn't even have coasters.'"

Well, shit. I guess I am.

"This has nothing to do with the bed frame," I say, kicking off my shoes. "You just didn't strike me as a girl who would have a barely decorated apartment. I'm not judging. It just surprised me."

She takes a bite of her pizza before answering. "I have my reasons."

"I'd love to hear them."

I realize now how much about Sadie I still don't know. I know what side of the bed she likes to sleep on. I know her Chinese food order. I know the spot to kiss when I want to make her squirm. It's things like this, though, me here tonight, in her space, going behind the curtain, that is still foreign territory to me.

"If you didn't know by now, I'm a bit of a workaholic," she begins.

"Yes, I do," I say, taking a second to brush my fingers down the line of her face. "It's a very attractive quality."

She laughs. "Well, you are the first guy to ever think that. It's why I don't date. I tried a few times, but none of them could handle my irregular hours, or the fact that I'm always on call, so none of them proceeded to the level of 'want to come over.' As for friends, I have a few, other reporters, but none of them ever come over here. I'll go to their houses or we'll meet for dinner or drinks. It's just me and my job. And this apartment works for that. I have my desk. And a spot at my kitchen counter. That's all I need. The other stuff isn't necessary."

She tries to say that last part with vibrato, but I'm not buying it. I doubt she talks about this often, or to anyone, and I love the fact that she trusts me with this part of her. I could break the silence, but I'm not going to. Instead, I tuck a loose strand of hair behind her ear, hoping that my touch eases her nerves.

"I guess I just never felt the need to decorate for just myself," she continues, her voice now a bit more somber. "When it's just me and my laptop, what's the point? Until tonight, it's not like I had anyone to impress."

I hear the sadness in her voice, and then it hits me. Did she say what I just think she did? "Are you telling me that I'm the first person to be in your apartment?"

She nods and a bitter laugh comes out. "Pathetic, right? I've lived in Nashville for five years and you are my first house guest. Only tonight did it even hit me that maybe I should have a plant, or coasters, or... I don't know, a basic Live, Laugh, Love sign or something."

The way she says those words breaks my heart a little. This girl is so strong on the outside. She'll go toe to toe with doubters and Internet trolls all day. She'll work her ass off to prove her worth to everyone she can. She has given so much of herself to be the best reporter she can be, that she doesn't know who she is when she's *not* doing that. I know a few decorations isn't a big deal on a grand scale, but it's just one of I'm sure a dozen ways she's put herself on the back burner in the name of her career.

Well, that ends tonight, if I have my way.

"Come here," I say, putting down my plate so I can bring her in my arms. She immediately melts against my chest. "You know you aren't pathetic, right? I could come up with a hundred words to describe you, and that one wouldn't even cross my mind."

She shrugs. "I'm twenty-seven years old and I don't have coasters. Are you sure this is what you want out of a girlfriend?"

I lift her chin so she's looking at me. I know she's trying to use humor to deflect, but I'm not having that. "I couldn't give two shits about your coasters. In fact, until tonight, I've never had so many conversations about coasters. I just want you to be happy. If you want plants and decorations, then tomorrow we go shopping. If you want to keep your place like this, then that is your right. But don't think you have to do this to impress me. You impress me every day."

She gives me a small smile. "Well, that's good. I'd hate for this to end because I've never been to HomeGoods."

I laugh and kiss her forehead. "I do have one important question, though."

"What's that?"

"How is your bedroom decorated?"

She smiles and slowly stands up while taking my hand. "Let me show you."

21

SADIE

IT WAS the hair tuck behind the ear.

That is what did me in. That's what made all my rational decision making go away. That's the only reason I can come up with that I spilled all of that emotional baggage onto Hunter's lap. I can't believe I told him all that. I've never admitted my loneliness to anyone. That in the process of advancing my career, I put myself second in every facet of my life.

Then, he brought me onto his lap. At that moment, I knew he was the one I was supposed to admit that to. That he was supposed to be the first person ever to be in my apartment. That he was supposed to be the first person to see my bedroom.

That he is supposed to be the first person to have me in my bed.

I lead Hunter out of my living room and take the ten steps required to get to my bedroom. By step nine, Hunter's mouth is already on the back of my neck, gently kissing the exposed skin as his arms wrap around my waist.

"You could have at least waited until I stopped walking," I say, though I'm not really mad about the journey his lips are taking.

He doesn't say anything, instead mumbling something that I think sounded like "didn't want to."

I don't stop him. His mouth feels too good on me. His hands are now working their way up my front until they reach my breasts. He takes one in each hand, kneading them as he continues to spread kisses around my neck and shoulders.

"God, I've missed you," I say breathlessly. And I have. Who knew you could get so used to someone in such a short amount of time? Not seeing him these past few days has been torture. But our days were insanely long. It was the responsible decision to make.

Now I'm ready to make up for lost time.

"Well, then, we should reacquaint ourselves," he says as he slowly walks me the rest of the way into my room.

He lets go just long enough for me to turn around, and before I know it, he has me lying on my bed.

My room is dark, save for the light coming in through the hallway. It's just enough so I can see him. The square line of his jaw. The fire in his blue eyes. The smile that promises dirty and amazing things are about to happen.

Hunter slowly begins taking off his shirt, his broad chest now on display for me. His body is built like he still plays football. His pecs and abs make it clear he never misses a workout. His arms are perfectly defined, and all I want to do is grab on to his biceps as he enters me. He unzips his pants, his hard cock straining against his boxer briefs.

"See something you like?" he says, moving next to me on the bed. "Or has it been so long that you forgot how hard you make me?"

I want to say something sexy. I want to speak dirty, dirty things to this man because he brings out a sexual side of me I didn't know I had. But I don't say anything. I raise to my knees and take off my shirt, thankful I didn't wear the plain white cotton bra today.

"Fuck, Sadie," Hunter says, moving his hand down to his cock.

His words spur me on. I sit back and begin taking down my leggings. I don't know if I'm giving Hunter the show he gave me, but considering somehow his briefs are off and he is full-on stroking himself while he watches me, I think I'm doing a fine job.

Next comes my black lace panties, and finally, the matching bra. I'm back kneeling on the bed, naked and on display for Hunter.

"I need you." Those are the only words he says as he falls into bed with me. I don't know how he does it, but in one motion, I'm underneath him and his mouth is on me in a million places. His kisses are wet and hungry, and my body has never felt more alive.

He settles in on one of my breasts, sucking it so hard I'm sure it will leave a bruise, but I don't care. It's only fitting that he leaves a mark on me. He left a mark on me the first day we met.

He switches sides, but now his hand has made its way to my center. He pushes in one finger, and while it feels amazing, it's not enough. I need him. All of him.

"Hunter... more," I say as my hips rotate against his hand, my orgasm is building, begging to be released.

He doesn't make me wait. He rolls away for the three seconds it takes to grab a condom and is back kneeling on my bed before I blink. My legs are on both sides of him, my center wet and open for whatever he wants to give me. Our eyes stay locked as he covers himself, and holy hell, this is the hottest moment of my life.

"Do you know what it does to me knowing that I'm the first one to have you in this bed?" Hunter asks with an intensity in his voice I didn't know he had.

"You're the only one."

"Say it again."

"You're the only one."

My breathy words are barely out of my mouth before Hunter is entering me, his chest falling onto mine as he pushes in and out of me. Our lips find each other, and for I don't know how long, all we are is a mixture of thrusts, kisses, and touches. We are so close in this moment; I don't know where I end and he begins.

His mouth is back on my neck, leaving sloppy kisses as he moves in and out of me. I wrap my legs around his ass, and the slight change of position is exactly what I need.

"Yes, Hunter. Right there. More."

My words spur him on. Before I know it, he has one of my legs on his shoulder and... oh fuck me, does that feel good.

"I'm... I'm not going to last."

I don't mean my words to come out as a challenge, but that's how he takes it as he buries himself deeper. In one thrust, I come undone, my body quaking from my head to my toes.

"Sadie! Fuck!"

Hunter follows right behind me. He drops my leg as he spills himself into the condom. Before I know it, he is collapsing on top of me.

I don't know how long we lie there. I don't care either. I love the feeling of his weight on top of me. I don't feel smothered or confined. I feel treasured and safe.

And there's another word I could add to what I'm feeling that I'm not ready to admit yet.

22

HUNTER

"I CAN'T BELIEVE you didn't buy the decorative bowl," I say, dropping the shopping bags on the floor of her apartment.

She shoots daggers at me as she puts down her bags and keys. Because yes, to make it in one trip from her car, we both had to have our arms full of the newly purchased home décor and kitchen gadgets. "One, never say the words 'decorative bowl' again. It just sounds weird. Two, I'm not rolling in the cash like some of us who signed a huge contract because they are some big shot coordinator. And three, I *refuse* to pay twenty-five dollars for a bowl to sit on my counter."

"But it would go so well next to your new Instant Pot," I say, trying to lighten the mood with a bit of teasing. "Or, you could have put it next to your new wine rack. For the wine you don't drink."

A new set of eye daggers hit me. "I'm trying to become an adult. Which, by the way, this is *all* your fault. I was perfectly fine being a barely functioning adult until you strutted in here with your perfectly decorated condo and matching dishes and snarky comments."

I want to laugh at her rant, but I know that will just earn me another death glare. Instead, I walk over to her in her kitchen and wrap her in my arms. I lean down for a kiss, which she resists at first. But not for long. Within seconds, her head is against my chest and we are standing in her kitchen, surrounded by bags from Target.

"You know I don't care about this stuff," I say softly, hoping to put her at ease. "You also know that I had nothing to do with decorating my condo. That was all my mother and sister."

She looks up and gives me a pouty look. I kiss that away immediately.

Today's shopping trip was brought on by what was meant to be a harmless joke. A little playful banter, if you will.

Since the draft is over and I only have limited meetings, we've been able to spend most nights together. Last night, we were at my condo, laying on the couch watching television, when she shivered. So, I did what any good boyfriend would do. I reached behind me and grabbed a blanket that I have laying on the top of my couch and covered her up.

I should have stopped there. She was happy and snuggling into me. Her ass was doing that wiggle against my dick that makes me hard every time.

Then, I had to open up my mouth. This is where I know I made the mistake.

"What do you do when you're on your couch at your apartment and you get cold?"

She turns her head to look up at me, like she didn't understand the question. "I get up and get a blanket."

I wrinkle my nose at her response. "That seems like so much work. If you had a blanket that you used for decoration and warmth, you wouldn't need to get up. It would be right there. But we know that you don't have that because you are anti-decorations."

She withheld sex last night. And dragged me to Target today, where she bought every item in the home goods section. The Target an hour outside of Nashville to give us a better chance of not being recognized.

I understand all of her decisions.

We bought blankets. And an area rug. And curtains. And decorative pillows.

And yes, we bought coasters.

She didn't stop there. At one point I think she became a woman possessed. I believe I heard the words, "if I'm going to be a fucking adult, I'm going to do it right." Next thing I know, we were in the kitchen department buying things that she can learn to cook with.

Every day being with Sadie I learn something new. Today's lesson: when she does something, she does not half-ass it.

Not one bit.

"I know you were teasing about the blanket. And the bowl," she says, her fingers now playing with the hair on the back of my neck. "But you were right. I've avoided all of that stuff for too long. I don't want to be embarrassed or self-conscious when you come over. Heck, maybe I'll even invite my family over. Now I won't have to worry about Bethany wanting to decorate my apartment in glitter."

I kiss her on the nose. "We should probably start putting this stuff away."

She leans up and gives me one more peck on the cheek. "Sounds good. You can start by hanging the curtain rods for me, and I'll start organizing the kitchen."

The next half hour is so... domestic. Easy. I don't have much experience with adult relationships... the last time I had a serious girlfriend was in college, but I'd have to guess that spending a Saturday shopping for household items and hanging curtain rods is about as domestic as you can get.

This is how it's been for Sadie and me. Well, not the

shopping. But the easiness of everything. We spend nearly every night together. We both know once the season starts in July, our time together will be minimal, at best. So, we are taking every moment we can to be together over the next few months.

"Do you want to stay here for dinner tonight?" she asks from the kitchen. "Since your car isn't here and no one saw you come in, it's safe to stay here tonight."

At that moment, my phone rings with a FaceTime request. I tell her that's fine, and I put down the curtain to pick up my phone and answer it, not bothering to see who it is.

That's the second bad decision I've made in the last twenty-four hours.

"Hunter Michael. Now, son, I know you are busy coaching and getting those boys into shape and I am so proud of you but how dare you not call me all week! I am your mother for goodness' sake!"

"Hey, Mom!" I say nervously and a little louder than my normal tone. I take a second to look across the apartment to Sadie, whose face has gone a very bright shade of white.

Shit. I shouldn't have answered, even though I would have had to hear about it from her later. It would have been one thing if it was a phone call, but my mom helped me move into my Nashville condo. Just one look at the exposed brick in Sadie's apartment, and she will know I'm not at home.

Fuck, fuck, fuck.

"How are you?" I say quickly, trying to find a non-discreet angle, if that's possible.

"I'm fine. Your sister is trying to send me to an early grave, but that's nothing new." Just when I think I'm in the clear, she starts looking around, tilting her head and the phone screen like she'll be able to see more if she moves a little more to the right.

"Where are you, Hunter? That doesn't look like your house."

"I'm at Davis's place," I say, again a bit too loudly. "He needed some help moving furniture."

I take that second to look up at Sadie. I wish I hadn't. All I see is the sadness on her face before she walks into her bedroom, shutting the door behind her.

Fuck. I hate being the one who put that look on her face. I hate that I can't tell my mom about us. Don't get me wrong, I could. She'd be ecstatic. She'd probably start planning our wedding.

But if I tell my mom, then Dad finds out. And like everything else in my life, I know he'd have an opinion. I'm sure he will have plenty to say when he finds out I am dating the reporter who told him he was basically too old to run my offense.

Yeah, that would go over swimmingly.

So, I lie to my mom. She talks for a few minutes, and I answer when appropriate. She tells me that she and Dad have secured season tickets for the Fury's home games next year, and that she wants to make a visit before the season starts.

Finally, we say our goodbyes, and before I've even hung up, I'm making my way to Sadie's bedroom. What I see when I open the door breaks my damn heart.

She's sitting on the middle of her bed, holding a pillow against her chest. She's looking away from the door toward her window, but I don't think she's looking at anything. As I sit next to her, that's when I see a tear falling down her face.

"Sadie." My voice is hoarse as I bring her into my arms. "I'm so fucking sorry."

"It's okay." Her voice sounds anything but okay. "I understand. Not like I've told my family yet. But I haven't had to lie to them, either."

For the next few minutes, I just hold her. She has let go of the pillow and she has wrapped her arms around mine as we slowly rock back and forth.

"I hate lying to her," I say. And it's the truth.

"I know. And I get why you have to. It just..." her voice trails off for a second. When I hear her swallow, I then realize it is because she's holding back tears. "It just sucks, Hunter."

Silence falls back on us again. This isn't the first time we've been in this situation. But it is the first time we've actually talked about it.

A few weeks ago, there was a black-tie dinner for advertisers and season ticket holders. I had to go and schmooze. She was there covering the event. I was there in a custom-made suit, and she was standing off to the side in her everyday clothes. I tried to be very specific with who I talked to that night, but out of nowhere, the team owner came up to me, making sure to introduce me to his daughter. His daughter who is twenty-five and was just offered a modeling contract. I had to play nice and talk to her. The whole time I could feel Sadie's eyes on me.

By the time I ended the conversation, the reporters were gone. I tried texting her, but she wouldn't respond. The second I could leave, I hurried back to my condo. Luckily, she still came over. When I found her in my bed she was asleep. Though I'm pretty sure she had been crying. I didn't want to wake her up, so I just laid next to her and brought her into my arms.

The next morning we pretended like nothing happened.

"You know I wish I could tell everyone about you," I say, squeezing her a little tighter into me.

"I know. When we decided to do this, six months didn't feel like that long. It's barely been two, and I feel like it's never going to end."

Damn. When she says it like that, it does make it seem more daunting.

The two months we have spent together have been amazing. But we've been secluded. We have been so worried about being noticed, that every date night is spent at my house. Besides Memphis, we've never been on an actual date.

That ends now.

"Can you do me a favor?"

She looks back over her shoulder at me. "What's that?"

"Can you put on a sexy dress and be ready at seven?"

Her eyebrow lifts up, which I can't blame her for. "And why is that?"

I lean down and give her a quick kiss before I get off her bed. "Because I am taking my girlfriend on a date."

23

SADIE

I HAVE NEVER BEEN MORE focused on anything in my entire life.

"Baby, you look so sexy in that skirt. I wish I could just take you home and bend you over my bed. You know I love taking you from behind."

Unsweet tea.

Ear wax.

The smell of a locker room after a game.

I ignore Hunter's words. I know he's just trying to get in my head. He thinks if he keeps talking about sexy things that he will distract me from my target.

Not a chance in hell, McAvoy.

I take three steps and slowly bring the ball back behind me, and after another two I heave it forward, saying a silent prayer as my bowling ball rolls down the alley.

I swear I watch it play out in slow motion. I also hear Hunter behind me trying to will the ball into the gutter with just the sound of his voice.

After what feels like hours, my ball finally connects with the pins, knocking all ten down one by glorious one.

Strike.

Game.

Set.

Match.

"Woohoo!" I can't help but let out a little cry of celebration as I do a little shimmy back to where Hunter is sitting.

"You cheated," he says, looking up at the scoreboard to make sure that the computer did the math right. "There's no way in hell you beat me."

I take a seat across his lap, wrapping my arms around his neck. "Is someone a sore loser? Or does someone not like getting beat by his *girlfriend?*"

The look he gives me is priceless, and I can't help but let out a loud laugh. It's a mix of mock anger, real confusion, and a little bit of hurt pride. Poor baby.

"What are you laughing at?" His pouty question makes me laugh even harder.

"You. Your face." I can barely get the words out. This man really is pouting because he lost to me. "I need a picture. I need to document this moment."

I slide off of Hunter's lap to retrieve my phone from my purse. That's right. I left my phone in my purse. I wasn't letting any distractions get in the way of our first official date as a couple.

This is uncharted territory for me. I put my work aside to enjoy life.

Life with my boyfriend.

When Hunter suggested date night, I knew he was trying to make me feel better. I hated the way I reacted when his mom called, but I couldn't help it. Another example of my emotions being too big for me to handle when it comes to Hunter.

The second that he showed up at my door, dressed in dark jeans and a fitted polo, I forgot about the events that led up to this moment. My boyfriend was picking me up for a date. And I was not about to let anything ruin it.

Not only was it our first date, but it was the most cliché first date ever. Dinner and bowling. Honestly, though? It was perfect. He found a restaurant just outside of the Nashville city limits, hoping that it would give us a little more anonymity, before a night of bowling.

It is casual. And fun. And everything I needed.

"I still can't believe you didn't tell me you were a junior bowling champion," Hunter grumbles as I make my way back to his lap, cell phone in hand. "That would have been good information to know."

"You didn't ask," I say, bringing up the camera and setting the timer. "Now smile and say, 'My girlfriend just kicked my ass!'"

He does no such thing. His lips attack my neck, making me shriek. My body is thrashing on his lap as I try to break away, which just makes his hold on me that much stronger. The bowling alley only has about ten people in it right now, so I'm sure we are causing quite the scene. I'm not even paying attention to the camera when I hear it go off.

"Hunter," I say, trying to catch my breath. "Hunter, stop!"

He puts one more sloppy kiss on my cheek before I bring my phone up to look at the picture. It wasn't the one I was going for.

It's better.

I'm laughing. And smiling. And enjoying this impromptu moment with the man I adore.

As for Hunter? The camera caught the one moment his lips weren't buried in my neck. It caught the moment when he's looking at me with... is that love? If it is, until now I wasn't sure what it looked like. But for some reason, that's the only word that comes to mind. I don't know if I'm right, but if he looked at me like that every day for the rest of our lives, I wouldn't be mad.

All in all, this is the perfect picture.

One I can't help but make the new background of my phone. Why not? I'm not going to be around any of the other reporters for a few more months. I spend most of my free time with Hunter these days. Why can't I?

So, I do. It's scary how sometimes the smallest things can be the most freeing.

"Do you want one more game for redemption? Or have you had enough ass kicking for the night?"

He goes in for one more neck kiss before moving me off his lap to take off his rental shoes. "My ego has had enough. Plus, I've been watching you bowl all night in a dress. There's only so much a man can take, woman. I've had enough torture."

"Hey, that last part is your fault," I say, sitting back down to take off the hideous bowling lane shoes as Hunter returns our balls to the racks. "I was just following your directions."

"Yes you did," Hunter says, holding his arm out for me so I'm able to slip right into his embrace. We walk side by side to the counter to return our shoes when he leans down and whispers in my ear, "I wonder if you'll follow directions tonight when I tell you to come for me."

I don't even have a second to be turned on by his words, because before I know it, he's pinching my side and tickling my waist. The action makes me laugh obnoxiously loud, which then Hunter takes advantage of. He brings me into his side a little tighter before placing a kiss on my hair.

With all of this flirting and dirty talk, I need this man to get me home. Immediately.

"Oh my God! You're Hunter McAvoy! Babe! Look! He's a Fury coach!"

Hunter and I freeze when we hear the words. I'm not shocked that he was noticed, considering who he is, it makes sense. All I can do is hope the man doesn't recognize me. I know the chances are slim, but they are still there. My picture is in the newspaper and online so I'm not anonymous.

"Hey, man. How are you tonight?" Hunter asks in a polite tone as we place our shoes up on the counter.

"I'm great. Just great," the man is bouncing on his toes like he's meeting Santa on Christmas Eve. "I'm a big fan. Also, a 'Bama fan. Roll Tide."

Hunter smiles his fake-polite smile. It's the one the media gets most of the time. It's like the fake smile you give a relative on Christmas Day when they get you a shitty present. "Roll Tide. Have a good night."

"Wait! Can I have your autograph?"

Hunter looks down at me, and I give him a small nod that it's okay. It's not like there are a slew of people here. It's a guy who hasn't looked at me once because he is all but drooling over Hunter. And by the looks of it, an annoyed wife or girlfriend who can't believe her man is fan-boying over a football coach like he's in a boy band.

"Sure. No problem." Hunter asks the bowling alley worker for a pen and paper and begins signing the small piece of paper.

"Sorry about that," the girlfriend/wife says to me. "As soon as he saw you two, he was freaking out so much I told him just to suck it up and say hello. I'm sorry if we're ruining your night."

I shake my head. "It's no problem. We were on our way out. The alley is yours."

"He is a big fan of yours too."

My eyes go wide at her words. "Excuse me?"

She leans a little closer, her words a little lower. "I know you're Sadie Benson. I've read your stuff for years. So does my jackass of a husband. But he's too starstruck to realize right now who you are. Please, don't take offense."

I'm speechless. Completely and utterly speechless.

"I'm... it's... we're..."

"It's none of my business," she says, now averting her eyes as to not draw attention to us. "All I see here are two adults spending a fun night together at a bowling alley. Who am I to judge anything about that?"

I feel the wetness pooling in my eyes, which is ridiculous. "Thank you. I appreciate that."

She gives me a nod and a smile. "No worries. Now get your man out of here before mine tries to kidnap him."

I turn back to Hunter, who is handing his autograph to the fan. "Here you go. Have a good night."

"Thanks, man! You, too!"

We hurry to Hunter's truck, not saying a word until we're back on the road.

"That was close," Hunter says, giving my hand a squeeze as we make our way back to his condo.

It was close. Too close.

That woman didn't care. Unfortunately, though, she is one of the rare people who won't.

"So, I guess that was our first and last public date within an hour of the Nashville city limits," I say. We got lucky this time. I doubt we'll get lucky again.

Hunter brings my hand to his mouth, and I know it's to soothe my anxiety. "I'm sorry, Sadie."

"It's not your fault. We knew this could happen."

He lets out a defeated sigh. "I wish we could go somewhere where no one would recognize us."

"And where in the continental United States can Hunter McAvoy go without being recognized?"

"I doubt people would know me out West. They hate the SEC. And they don't like to acknowledge any pro teams on the wrong side of the Rockies."

I laugh, but then get an idea.

Can I?

Is it too soon?

What if he says no?

What if he says yes?

"What's going on in that brain of yours?"

I have no idea how he knows my wheels are turning as he has both eyes on the road.

"Just an idea. But it's stupid."

This gets his attention. "No idea you could have is stupid. Lay it on me."

I take a big breath for courage. Because I can't believe I'm about to ask this.

"Next month I had a vacation scheduled in San Francisco. What if… would you like to… I was thinking maybe…"

In a case of perfect timing, we come up to a red light, which allows Hunter to turn to me. And when he does, I'm greeted with the best and brightest of all of the Hunter McAvoy smiles.

"Are you asking me to go on vacation with you?"

"That depends."

"On what?"

"If you're saying yes."

This earns me a laugh. "Oh, Sadie. Don't you know?"

I quirk an eyebrow at him. "Know what?"

He leans down and gives me a quick kiss before the light turns green. "You could ask me to go to the moon with you and I'd do it. I'm crazy about you. Let's go to San Francisco."

24

SADIE

"TOOTHBRUSH?"

I laugh because my father is nothing but predictable. That is always his first reminder. "Got it."

"Tennis shoes because you'll be walking a lot?"

"Packed before anything else."

"Did you remember to get your sunglasses out of your car?"

That reminder comes from Helen. They love doing these reminders on speakerphone. "I put them in my purse last night."

"How about your laptop charger?"

"I'm not taking it, so I don't need the charger."

My admission stuns Dad and Helen silent. It was the same reaction John had when I told him. I've never gone on a vacation, or any trip, without my laptop. I've always been scared that something would happen, and I'd need to jump online to write a story.

Not this trip. This trip I'm determined to enjoy the moments, enjoy the scenery, and enjoy time with Hunter.

That means breaking news can wait.

I never thought I'd say those words out loud.

"I... I don't know what to say." Dad finally finds his words after at least a minute of silence. "What made you decide that? I mean, I'm happy. Don't get me wrong. I've always said you work too much. It's just… I never thought I'd see the day."

Me neither, Dad. Me neither.

I look down at my open suitcase and notice the clothes that are not generally packed for one of my trips. Dad would never think to ask if I have packed these things.

New bikini? *Check.*

New lingerie? *Check.*

New dress that I've been promised by Bethany will make Hunter's eyes pop out of his head? *Check.*

Ted, because I had a very dirty fantasy about using that with Hunter? *Double check.*

These are definitely *not* my normal vacation items. And ones that he *definitely* does not need to know about. I wouldn't have told him about those items regardless of whether he knew about me and Hunter or not.

Which he doesn't.

Because I've been too scared to tell him. I know I said I didn't want to lie to him, but the thought of telling him has been worse, so I haven't said anything. The only person who knows is Bethany.

"Well, I for one am glad that you are leaving work behind," Helen says, breaking the silence. "Though, I still hate the thought of you going around that big city all alone."

"I'll be fine," I say, trying to figure out a way to turn this conversation. I wish I could tell them I won't be alone. That for the first time in my life, I'm looking forward to a vacation. That I'm thrilled that I'm leaving my laptop behind because I'm going on a vacation with my boyfriend who I am head over heels for.

But I can't. Not yet. Maybe when I get back from San Francisco. And even then, it's not a conversation you have over the phone. If I'm telling Dad and Helen that I'm not only seeing someone, but it's Hunter, that needs to be an in-person conversation.

Preferably with beer.

I'm barely listening to the list that my dad and Helen are saying when I hear the door to my apartment open and shut. I take a quick glance at my watch and realize that Hunter is a half-hour early to pick me up.

He pops his head inside my bedroom door, and I hold a finger up. The last thing I need him to do is announce his presence as I'm on the phone with my dad.

I thought that was the universal signal for "give me a minute." Apparently, Hunter either doesn't know that or doesn't care, because before I know it, he's inside my bedroom with his arms wrapped around my stomach, placing quiet kisses on the back of my neck.

Fuck, that feels good.

"Sadie! Are you listening to me? You know I'm not helping you pack for my own benefit!"

My dad's words break me from the spell that Hunter was trying to put me under. "Sorry. I was distracted. I was... zipping my suitcase."

"Zipping your suitcase distracts you?"

I reluctantly nudge Hunter away from my body so I can actually zip my suitcase and not make me out to be a bigger liar to my father than I already am.

"I had other things on my mind. Sorry. But thanks for helping me pack as always. But it's time for me to go."

"No, it's not," Helen says. "Your plane doesn't leave for another three hours and your alarm didn't go off. I would know the sound of that blasted thing anywhere."

"I..." Shit. I have no idea what to say. I'm breaking under the pressure. I can still feel Hunter behind me and all I can think about is if we have time for a quickie before we leave for the airport.

"Sadie? Is everything okay?"

"I have to go to the bathroom!" I say a little too loudly. "You know. Hate to do that in the airport. Better to do it now."

If there is any way to kill a mood, it's talking about bathroom usage. Because as soon as the words leave my mouth, I feel Hunter step away from me. When I turn to look at him, all I hear are gasps of air as Hunter is trying not to break into a fit of laughter. His face is beet red, and he looks like he's about to explode.

I don't care. It's his fault that he's early and got me all hot and bothered.

"That's smart. Have a safe trip, slugger," Dad says. "Bring us back something fun."

"You know I will. Love you both."

I have barely hung up the phone when Hunter's laugh erupts from his body.

"This is not funny," I say, tossing a pillow at him that he successfully dodges.

"Oh, but it was. You should have seen your face."

I lean over to zip my carry-on while Hunter continues to laugh at what he must think is the world's funniest joke. "This is all your fault. If you weren't early, then I wouldn't have had to lie."

Still laughing, he sits down on my bed next to my suitcase. "If I wasn't early, then I wouldn't have time to do this."

He brings me in for a kiss, and before I know it, I'm straddling his lap and my arms are looped around his neck.

I figured after three months I'd be tired of kissing Hunter whenever I can. That couldn't be further from the truth. Each time we kiss, it's a new experience. I fall for him a little bit more every time our lips touch.

And each time we kiss, I fall closer and closer to that L-word that I never thought I'd say.

He breaks the kiss first, but not before giving me a small

peck on the corner of my lips. "See now why I came over early? We have a long flight, and I'm not going to get to do that for hours."

I check my watch. We still have three hours before our flight takes off. And it only takes twenty minutes to get to the airport.

"Do we have time for anything else?" I ask, my hips rotating on his lap for emphasis.

His eyes go a shade darker at my question. "It's like you can read my mind."

25

HUNTER

"WELCOME TO THE ROCK!"

Sadie doesn't even laugh at my horrible Sean Connery impression as she collapses onto the bed. "How long are you going to be saying that?"

I plop down next to her, completely spent from our day touring the famous prison. "At least for the rest of the trip. And probably every time I look at the pictures from today."

I take out my phone and flip through the pictures. We have been the definition of tourists this week. We've been to the Golden Gate Bridge and Fisherman's Wharf. We rode the cable cars and walked through the streets of San Francisco. Today we toured Alcatraz, and tomorrow we are on a mission to find the house from the opening of the television show *Full House*. She thinks she's "dragging" me to find it. Little does she know my childhood crush was D.J. Tanner.

Tonight I made reservations at a Michelin-star restaurant that I have been told will change my life and will make me never want to order a steak from another restaurant ever again.

We are living our best vacation life. And we've been able to do it without feeling guilty or having to hide.

"We're going to fall asleep if we keep lying here," I say drowsily.

"Is that a bad thing?" she says, snuggling next to me.

I kiss the top of her head because no, a nap does not sound bad. Except I am bound and determined to see her in the dress that she's been hiding from me all week.

"You take a nap. I'm jumping in the shower," I say, kissing her cheek before I get up. "Unless you want to join me?"

She shakes her head, further burrowing it into the bed. "Can't move. Too sleepy."

I laugh and make my way into the bathroom. I don't blame her. We are on day five of seven, and we have been running ourselves ragged, determined to do and see everything we wanted on this trip.

We've caught the attractions. We've eaten everything in sight. We've drunk to our heart's content. We've lounged at the pool. And each night, we end up back in this bed and make love until we pass out.

And yes, we make love. Calling it sex anymore feels wrong.

As I step into the hot shower, I let that thought pass over my mind. It does feel wrong to call it sex. It's so much more than that. Honestly, it was never just sex with us. From the first kiss, I knew it was something more with Sadie.

I didn't admit it to myself then, but I knew I was in denial. And as the days continue, I know I can't deny it for much longer.

I'm in love with this woman.

I'm not exactly sure when it happened, but somewhere along the way I fell in love with Sadie Benson.

I take that back. I know exactly the moment it happened. It happened on Beale Street.

This week getting to be together, not having to hide ourselves from the public, has been freeing. I didn't realize how much of a bubble we were staying in while living in

Nashville until we got to experience complete freedom to be ourselves. To be a couple who is slowly falling in love with each other.

Well, I am. I hope she is as well.

I don't linger in the shower because I'm way too eager to climb back into bed and take a nap with Sadie before our reservations tonight. However, when I step out of the shower, I hear her talking to someone. She's obviously on the phone because I only hear one voice.

"It better be very important if you're calling me on a vacation that you said I wasn't allowed to work on."

Silence.

"Are you serious?"

Longer silence.

"And you couldn't wait to tell me this until I got back? You know I'm going to freak out until then."

Another round of silence.

"Thanks, John. I appreciate this. I'll call you when I'm back in town and we can talk more. Thanks. Bye."

I wait a second before stepping out of the bathroom. Immediately, I can tell Sadie is in her brain in some far-off place that's not our hotel room in San Francisco.

"Who was that?" I ask, sitting across from her on the bed.

"John. My boss. He… he had some news for me."

"Good news?" I ask, taking her hand in mine.

She nods. "A few months ago, he told me there was a possibility of a job opening at *US Daily.* But then it was just a rumor. Turns out that the job is real. And they want me to interview for it."

Shit. I'm not even in the media and I know that *US Daily* is a big deal. When I was at Alabama, they were the only ones to get access that no other media outlet got. They are the top dogs.

"Sadie. That's amazing."

"It would be," she says, a smile finally coming through. "I've always wanted to work for them. Your goal is to one day coach your own team? Mine is to work for *US Daily*."

My heart is swelling with pride right now. I've witnessed firsthand how hard she works. She absolutely deserves this chance.

I can't help but think about what this means for us. She wouldn't be covering the Fury anymore, which would be a good thing. But if they make her a national writer, does she have to move? Is that better or worse for us? Am I selfish for thinking like that?

"You know you make fun of me for thinking out loud, but you do the same thing," she says, her smile teasing. "What's going on in that brain, McAvoy?"

I let out a small laugh. "One of these days I'm going to be able to hide an emotion from you."

She shakes her head. "Today isn't that day. Spill it."

"I'm just curious, what would happen if you got the job?"

"I can ask the same thing about you."

This takes me off guard. "What do you mean?"

She takes her free hand in mine. "Hunter, I'm not naïve enough to think that you will be coaching in Nashville forever. If things go well in a few years, teams will be calling you to be a head coach. Maybe that's in Nashville? Maybe it isn't. I knew that when we started this. And as for me? I'm not sure where they will want me. A few of the national writers live wherever they'd like. A few they have asked to move to certain parts of the country to make travel easier. I won't know anything until I talk to them. And even if they like me, I'd probably not get it. I feel like I'm one major breaking news story away from them seriously considering me. And stories like that don't come around every day."

I let her words sink in. She's right. Here I am freaking out about her job when I'm the one who could be moving sooner rather than later. Just because I'm a coordinator now doesn't mean I'm setting down permanent roots. If a team calls me next year offering me a head coaching job, especially if and when we make the playoffs, there's a very good chance I will take it.

And where would that leave me and Sadie? If she gets the *US Daily* job, feasibly, she could come with me. If she doesn't, well, then I guess we cross that bridge when we get there.

"You know we don't have to figure out everything right now."

Her words are soft and put me a little more at ease. "You're right. But we should celebrate."

This gets me a smile, followed quickly by a yawn. "Can we take a nap first? John woke me up and I'm not about to fall asleep face-first in my steak tonight."

I laugh as we move under the sheets, cuddling together for a mid-afternoon nap.

Well, she takes a nap. I can't help but think about all of the scenarios for the future.

And there is not one I can think of that doesn't have Sadie by my side.

26

HUNTER

I NOW KNOW why Sadie was hiding this particular dress from me all week.

She knew that if I saw her in it, we would not have left the hotel.

She knows me too well.

When she stepped into the sitting area of our suite, I just stared at her. She looked stunning. Her hair was down and styled with soft curls. Her makeup was bolder than I had ever seen it, making her hazel eyes even brighter. She's also wearing red lipstick, which is a first for her. As soon as I saw that, all I could think of was a ring of red around my cock later.

And that dress? I want to write a thank-you card to whoever designed it. Because they had to have done it with Sadie in mind.

The black fabric clings to every one of her curves. There isn't an ounce of cleavage showing, yet the dress is so tight that it's making my mouth water when I look at her full tits pressing against the fabric. And her ass? Kill me right fucking now.

I wanted to punch every man who tried to get a glimpse of

her as we walked through the restaurant. I almost slapped our waiter who stared a bit too long when he was delivering our drinks. And now that our meals are done? All I want to do is get her back to our room and slowly peel that dress off of her.

"You're staring again," she says before taking a sip of her cocktail.

"I can't help it. You're a vision."

I know it probably sounded cheesy leaving my tongue, but I can't think of any other words.

"If I knew doing my hair and makeup would get this kind of reaction from you, I would have done it a lot sooner."

She sets her glass down and I take her hand from across the table. "You know that I couldn't give two shits whether you were wearing makeup or not, right? And hell, I can spot you easier when your hair is on the top of your head."

This makes her laugh a little, but the heaviness isn't gone yet. "I know you don't care. Which kind of shocked me at first. I figured you'd be one of those football guys who was used to having the hot girl on his arm with the perfect makeup and perfect outfit. It's kind of why I was surprised when you flirted with me that first day."

"So you noticed I was flirting." I move my eyebrows up and down to try to make her laugh. It works a little. "That first day I saw you, it was like a punch in the gut. I couldn't take my eyes off you. And I remember thinking to myself how gorgeous you were without a drop of makeup on. I remember wishing that I would get this job so I could move to Nashville and take you out to dinner. Little did I know that you would turn my world upside down that day."

Now that gets me a real smile. "You turned my world upside down, too, McAvoy."

Our waiter breaks the moment by coming back and giving me the check; I give him my credit card immediately. I need to get her back to the hotel. I need to worship her body. I need to show her she is the only woman I will ever want.

"What are you staring at?" she asks as we stand to leave the restaurant. "Do I have something on me?"

I grab her hand and pull her into me. I don't care if we have an audience. I need to kiss her.

And I do.

It's hard and fast and leaves her breathless.

"I'm staring at you. Only you. Now, let's go back to the room so I can remind you how much you drive me fucking crazy."

———

TELLING Sadie that she drives me crazy may not have been my best idea.

She has been taking my words quite literally from the moment we stepped out of the restaurant and into our Uber.

She sat flush against me in the back seat, her hand resting on my thigh. Her touch alone was enough to make me hard. Every time I squirmed a bit to adjust myself, for the sheer fact that my cock was beginning to feel uncomfortable, the vixen moved her hand up.

By the time we stepped onto the elevator, I was hard as stone for her. Unfortunately, we weren't the only ones in the car, so I couldn't kiss her the way I wanted to. Instead, she decided to take that opportunity to stand in front of me, slowly moving her ass back and forth over my dick.

She was teasing me in the best possible way.

Now it's payback.

"Bed. Now," I demand the second we walk into our hotel suite.

"I didn't know you could get so caveman," she says as she makes her way back to the bedroom. "I kind of like it."

"Oh, you do? Then you're going to love what I have in mind," I say, pulling her into my arms. I don't ask for permission. I don't go in slowly. I take her mouth, claiming it as mine. Because it is. I kiss her hard and rough, because if there is one thing she needs to know at the end of tonight, it's that no other woman brings this out in me.

Only Sadie.

We stumble to the bed, ungracefully falling onto the soft mattress. We are a mess of lips and limbs and it's perfect. Our hands are grabbing at clothes, doing our best to shed them as quickly as possible. I think I heard a tear. I don't know if it was her clothing or mine.

This is wild. Insane. Crazy.

It's fitting. We are crazy about each other. We are crazy for each other.

I release her lips only because I have more skin that I need to taste. I don't know what kind of perfume she wore tonight, but it's new and intoxicating, and I'm determined to lick it off of wherever I taste it.

"Mmm." Her moan only spurs me on, and I take one of her tits into my mouth, letting my other hand travel down to her center.

"Fuck, baby. You're fucking soaked."

"Only for you, Hunter. Only for you."

Damn right only for me.

My mouth switches to the other, and Sadie's hands are now in my hair, pulling me farther into her chest. Holy hell, this woman... she's just as unhinged right now as I am.

"Hunter... suitcase."

Did I hear her right?

"Whatever you need can wait."

I continue where I left off before she lifts me off of her. "In my suitcase is my vibrator. I thought we could..."

Holy. Fucking. Hell.

"Don't move an inch," I say, giving her nipple one last suck before I nearly sprint to her suitcase. First, she hid the dress from me all week. Now I find out she's had this gem stowed away?

This woman is going to be the death of me.

Vibrator in hand, I make my way back to the bed. I allow myself a moment to take her in. Her eyes are dark and full of heat. Her lipstick is smeared, and her hair is wild. I love seeing her like this. She's so deliberate in everything else she does. But with me? With me, she lets herself be free.

"See something you like?" She parts her legs for me as her hand travels down to her center.

"A few things."

I flip on her toy and I can feel it hum in my hand.

"Where do you want this?" I'm unable to hide the lust in my voice. This is turning me on so fucking much.

"On my pussy," she says.

She's already so turned on, the words barely come out of her mouth. I move to stand next to her and lower the toy to her center. I barely touch her, and her hips shoot off of the bed.

"Yes. Fuck, yes."

God, this is hot. Watching her come undone like this? I can't help but start stroking myself. I move the vibrator slowly over her folds, keeping a close eye on what movements make her moan more than others. But that's not enough for me. I let go of my cock and lean down, taking her tit into my mouth.

"Oh God, Hunter. I... I'm not going to be able to last."

As much as I love seeing her come unraveled like this, she's coming on my cock. There are no other alternatives tonight. I flip the vibrator off and toss it to the bed as I climb on top of her.

"Fuck. Condom." I forgot to grab it out of my pants. I start to roll off of her when she puts a hand on my arm, stopping me.

"I'm safe. And clean. I want to feel all of you, Hunter."

Fuccccck.

"Are you sure?" We've always used a condom. *I've* always used a condom.

"Yes, Hunter. Will you?"

The fact that she even has to ask me that is absurd. This woman could tell me to rob the hotel right now and I would.

I lean down and press another kiss to her lips. "I'll give you anything you want."

And with one thrust, I'm inside her. And holy fuck, I have never felt anything better in my entire life.

She's hot and wet and tight and fucking perfect.

My pace starts as slow and intentional. It's like my body knows I will want to memorize every minute of this. Sadie and I have been together countless times, but this, this is different. This is... love.

I fucking love this woman.

"More, Hunter. I need you to move."

She doesn't have to ask me twice. I slowly begin to increase my speed, and Sadie meets me thrust for thrust. Our pace soon becomes frantic. Her arms are gripping my biceps like she needs an anchor to hold on to.

"Hunter, I'm close. Make me come, Hunter."

I'll never get tired of hearing those words.

I take her legs over my arms, tilting her hips up just enough to hit the spot I know she loves. The scream that comes out of her mouth is enough to send me over the edge, and all at once, I feel her contract around me as I let myself explode inside her.

I am breathless as I fall on the bed next to her, doing my best to keep my weight off of her. But I crave her touch. I need to feel her body on me.

"That..." she says, her words barely able to come out of her mouth.

"Yeah," I say, kissing her neck as I slowly pull myself out of her. "That."

She pushes a piece of sweaty hair off of my forehead. "Is it always supposed to be like that?"

I take her hand, placing a kiss on her palm.

"No, gorgeous. That's just because it's us."

27

SADIE

"ARE you sure you're okay? We don't have to do this. You can drop me off then turn around and—"

Hunter turns down the volume of the radio and gives me a quick *you have got to be kidding me* look as we make our way through the suburbs of Nashville on our way to my dad's house.

I don't blame the look, though. I'd probably give it to me too. I've asked that question in some form no less than thirty times today.

"For the last time, because according to my GPS we are five minutes away, I'm excited to meet your dad. And Helen and Bethany. You know I *have* met parents before, right? I'm not a complete boyfriend virgin. Parents love me."

He's right. I'm being ridiculous. I know they will love him. I can't think of a better guy to bring home to meet my family than Hunter. And considering he's the first guy I've ever brought home, not counting random prom dates in high school, I have nothing to worry about.

At least, I hope.

I knew after we got back from San Francisco that I wanted to figure out how to tell them. I knew they'd be overjoyed about me dating someone. I just didn't know how they'd react to it being Hunter. At least, my dad. Helen would probably be like Bethany and not understand the true significance of this. But my dad would.

And that's what I was most afraid of.

So, I weighed my options of how to tell them. At one point I considered just randomly showing up at the house with him and yelling, "Surprise!" and letting the cards fall where they may. I also considered the opposite, never telling them.

Both had solid points in the pro column.

Then, I got back from San Francisco. And little did I know that Helen would back me into a corner so much that I had no choice but to admit the secret.

"Why didn't you post any pictures?" Helen asks at the first Monday night dinner after my return. "I was looking on your Instagram every day hoping to see your trip, and I didn't see anything! After dinner you need to show me."

"Oh..." I don't know what to say. Shit. I didn't post anything because every picture was of me and Hunter together. "I just didn't want to publicize where I was. And I really didn't take that many."

She scrunches her nose at me, so I quickly look away. If I make eye contact with her, I might break. This doesn't stop her from wondering out loud.

"Well, that makes no sense. You posted pictures from Memphis. And last year when you went to Savannah. What was different this year? And if you didn't take pictures from the Golden Gate Bridge, I don't even know why you went."

"Mom, give her a break," Bethany chimes in while simultaneously reaching for the potatoes. "Maybe she wanted some privacy. Or maybe she met a guy and had a wild tryst and they never left the hotel room."

I shoot Bethany a look because she knows that Hunter was with me. Why is she stirring the pot? I thought she was on my side. The evil grin she is giving me right now means she knows EXACTLY what she is doing.

"*I'd rather not hear about that if she did,*" Dad says, taking the potatoes from Bethany.

"*Nonsense. We'd know if Sadie was seeing someone. Or if she met someone. She wouldn't hide that from us. Now would you, Sadie?*"

That's when I make my mistake. I look up from methodically placing roast beef on my plate to two sets of eyes looking at me in curiosity. The other set is all of a sudden very interested in her dinner.

And then I break.

"*I've been secretly dating a coach of the Fury for three months and we went on vacation together!*"

I crumbled at the guilt. I'd be a horrible CIA agent, handing over all the nation's secrets with just a side eye and a few cupcake questions.

So, I told them. Well, not everything. I told them that for the past three months I had been seeing Hunter. I told them that I hadn't told anyone due to the nature of our jobs, hoping that would smooth over my secret keeping. Bethany pretended this was new information. Helen was so excited she all but demanded I bring Hunter to the next Monday dinner.

My dad didn't say anything. And he hasn't since I left their house last week.

"Hey, you okay?" Hunter asks, and I realize then that I was so zoned out that we are now in the driveway of my childhood home.

"Yeah," I say, giving my head a little shake. "I'm fine."

Hunter reaches for my hand and brings it to his lips. I don't know why this relaxes me so much, but whenever he does it, an instant sense of calm overtakes me.

He pins me with his stare. I feel like I'm about to get a pep talk like he'd give one of his players.

"The hard part is over. They know about us. You played defense and got me the ball. Now it's my job to make them fall in love with me. I got this, gorgeous. Don't worry about anything."

Hunter gets out of the truck and I put my phone in my purse as I wait for him to open the door for me. I've learned my lesson over the past few months. I am not, under any circumstances, to open my own door.

At first, I thought it was ridiculous. Now, I kind of love it.

Hunter takes my hand as I step down from his truck and doesn't let go as we make our way up the driveway. Before we are even on the front porch, the door opens, and standing there are Helen and my dad.

The smile on Helen's face is one I've never seen on her before. Not even on her and my dad's wedding day.

My dad, on the other hand? I wouldn't necessarily call his expression a smile. It's more like a grimace. It's stern. What I would expect him to give his class of English students if they all failed a test.

Hunter gives my hand one more squeeze before he drops it to put his hand on the small of my back, leading me up the few stairs to the door.

"Hi, Dad. Helen. This is Hunter."

"Mr. Benson. Mrs. Benson, it's a pleasure to meet you," Hunter says, extending his hand.

"Hunter. It's nice to meet you. I'm Mike Benson," my dad says, meeting his hand for a shake. "Come inside. We have a lot to talk about."

———

I LOST MY BOYFRIEND TONIGHT.

I never had a chance. Really, I should have known this would happen.

"What do you mean, the Alabama-Auburn rivalry is better? Tennessee-Alabama is a tradition that you can literally set your calendar for every year!"

"Mr. Benson, while I appreciate your passion about the

discussion, take it from a man who *played* in the rivalries. There is nothing like an Iron Bowl when the season is on the line. I'm sorry."

"What did I tell you about calling me Mr. Benson. It's Mike. And fine, that game does have more meaning being at the end of the season. But let's talk about the Peyton Manning years. Now *those* were some classic games."

This is all I hear from the back patio as my dad and Hunter continue to argue and debate the ranking of college football rivalries.

Honestly, there hasn't been a football topic they *haven't* discussed.

Once Dad got Hunter in his clutches, he was a goner. That is, after Dad let it be known that he was "willing to look past" me dating an Alabama graduate.

Apparently, *that* was what gave Dad pause last week. Not that he's a coach. Not that I felt the need to sneak around. It's the fact that he went to the school that my dad considers his college football enemy.

I shouldn't be surprised. This is the South and college football.

But he loves him. I can tell. Which makes my heart so full it could burst.

"And to think you were worried," Helen says as she passes me a dish to load into the dishwasher. We are both staring out the back window, watching the two men we love have a friendly argument about uniform combinations.

Because yes, I'm in love with Hunter McAvoy.

It's been on the tip of my tongue for a while now. I almost said it in San Francisco. Now that I see Hunter interacting with my family like this, I don't know how long I'm going to be able to keep it in.

I can only hope that he feels the same way.

"I wasn't worried," I fib. "I wasn't worried at all."

"That's some bull crap, and you know it. You only told us because you got busted," Bethany whispers, bringing in the last of the serving platters from the dining room.

She's right. I didn't want to tell them. Who could blame me? We have to worry about what the Fury and *The Banner* will think when we tell them. I really have to worry about my reputation to my readers and the fans.

It just made sense in my head to lump my family in with the rest of those people.

But they don't care who Hunter is. All they care about is that Hunter treats me right and that I'm happy.

He does. And I am.

"He's a very nice young man," Helen says, handing me a pan to load.

"He's very nice to look at too," Bethany adds, her eyebrows going up and down.

"Bethany! Be nice."

"I am! I'm complimenting my stepsister on her hunk of a boyfriend, and I'm using this opportunity to ask if he has any single friends. Or maybe a brother who doesn't fall too far from the family tree, or maybe a family friend who is clinging onto a branch with biceps the same shape as Hunter's?"

I laugh, closing the dishwasher. "Only a sister, so sorry on that one. And… well, I haven't met any of his friends. Because we have to keep things a secret, not many people know. In fact, besides a random couple at the bowling alley, you three are the first to know."

This causes the mood to turn somber. I told them that Hunter and I weren't telling people about our relationship, but I don't think they truly realized to what extent that meant.

"Are you okay with that?" Helen asks, concern heavy in her voice.

Am I? At first, I was. It was nice getting to know Hunter and figuring out the dynamics of our relationship without having outside interference. Now that we are a few months in? There are times I wish we could be a normal couple. I wish I could ask him if he has anyone to set Bethany up with. I wish we could be more open.

But this is our reality. Training camp starts in a few weeks, and before we know it, the season will be upon us. We only have a few more months to go.

"I have to be," I say, unable to hold in the honesty. "It's only for a few more months. The reward will be worth it."

As the words leave my mouth, Hunter and Dad open the screen door and make their way back inside.

"Slugger, your boyfriend here thinks he knows more pro football facts than I do. Tell him that he might be a big, hotshot coach, but when it comes to random factoids, no one will beat me."

I can't help but laugh at Dad's bravado as I walk over to stand next to Hunter, who promptly puts his arm around my shoulders to bring me to his side as he places a kiss to my temple.

"Sorry, babe. Dad here has made it his life's mission to remember every small fact he can. I think he's got you."

"I refuse to believe this," Hunter says. "Next time we come over, Sadie will quiz us. Twenty bucks says I'll win."

"You're on. And make it fifty, that's how confident I am that I'll smoke you," Dad says, reaching his hand out to shake Hunter's.

I don't know why, but this small gesture makes tears well in my eyes.

I really need to get this crying thing under control.

One hour and one more football debate later, Hunter and I begin saying our goodbyes. There are only five of us so I didn't think it would take long. However, I didn't count on Bethany cornering Hunter about his single friends.

"That's a good one you got there," Dad says as he brings me in for a hug.

"I was so nervous to tell you all," I admit, squeezing him a little tighter. "I'm sorry I didn't. Please know I wanted to."

He kisses me on the top of my head like he did when I was little. I can't believe I was hesitant to tell him. This is the man who told me I could do and be anything I wanted. He let me fall so I could learn to get back up. He supported me in every decision I have ever made.

I should have known this was going to be no different.

"I know you did, slugger. And I know what's on the line for you," he says, releasing me from the hug but keeping his arm around my shoulder. "I also know that you wouldn't have even started this if you didn't think he was worth it. And he is."

If I had any reservations about Hunter before, with my dad's words, they all disappear.

28

HUNTER

I SHOULD BE WORRIED.

Okay. I am worried.

Why is Sadie's car in my driveway?

Don't get me wrong, she is welcome over whenever she wants. It's why I gave her a key. However, she has never once used it. She said she felt uncomfortable being at my place without me there.

So why tonight?

When I talked to her earlier today, I told her I'd be home a little after six, which she then promptly said she'd be over by seven. Our plan was to spend the night relaxing since training camp opens tomorrow.

Also known as the time of the year where our relationship is going to be put through tests we have yet to face.

Both of our jobs are about to go from zero to sixty, literally overnight. And we know this. I'll be trying to install a new offense with players who have never worked with me before. She's working her ass off knowing that the *US Daily* job could be hers.

It's a busy time for both of us. And we know what that means.

Less time together. Less time being us.

Neither of us has said it, but we both know it.

Tonight is supposed to be our last night of normal. We had plans to order in, throw on our latest Netflix binge, and just spend the night wrapped in each other's arms.

So Sadie beating me here has my spidey senses on alert.

They perk up even more when I walk into my condo to hear music playing and the smell of spaghetti sauce tickling my nose.

What is she up to?

I drop my keys and wallet on my front table and make my way back to the kitchen. If she heard me, she hasn't acknowledged me yet. Which is good. That gives me a chance to take her in.

She's wearing black leggings and a tank top that hugs all of her curves. Her hair is on the top of her head as always. I've learned that I like her hair up like that, it gives me a view of the line where her neck meets her shoulders. I love putting my mouth on the spot that sends shivers down her spine.

She has music connected to the speaker in the kitchen, and she's dancing back and forth. Nothing big, just swaying her hips to the sound. And then I get a glimpse of what she's doing.

Spaghetti noodles are in water on the stove, just waiting to be cooked. There's a pot of sauce next to it based on the smell. She's chopping vegetables and placing them into a salad bowl.

Holy shit. Sadie Benson is cooking for me. More importantly, Sadie Benson is cooking and it's not burning.

The gesture hits me square in the heart. This woman doesn't cook for herself. Well, not since the failed attempts at grilled cheese. She returned half of the kitchen items we bought as she came to terms that she was not meant to be a cook.

But here she is. In my home, cooking us dinner for two. The

gesture might not be grand in size, but in meaning? There isn't one bigger.

I fucking love this woman so damn much.

Without saying a word, I walk into my kitchen and slip my arms around her waist. She jumps a bit, but as my lips kiss her neck, she melts into me like she always does.

"You scared me," she says, putting her arms around mine to squeeze a little tighter.

"I could say the same thing about you. I didn't know what to think when I saw your car in the driveway."

I turn her around, and her hands immediately go around my neck. "I hope it's okay. I wanted to surprise you."

I kiss her nose, because I know if I kiss her lips I won't stop. "I loved seeing your car here. You didn't have to do this all for me."

"I wanted to. I thought it would be nice since this is probably our last date night for a while."

"You know we will see each other when the season starts."

She lets out a small sigh. "I know. But it won't be the same. It will be a lot of late nights and long days. Which is why I wanted one more special night. It doesn't get much more special than me cooking."

We both laugh, knowing no truer words have been spoken. "It smells amazing"

"You have to thank Helen for this one. She talked me through everything."

"I'll have to make sure to thank her at the next dinner," I say in a low tone, the intimacy of the moment getting to me.

At that moment, the song on the speaker changes. It's slow. Familiar.

Where have I heard this?

I instinctively pull Sadie closer to me, taking her hand in mine, my other brings her in close to me so her head can lay on my chest. Slowly, our bodies start swaying with the song.

Like a lightning bolt it hits me.

This is the song.

The song that we danced to on Beale Street.

The song that was playing the moment I knew that I had something special right in my arms.

The song that was playing the first time I knew I could love this woman forever.

"It's our song," she says in a whisper.

"It is. You know I couldn't remember the words that night."

"It's Elvis," she says, and even though I can't see her, I can feel her smile against me. "How can you not remember Elvis?"

I lean down and place my lips on her hair as I let the words of the song run through me.

Words about fools rushing in. Words about not being able to help but falling in love.

"I love you."

She raises her head off my chest, her hazel eyes finding mine.

"What did you just say?"

I can't help but smile before leaning down and kissing her. Nothing deep. Just a soft kiss to let her know that yes, I did just say that.

And no, I don't regret it.

"I love you, Sadie Benson. I think I loved you the first time we danced to this song. You are strong, and kind, and smart, and funny, and I thank my lucky stars every day that you came into my life."

"You haven't tried the spaghetti sauce yet."

"Woman, let me finish," I say, giving her hips a squeeze, which makes her laugh. Of course, she would throw in a joke right now. "I love you. I know it's probably too soon, but things are about to get crazy and I just wanted to let you know that—"

"I love you too," she says, cutting me off. "I love the man you are. I love the man you want to be. I love every single thing about you, Hunter McAvoy."

What else is there to say? Nothing. Which is why I scoop her up into my arms and take her to my bedroom.

The sauce can wait.

Making love to Sadie can't.

29

SADIE

"KNOCK-KNOCK! YOO-HOO? BOYFRIEND? ANYONE HOME?"

I'm surprised when I don't get an answer. His truck is in the driveway and he's not outside. He was the one who texted me to come over tonight and to pick up the pizza he ordered.

I have the pizza. I even picked up a six-pack of beer that he likes.

Now I just need to find him.

I check all the rooms in his condo, this time not feeling like a creep like I did that first night when I was checking out if he had a bed frame or not, but I can't find him. I shoot him a text, wondering where he is before settling on the sectional with my laptop. I figured he would have to work a bit tonight, so I brought my computer as well to get some work done.

The second week of training camp has ended. I don't even need two hands to keep track of how many times I've talked to Hunter. It's even less when you count how many times we've spent the night with each other.

To say that the official start of the season has been a rude awakening for us is an understatement. I knew it would be hard, but I didn't think it would be like this.

He is at the Fury facility from morning until night. I'm there every day as well, but not as long as him. This is an important part of the season for him. This is the first time he really gets to work with his players and install his offense. I know how much pressure he is putting on himself. I know how hard he has been working.

Which is why I have been giving him his space and not freaking out when he says that I should stay at my place because he won't be home until late. I want to make sure he has all the space he needs to get his feet under him as the season begins. I want him to excel. He is so determined to be the best, and I'm going to do everything possible to help him get there.

Even if that means I'm pushed to the back seat for a while.

Most days I at least get to physically see him. Though that comes from the limited viewing the media has of practices. And every time I catch a glimpse of him, it takes all my willpower not to stare at him the whole time.

The few times I have allowed myself to watch him, I have an overwhelming sense of pride in my heart. He's in his element. He's firm with his players, but you can tell there is a respect there. He knows what he wants, and he is not afraid to get his hands dirty and show the players what he means.

And if I must say, no man should make basketball shorts and a T-shirt look that good.

Today was a day off for the team, so there was no reason for the media to go to the facility. That doesn't mean the coaches got the day off. Needless to say, it was a pleasant surprise when Hunter texted me asking me to come over and to pick up pizza on the way.

Which makes it even more strange that he isn't home. Why would he have texted me? And why is his truck here, but he isn't?

I check my phone and see no reply, so I boot up my computer and throw my earbuds in. Today's mission: find the best stories I've ever written and send them to *US Daily* while jamming out to some Boyband Radio.

I exchanged emails with the editor, and they want to have a phone interview with me next week. They also want me to send them what I feel are my best stories. They also specifically asked for everything that I wrote about Hunter to see how I reported his hiring.

I can't help but smile as I go back and read all of those early stories. Then he was just a coach, a good-looking coach whom I had a reluctant crush on, but a coach, nonetheless. How funny that in such a short amount of time he has become so much a part of my life.

He's not just a part of my life. He's the love of my life. I don't know how I know that, I just do. I don't know what will happen in the future. I don't know if we'll survive this season, and I don't know what will happen when we are finally able to tell people about us. But I do know that even if this crumbles and fails, that when I'm eighty years old, I'll look back at these months with Hunter and smile because they happened.

"Dude! I have never seen your place. Plus, I have to take a piss. I'll be five minutes."

"Can't you hold—"

Hunter's voice is cut off when Davis, one of the Fury coaches, comes bursting through the front door. We're both frozen when we catch sight of each other. I'm sure he wasn't expecting me, and I sure as hell wasn't expecting him.

"Whoa! What are you doing here? Did you break in or something?"

His confused eyes look back and forth from me to Hunter. What he sees on both of our faces are looks of straight guilt.

We have been officially busted.

"I… I need to take a piss… so I'm…"

"Up the stairs. First door on the right," Hunter instructs, a resignation to his voice.

Davis gives me one more confused look before making his way up the stairs. Before I can say anything, Hunter is on the couch next to me, taking my hands in his.

"I'm so sorry," he says, bringing my knuckles to his lips. "I just got home and texted you when he messaged that he was on his way over and he needed my help with something back at the facility. I said I'd drive, but he was apparently not far from here. I couldn't think quick enough to make an excuse. And then I forgot my phone in my bedroom. I plugged it in to charge. I am so sorry, Sadie."

I don't even have the chance to respond before Davis is coming back down the stairs, his eyes glued to us on the couch.

"Davis—" Hunter says, but he holds up his hands, effectively cutting Hunter off.

"I won't say anything," he says, making sure to make eye contact with both of us. "As long as you both promise me that nothing shady is going on, I'll keep my mouth shut. This is none of my business. But I must say, everything now makes a hell of a lot more sense."

I nod in thanks, though I'm confused by that last part. Before I can ask what he means, Hunter is leading him out of the condo. I don't know what else he says. I think I hear something about "calling dibs" and Hunter giving him a slap on the back of the head as they step out of the condo.

I put my computer away and fall back onto the cushions of Hunter's sectional. I knew at some point we'd be found out. I just never thought it would be like this.

"So that happened," Hunter says, collapsing next to me. His head goes immediately to my lap. The man has a thing for me playing with his hair. Especially when he's on edge.

"What was that about calling dibs?" I ask, trying to lighten the mood. Hunter laughs, so mission accomplished.

"He was with me the day I saw you at Sandwich City after

Memphis. Let's just say I didn't react well when he said that you were hot."

This makes me laugh. "So, you called dibs?"

He nuzzles into my lap a little more. "More or less."

We sit there for a few minutes in complete silence. For a second, I think I've put him to sleep. It wouldn't be the first time he's fallen asleep on my lap when I'm playing with his hair. Then, he speaks, and his words nearly break my heart.

"I've missed you so damn much."

I lean down and place a kiss on his head. "I've missed you too."

"I don't like you not sleeping here. I know why you haven't, but that doesn't mean I have to like it. I feel like we never talk. Or see each other. I fucking hate it."

I let out a sigh. I haven't liked it either. "I know you've had long days. I just don't want to be in the way. So I haven't wanted to bother you."

This makes him sit up. "I have been a miserable bastard to my coaches and players, and it's because I have to see you almost every day, and know that I didn't get to kiss you that morning. Our days have been long, and at first I thought it would be best if some nights we stayed apart, but I was wrong. Dead wrong. I don't care if I've been working for thirty-six straight hours, I need to see you when I get home. Hell, if you started moving your stuff in here, I would be over the moon."

My eyes go wide. "You... you want me to move in?"

He gives me a shrug, and for the first time in God knows how long, I'm greeted by my favorite small smile. "I know we can't right now. We have to wait until we're free to be out in the open. But I just want to let you know that if you were here every day, and a few of your clothes happened to make their way over here, I wouldn't be upset."

I can't help myself anymore. I adjust myself so I'm straddling him because I need to feel as much of him as possible against me. I bring our lips together, and as soon as they connect, I feel like I'm home. That the weirdness of the past two weeks was just another milestone and building block in our relationship.

Hunter eventually breaks our kiss, but his hands don't leave my body. "Promise me no more staying away when we are in Nashville. I know when we're on the road we'll need to keep our distance. But if we are here, it doesn't matter how long our days have been, or how early we have to be up in the morning, from now on we are beginning and ending each day together."

"Promise," I say, leaning down and giving him one kiss. "Did you really call dibs on me?"

"Hell yeah, I did," he says as he stands up, still holding me so my legs wrap around his body. "And I'd do it all over again."

30

HUNTER

"IT'S his first game as a pro. You need to give him some breathing room. He's a fucking rookie, Hunter."

Davis's words run through me as I slam my now-empty beer can down on the small patio outside my hotel room in Miami. I unceremoniously toss it on the ground, joining the now five other empty cans.

All from me.

"I know he's a fucking rookie," I say, cracking open another beer. "It doesn't give him the excuse to forget how to throw a damn pass. Or to act like he doesn't give a fuck."

I should be quieter. It's nearing midnight. I don't know if the Fury has every room on this floor booked or not.

I can't find it in me to care, though.

We had our first preseason game tonight.

We got our asses beat.

And when I say we, I mean the offense.

I've never felt like such a failure in my life.

The offense completely crumbled. Bryce Donald, our quarterback of the future, was a deer in headlights. He didn't complete one pass. It was like he wasn't even in the same stadium as the rest of us. Every play we ran was a failure. Luckily, we went into the game only planning to play our starters in the first quarter. That was the only thing that stopped the bleeding.

I didn't speak to anyone after the game. I immediately came to my hotel room and planned on sulking here, alone, until Davis showed up with a case of beer. Thankfully, I don't have to put on a brave or happy face around Sadie. She's staying at a different hotel, and I know she's still working.

Just as well. I'm shit company tonight. And I don't want her to see me like this.

"Why are you taking this so hard?" Davis asks. "It's the first preseason game. Everyone knows preseason games don't mean shit."

"Because we are not where we need to be as an offense, and tonight proved it."

I had a sinking feeling in my gut for the past few weeks that what I was trying to do with the Fury wasn't working. Practices have been horrible. The defense was kicking our ass every day during intra-squad scrimmages. But I wasn't letting it get to me. I was a new coach, and these guys had never worked with me before. It was going to take some time for us to hit our stride.

Tonight was a rude awakening and confirmed every doubt I was having. Was I too tough? Was I not tough enough? Was my offense too complex? Was I not a good coach or teacher?

Every time I let my mind go down these rabbit holes, I only hear one voice in the back of my mind fueling my doubt. And his voice is getting louder with each passing day.

"All tonight proved was that we still have work to do," Davis says as I hear my message alert go off from my phone inside my hotel suite.

I walk through the patio doors and grab my phone off the charger to see a text from Sadie.

Girlfriend: I'm on my way back to my hotel. I'll call you in an hour if that's OK?

Boyfriend: Great.

I know my response is short, but I'm worried that between my piss-poor attitude and the fact that I'm drunk will lead to a text message I might regret. Still, just seeing her name on my phone slightly brightens my mood as I take back my seat on the patio, phone in hand.

"Remind me to thank Sadie next time I see her. At least now I know how to get you out of a mental spiral," Davis jokes. "How's that going?"

His question is sincere. It also catches me off guard. That's not an uncommon question for friends to ask one another. But because no one knew about me and Sadie, no one has ever asked me that.

"She's great," I say, my tone a little lighter now that I'm not talking about football. "It's been a little hard since the season started, but we're getting by. Thanks again by the way for not saying anything to anyone about us. It's... it's complicated."

"No problem, man." My phone starts ringing in my hand, and Davis slaps my shoulder as he stands. "I'm sure that's her. Take the call. Try to forget about tonight. We'll get back to the drawing board when we're back in Nashville."

I swipe the phone to answer as Davis leaves the room, not even looking down to see who called. "I thought you weren't calling me for another hour, gorgeous."

"I'm ignoring the gorgeous comment. And you're lucky I didn't call you the second that putrid excuse for a game was over."

Fucking wonderful.

I lean down and grab another beer out of the case that Davis left. That is the only way I will get through this phone call with my father.

"To what do I owe the pleasure, Dad?"

"Don't get salty with me, Hunter. I wouldn't be calling you if it wasn't clear that you need my help."

His help! He has got to be fucking kidding me.

"Your help? Your help! What in God's name makes you think that I want, or need, your help?"

"Hunter, don't be stubborn." His voice is stern, like he's lecturing me when he was teaching me how to drive. "You clearly need some help. Your players looked horrible tonight. Now, I don't know why you insist on running that convoluted offense, but I think if you simplify it down…"

I tune him out. I have no clue what he's saying, and I honestly don't give a flying fuck. My entire life my father has believed that he is God's gift to football. Don't get me wrong, in his day, he was great. One of the best. I'll never argue about why he's in the Hall of Fame.

But he still thinks it's the late 1980s. Defenses were slower then. Offenses didn't need to have so many plays to be successful. He has never understood that the game has evolved over the countless decades since he was last on the field.

I really don't want to listen to him, but the last words he says catches my attention. "…and I don't understand why you think you have to reinvent the wheel with offenses. Just run the ball on first and second down, and then pass it on third. It's not that hard, Hunter. Back in my day, that's all I had to do, and look where it got me. I'm in the Hall of Fame. You keep this up, and you'll be unemployed by your bye week."

That's it. I'm about to fucking lose it.

"Shut the fuck up, Dad. Just shut… the fuck… up."

"Excuse me? Don't use that tone with me, Hunter."

"No. You don't get to call and tell me how to do my job." I'm now standing on the patio, pacing back and forth. I feel it. Years of rage and anger are about to bubble over. "Did my team have a bad night tonight? Yes. I won't argue with you on that. And if you ever *once* showed an interest or supported me in my career, then *maybe* I'd let you give me advice. But every time I hear you bash my profession, or bash my offenses, it's just another reminder of how bitter you are. That forward-thinking coaches like me, and new offenses, were the reason you had to retire early. You knew you couldn't hang. You knew you couldn't handle it. You were a coward. You were a damn coward and you quit. Well, guess what, Dad? You don't get to take that anger out on me."

Silence is heavy on the line. I have never in my life talked to my dad that way. Hell, the whole part of him retiring early and being a coward, I don't even know where that came from. I've thought about that from time to time, but it was always just my conspiracy theory as to why he retired in the prime of his career.

Now it's out there in the open. And I can't take it back.

I don't want to take it back either.

"Well, I think you've said all there is to say," he says, a defeat to his voice I've never heard before. "Call your mother soon. She misses you."

Click.

I stare at the phone, still in shock about what just transpired. The game tonight. Bryce's performance. My dad. Everything is spinning out of control right now.

I just unleashed years of pent-up anger at my dad, but he's right. Something isn't working in the offense. And I don't know how to fix it. What if he's right? What if I'm not cut out for this? What if I'm a failure?

I feel the doubt starting to slowly seep into my veins.

I shake my head, trying to snap myself out of this. Giving into these feelings of doubt means he wins. I won't let that happen. Then I take my phone and bring back up the last text I received.

Boyfriend: Are you back at your hotel yet?
Girlfriend: Halfway. Why?

Boyfriend: I had a blowup with Bo.

Girlfriend: I'll be right there.

I know this is risky. Someone could see her coming into the hotel. At this point, I don't care. Let them find out.

I need calm. I need my center.

I need Sadie.

31

SADIE

GIRLFRIEND: *I'll probably come over to your place around six, if that works?*

Boyfriend: I won't be home till late. Probably past ten. Maybe best if you stay at your place tonight. I'm sorry.

Girlfriend: OK. Miss you. <3

And like I predicted, no response. No I miss you too. No I love you.

Nothing.

The sad thing is that I'm not shocked by this. This isn't the first time this kind of message exchange has happened since we returned from Miami. Or what I like to call, our last good night.

That was five weeks ago.

I hate that I associate that night with good when it was horrible for Hunter. The fight with his dad shook him in ways he wasn't ready for. I'll never admit I saw this, but he fell asleep crying on my lap.

My heart broke for him.

But we were together. We were a team.

Since he came back, he's been a man possessed trying to turn this offense around. And he's on a solo mission to do so. He tried easing up on the playbook. He tried adding new plays. He tried becoming a straight asshole to the players. He tried being their friend.

Nothing has worked.

We're now two weeks into the regular season, and the Fury has yet to win. Or even score a touchdown.

The offense has been putrid. Bryce can't figure out how to run the offense. Nothing is gelling. And Hunter is taking the brunt of it from the media.

Including me.

And here lies the other component of why my boyfriend has been avoiding me. Yes, he promised me during preseason that we would spend every night together. But would you want to share a bed with a woman who is writing daily articles about how bad your offense is? I wouldn't want to see me either.

Funny how I never thought about this scenario when we started dating. It's my job as a reporter to talk about why things are or aren't working with a team. I did it last year leading up to Bancroft getting fired. I had to speculate daily on his job security and his future. I pulled no punches. I told it like it was.

I never thought I'd have to do that with Hunter. Especially this early into his season. Every time I write a story about "what's wrong with Hunter McAvoy's offense" it kills me a little inside.

I know Hunter's text about being there late isn't a lie or a cop out. The Fury staff has been pulling all-nighters trying to figure out what's wrong. I give them credit; they aren't just waiting for the ship to right itself. That means I've been spending many nights alone.

And many nights wondering if Hunter and I will survive this.

I can't do this another night. I'm driving myself crazy with "what ifs." What if Hunter breaks up with me because of a story I write? What if the Fury has to fire Hunter this season and he has to move? What if I get fired because I let my feelings for Hunter get in the way of my reporting?

"AAAAAHHHHHHHHH!" I scream to no one, because I can't hold it in anymore.

I grab my phone off the charger and bring up my contacts. I need to talk to someone or I might go insane.

"Hello? Sadie?"

"Bethany, are you busy?"

"No. I'm just finishing up at the shop. Is everything okay? You sound upset."

"I..." I push back the tears. Damn Hunter McAvoy for turning me into a crier. "I'm going crazy and I might cry and I'm freaking out."

"I'll be there in an hour. Do you have wine?"

"You know I'm not a wine drinker." I pause to try and get a glimpse of something from the view in my living room. Boom. There it is.

"I have tequila."

"Even better. Call for pizza. I'll bring ice cream."

Fifty-eight minutes later, Bethany is standing in my apartment with three different kinds of ice cream and a bag full of limes.

"You are my hero," I say as I grab plates for the pizza that was delivered. "I hope you didn't have plans tonight."

She gives me a wave of her hand as she puts away the ice cream. "Not a one. I was with my last client when you texted, and I really didn't want to eat alone tonight. This worked out for everyone."

We load our plates and grab a drink before heading into my living room. I can't help but notice Bethany looking around, taking in every inch of my space.

"Your place is great," she says, taking a seat on one end of my couch. "I can't believe this is the first time I've been over here. I love this area rug."

I give her a sad smile, because now I'm reminded of Hunter and our shopping excursion to decorate my apartment. He picked this rug out.

"Oh gosh, what did I say?" She immediately puts her pizza down on the coffee table. "Sadie, talk to me. I've never seen you this upset."

I give my head a shake, determined not to cry. What is there to cry about? It's not like we are broken up. I just miss my boyfriend. That's all.

Right?

"Things with Hunter... well... they haven't been great as of late."

"Did you two break up?"

I shake my head. "No. At least, I don't think so. The season has been rough on him and it's kind of spilling over to us."

"Talk to me about it."

And I do. I spill everything. When my word vomit is over, I expect to see an *I told you so look* on Bethany's face. Hell, that's how I'd be looking at me.

Instead, I see my stepsister looking at me with kindness. Sympathy. There is not an ounce of judgment in her eyes. Even as she hands me a tissue, because at some point in this story, I started crying my eyes out.

Right here, right now, I've never been so thankful for my dad marrying Helen.

"Girl. I didn't realize this was going to get so heavy," Bethany says, standing up from the couch. "Be right back. Don't move."

I don't even look to see what she's doing. Before I know it, she has returned to the couch with two shot glasses, the bottle of tequila, and a cut-up lime.

"Here. We should have done this before we started."

I laugh but do what she says. I sling back the shot and suck on the lime. The tequila burns down my throat.

It's exactly what I needed.

"Thanks," I say, wiping my mouth with the tissue. "I'm a mess."

"Girl, if you weren't a mess right now, I'd wonder if there was something wrong with you."

I can't help but laugh. "I don't want to lose him, Bethany. I love him."

She takes my hand and gives it a squeeze. "I know, sis. I know."

32

HUNTER

"WHAT IN THE fuck is this shit?"

I didn't know my voice could reach this level, and I'm sure everyone in the Fury facility heard me. Hell, everyone in the metro Nashville limits heard me. Paul physically flinches at my outburst. Though my reaction shouldn't surprise him. If he didn't want me to react like this, then he shouldn't have shown me this morning's edition of *The Banner* with a huge headline:

Too much to handle? Hunter McAvoy in over his head as Fury offensive coordinator

You would think that if my girlfriend was writing an article wondering if the Fury made the right decision to hire me, that she would have given me some fucking notice.

Yes, that would require us speaking to each other more than a couple of times a week. We haven't spent the night with each other in... fuck, I don't know how long it's been. Most nights I don't even go home, choosing to sleep on my office couch. But still, a little bit of a heads-up would have been nice. Glad to know she has so much confidence in me. Though, based on the past few weeks of her articles, this shouldn't have been a shock. The woman has been busting my balls every day in her paper.

Though she's not wrong. Every word she is saying is right. Doesn't mean I have to like it.

"Did you know she was writing this?" I ask Paul as steam comes out of my ears. At least that's what it feels like.

He shakes his head. "The reporters don't exactly give me a daily rundown of what stories they are writing, Hunter. I just wanted you to see it before you have your weekly press conference."

Fuck me.

Of course, that's today. Just my luck. Not only do I have to answer questions about "am I in over my head," I have to do it looking at Sadie, who apparently thinks that I'm not cut out for this job.

Fucking great.

A rational person would understand where she's coming from. Right now, I am anything but rational. I'm pissed, confused, and frustrated. And it gets worse every day.

The beginning of this season has been awful. Things didn't get better after Miami. In fact, they got worse. We are now three games into the season, and we just scored our first touchdown last week. I've had to bench Bryce because he was just not getting it. The veteran backup has been doing all right, but he's not built for the offense that I built specifically for my first overall pick, quarterback prodigy.

Things are going downhill quick. I can't seem to make it stop.

Trying to figure out what the hell I'm doing wrong has been plaguing my mind every second of every day. I've been a bastard to be around, which is why I haven't seen Sadie. I can't be around her right now. Hell, I can't be around anyone. I need to figure this out.

If today's article is any indication, it's probably best I've kept her at arm's length. If she thinks I'm in over my head, I can only imagine what she would think if she saw me every night poring over plays and game film, trying to figure out where I've gone wrong.

She'd see that I'm struggling. That I'm lost. That I'm exactly what Bo thinks I am—not good enough and who only made it this far in life because of my last name.

"How much time do I have until I have to face The Mob?"

Paul checks his watch. "Less time than you'd like."

"Now?"

"Unfortunately. Let's get it over with."

————

"HUNTER, what's going on with the offense?"

"Is Bryce a bust?"

"Have you felt overwhelmed with the position?"

The questions are coming at me faster than I can answer them. As soon as I get the words out for one, another asshole reporter is throwing something else at me.

Except Sadie. Like always, she hasn't asked me a thing yet. She's probably waiting until the end, like always.

I wish she'd just ask. It would be better just to get it over with. Then I can hear in her voice how much of a failure she thinks I am.

I've never doubted my abilities so much like I have the past few months. Before, I had little voices in my head telling me I wasn't good enough, or that I was only getting jobs because of who my dad was. But I always shut those voices up by proving the doubters, and my father, wrong.

Those voices are getting louder. So loud that I can barely think anymore. And I didn't realize it, but they all sound like him.

"You're only coaching because you knew you couldn't hack it as a player."

"Why are you running this play?"

"Coaches are the guys who weren't good enough to make it."

"At least you won one championship."

I'm about to go down a long road of self-doubt when I hear her voice, though I don't have any idea what Sadie just asked.

"I'm sorry. Can you repeat the question?" I ask.

For the first time today, I allow myself to look at her. I feel like I haven't seen her in weeks. Months. She's still my beautiful girl. She's wearing her glasses today and, as always, her hair is on the top of her head. To anyone else, she probably looks fine.

I can see more. She looks… sad. Tired.

That's probably my fault as well.

I've never been so angry at a person, yet also want to take their pain away.

I love her, but I want to scream at her.

Right now, I can't do any of those things.

"My question is regarding Bryce," Sadie says, before clearing her throat. "Could his performance be a mental block stemming from a personal matter? Or has the transition to the pros been too much for him to handle?"

Too much for him to handle.

That was the headline on her fucking article today.

"It's funny… the phrase too much to handle," I begin, trying to keep the sarcasm and snark out of my voice. "You never know when you're going to be ready to handle something. All the signs could point to 'you're ready.' You could cross every t and dot every i to prepare for it. You could think of one thousand scenarios and think you have an answer for all of them. Everything could seem to be in perfect alignment. Then, BAM! Something happens. Maybe it's the reality of being in a live game. Maybe it's an injury. Maybe it's just something that you forgot to take into consideration. No matter what, though, that doesn't mean you give up on that person. We aren't giving up on Bryce. We aren't giving up on the season. This isn't too much for anyone to handle. We just have to figure out how to get the pieces back in order."

My words hang in the air as Paul dismisses the reporters. I know I probably said too much. It's all the truth.

It's true about Bryce. I'm not giving up on him.

The same can be said for me and Sadie. We thought we could handle this relationship. We thought we had a perfect game plan. Turns out we didn't.

And also, like Bryce, I'm not ready to give up on her. On us.

But we can't keep going on like this.

"Benson!" I yell, which causes all of the reporters who are exiting the room to look back at me in confusion. Coaches never directly address reporters. "Can I have a word with you?"

She doesn't say anything as she turns around to walk back toward me, but I can see the mix of emotion in her eyes. I'm sure it's exactly how mine look right now as well. Paul has left, thank God, and by the time Sadie reaches me, we are the only two in the interview room.

"Nice article today," I say, my sarcasm thick.

"Just doing my job," she replies matter-of-factly.

I let out a sigh and pinch the bridge of my nose because I want to yell at her. I want to kiss her. I want to scream at her. I want to break down in front of her and confess that I'm overwhelmed and confused. I want to fuck her over this chair.

But I can't do any of that.

"I'm coming over tonight. We need to talk."

She looks around quickly, making sure no one can hear. "You can't come over. It's a weekday. Someone might see you."

I lean in close. So close that if someone were to walk in right now, they might think I was kissing her.

If only.

"I don't give a flying fuck if anyone sees me. We have shit to figure out. Off the record."

33

SADIE

HUNTER DOESN'T EVEN KNOCK.

I didn't know what time to expect him. It's not like we've been seeing much of each other lately, and even before then, some nights were later than others. All I know is that I've been on pins and needles since I got home today.

Is he coming over to break up with me? I wouldn't blame him. I'd break up with me too for the story I wrote in today's paper.

I hated it. I didn't write the headline, that's my editor's job, but it's not like it was wrong or misleading. I did question whether or not he was in over his head. Because it's a logical question to ask, and I would have speculated it had it been any other coach. I can't show favorable treatment.

I cried as soon as I hit send on the article. I cried more than I ever have in my entire life. Every word I wrote broke another piece inside me.

I nearly didn't go to the Fury facility today. I have never taken a sick day, and I almost did. I wanted to hide in my bedroom and not have to see Hunter's face. When I came face-to-face with him, it made the pain come right back.

Normally, I'd stay and write at the facility after a press conference. I couldn't today. I couldn't be in the same building as him. I came back to my apartment. I don't even remember what I wrote. I've been on autopilot as I sat and stewed, waiting for Hunter to get here.

And now that he is, I have no idea what to think. Because he's not empty-handed.

"What in the world?"

Hunter doesn't acknowledge my question. Instead, he walks right to my kitchen counter and sets down a box of pizza, another to-go box which smells like chicken wings, and a six-pack of beer.

Is he feeding me before dumping me? I don't know whether to be happy or sad about that.

"I didn't know if you had eaten. We have a lot of shit to figure out, and I'm not trying to do it if you're hangry."

I don't know whether to be touched because he was thinking of me, or angry because he thought I couldn't have a rational discussion without food. He's not wrong... but still. Ouch.

I don't say a word as he fishes paper plates out of my cabinet and pulls out two beers before setting the rest of the bottles in the refrigerator.

"Here," he says. "Fix a plate."

I stare at the plate, then back up at him, my anger and frustration beginning to take over. "Are you fucking kidding me right now? We have barely spoken in weeks, and all you can say to me is 'fix a plate'?"

"What would you rather have me say?"

Is he... is he serious? What would I rather have him say?

Does he really need to fucking ask that?

"I would rather you say, 'Sadie, I'm an asshole for shutting you out.' I'd rather you say, 'Sadie, we need to end this because I can't be with someone who writes negative things about me.' Hell, I'd even rather you say, 'Let's tell everyone about us and rip the fucking Band-Aid off.' But in no universe do I want you to tell me to fix a goddamn plate when I have no idea where we stand!"

My breathing is heavy because damn, that felt really good. It's not nearly everything I have to tell Hunter tonight. Or make him tell me. But getting out that anger... yeah. That was needed.

When my breathing slows down, I take a look at Hunter. I expected him to yell back. I expected him to have some sort of rebuttal.

I didn't expect him to be standing in my kitchen looking like I just killed his puppy.

"You want to break up?"

I let out a shriek of frustration as I march back to my living room and sit down. He's been here five minutes and I already have a headache.

"No. I do not want to break up with you. But I don't want to keep going on like this. We aren't in a good spot, Hunter. And the longer you shut me out, the worse it will get."

He leaves his plate and beer in the kitchen before coming to sit by me. He immediately takes my hand in his. God, I have missed his touch.

"You're right. I have been shutting you out. And for that, I'm sorry. I promised you that no matter how tough things got, we would begin and end our days with each other, and I haven't kept that promise."

"You haven't." My words come out more defeated than I mean them to, but it's like right now, all the emotions and frustration of the past few weeks are crashing down on me.

"I knew this job would be tough. But I never expected this," he says, not looking at me, but brushing his thumb over my hand, I'm guessing needing the contact. "I've never not succeeded in something. Even the people who said I only got certain things because I was Bo's son, I was able to prove them wrong. Then, this season happens. My self-doubt came creeping in. All I could hear was my dad in my head telling me that I'd never make it."

I inch a little closer to him because while he never said this out loud, I had a sinking suspicion that Bo had a large part to do with this.

"I needed to fix it. I needed to prove to everyone that I could do this. So I cut myself off. I cut you off. But what has that gotten me? An offense that isn't getting any better, and a pissed-off girlfriend who writes articles about me doubting whether or not I should have been hired."

"In my defense, I would have written that about you even if we weren't dating. That wasn't because I was a scorned woman. That's because I'm a reporter and I have to write the story. No matter what. That's my job, Hunter, to report the news. You knew that when we got together."

He collapses back into my couch, letting out the most defeated sigh I've ever heard.

"I didn't mean to insinuate you wrote that because you were angry at me. Fuck, I can't even apologize correctly."

I shift my legs underneath me, which puts me an inch or two closer to Hunter. "If it counts for anything, I thought you'd come over here and just start screaming at me. The food threw me for a loop."

"Why would you think that?"

"Because of how you spoke to me today after the press conference. You were quite pissed."

He sits back up, his head now in his hands as his elbows rest on his knees. "I was. I'm not going to lie, I still am."

This I was expecting. This I'm ready for. "I'm not apologizing for doing my job, Hunter."

"And you shouldn't have to," he says, now looking back my way. "I don't want you to. I might not like it, but I don't blame you for what you wrote."

"You don't?"

He shakes his head. "I don't. I can *not* like it and also understand it all at once. When I saw you, Paul had just shown me the headline. It set me off. That's why I was angry before the interviews. And that's why I snapped at you afterward."

"So, what changed? Why were you spitting fire earlier, and then just a few hours later you bring me pizza?"

He turns back to me, now taking both of my hands in his. I can't help but look directly into his eyes. Earlier today I saw rage. Now? Now, I'm seeing remorse.

"The question you asked me today, that's what."

"I'm not following."

"You asked me about Bryce's headspace. The kid has more talent in his pinkie than I ever had. But you were right, there is something not right with him. So, I pulled him aside today and asked if he was okay. And not just physically. He didn't say much, but I feel like we had a breakthrough. And then I thought, maybe that's my problem? Maybe my problem is in my head as well. I was letting the voices of doubt get the best of me, and it was affecting everything around me. And not just my job. It was affecting my relationship with you. I don't know if I would have gotten there had you not pushed me along."

I look away, the compliment too much to take. "All I did was ask a question."

"No, gorgeous," he says, bringing my hands to his lips. "There's a good chance you saved the season."

He leans forward in search of my lips. I don't deny him.

It's been too long. I missed the feel of his mouth on me. I missed the feeling of his weight on me.

I missed him.

The rest of the night is a blur of kisses, apologies, agreements, and more kisses. Yes, we eat the pizza. Yes, we have amazing makeup sex.

In between all of that, Hunter and I agree that we can't let things fester. He now knows he can come to me if something is weighing on his mind, and he needs me to be a girlfriend and not a reporter. I promise him that if I'm going to tell Fury fans everywhere that he's doing a shitty job, that I'll give him a warning. We also come to the decision that after the bye week in New Orleans, we are getting away for a few days. Just the two of us.

And that night, after way too many nights apart, we end the day together. Just as promised.

34

SADIE

BOYFRIEND: *I miss you.*

Girlfriend: You just saw me two hours ago. And I am literally down the hall from you.

Boyfriend: This isn't my fault. It's yours. You can't wake me up the way you did today and not expect me to miss you.

Girlfriend: I just wanted to make sure you had something to remember me by since I won't see you for a few days. <3

Boyfriend: Mission accomplished. And what are you still doing here? Didn't the rest of The Mob go home?

Girlfriend: 1. You know I hate it when you call it that. 2. Yes, the rest of them went home. I'm just trying to get ahead so I don't have to work tomorrow. Plus, I have time to kill before I meet Bethany tonight for dinner.

Boyfriend: I'd like to eat you for dinner.

Girlfriend: Behave. <3

I can't help but smile reading Hunter's texts. Though, in my defense, all I seem to do lately is smile.

Since our heart-to-heart last week, everything seems to have gotten back on track.

Our relationship as well as the Fury's season.

After starting off 0-4, the team pulled out its first win. Bryce was put back in as starter, and he looked like a whole new quarterback. The offense set a franchise record in points scored in a game, and Bryce was named the league's rookie of the week.

No one could believe it. Hell, I think Hunter was even a little shocked at the one-eighty.

It's like everything is now right again with the world.

As for me and Hunter? Things are better than ever. I feel like we're back to the Sadie and Hunter of before the season. I can't wait to steal a few days away with him in New Orleans after this week's game.

Boyfriend: I don't like behaving. When do I get to see you again?

Girlfriend: Well, let's see. It's Friday. You leave with the team later this afternoon. I won't be in town until Saturday night, but unless you have another blowup with your father, I don't think we should chance me coming to the team hotel. Which, unfortunately, means you have to wait until Sunday night to see me.

Boyfriend: What I got from that is all I have to do is text Bo, have a fight, and you'll come over? I can do that. I mean, I haven't talked to him since Miami. I'm sure I've done plenty since then to irritate him.

Girlfriend: Don't pick a fight. You'll survive. See you Sunday. Love you.

Boyfriend: Love you more.

"Why are you smiling like a lunatic?" Tommy asks from over my shoulder, scaring the shit out of me. I hurry up and click off of the text message app and set my phone down. Just one more second, and he would have seen my background picture that is clearly me and Hunter.

"None of your business, old man," I say. "I didn't realize anyone else was still working today."

"You would have if you hadn't been glued to your phone for

the last fifteen minutes. If I didn't know better, I'd think you were texting your boyfriend."

My face goes white. My blood goes cold.

Does Tommy know? No. He couldn't. Could he?

"What do you mean?" I say hurriedly, turning back to my computer so I don't have to make eye contact with him.

Tommy takes a seat next to me. "It means you have the look on your face that my teenage daughter does every time her punk-ass boyfriend messages her."

"You calling me a teenager? Come on, Tommy. You can do better than that."

"You know that's not what I meant. Quit trying to deflect," he says.

I am. And I'm not being very good about it. I can tell him I'm dating someone, right? I just won't give names. At least then I'm not lying to him and I don't have to continue to look like I got caught with my hand in the cookie jar.

"Fine. I'm seeing someone. There. You happy?"

He leans back in his chair with a satisfied smile. "Yes. I am. And I'm happy for you. This business will kill you, and any semblance of a personal life, if you let it. Just ask my ex-wife. I've been worried about you. I know you put a lot of hours into your job. I'm glad you're realizing there is a world outside of reporting football."

I let Tommy's words sink in. He's right. For so many years, I didn't think I could have a relationship and a successful career. And I loved my job. I wasn't giving that up. So I just told myself that I didn't need love to be happy.

But my laptop doesn't keep me warm at night. One text from Hunter telling me that he loves me makes me feel a million times better than a random fan on Twitter telling me that he liked a story I wrote.

I love my job. I really do.

But I love Hunter more.

"Thanks, Tommy," I say, all of a sudden feeling very emotional. "He's a good guy."

"I hope I can meet him sometime."

Me, too, Tommy. Me, too.

"I mean, if you're still here, then I think I should come get a goodbye kiss."

Oh. Shit.

Fuck. Fuck. Fuckety-fuck.

I hear Hunter walking through the pressroom, each step getting closer to my desk area. You can't see my work station from the doorway. He has no idea that Tommy is sitting next to me as he makes his intentions to kiss me known.

He has no idea that he unintentionally just outed us. And not to family or friends.

To a man who has the ability to end this for us.

As soon as he rounds the corner, it's as if time stops. I'm staring at Hunter. Hunter is staring at Tommy. And Tommy? He's looking back and forth between us as he's slowly putting together the puzzle pieces.

"I can explain!" I blurt out at the same time as Hunter shouts, "That's not what I meant!"

If we didn't look guilty before, we do now.

Tommy turns to Hunter. "Have you given her any information that you shouldn't have?"

His tone is firm. Probably the most firm I've ever heard Tommy speak. It's almost like if my dad were asking Hunter what his intentions were with me.

"No, sir, I have not," Hunter replies.

Tommy turns back to face me. I was ready to see disappointment in his eyes. But his expression is blank, and I think that might be worse. Now I don't know what to think.

"Sadie, I would ask you if you've given him favorable treatment, but considering you all but said he might not be ready for this job just a few weeks ago, I can see you're not pulling any punches."

I laugh under my breath. "No. No favorable treatment. We've been careful."

Hunter closes the distance between us, and before I know it, he's next to me, reaching for my hand. "I know what you're probably thinking. And you're probably right on most of it. But this? It's not just a fling. I love her. She loves me. We know what's on the line for both of us."

Tommy weighs Hunter's words, and at this moment, I am so glad that Hunter's hand is keeping me grounded.

"Is he the one who was making you smile?" Tommy asks me.

I nod. "He was. He does. This isn't casual, Tommy. I love him. I also understand if you need to write about this. I'd never ask you to sit on a story."

I hate having to say that, but it's true. I know I'd at least consider writing about it. I don't know if I would, but I'd think about it.

Tommy shakes his head. "I'm not about to start writing sports gossip. As long as this stays fair. The second I see either one of you pulling punches on the other, or if she gets information I know came from you, I'm telling both of your superiors."

I nod. "I understand."

Tommy eyes Hunter again. "McAvoy."

Hunter straightens himself. "Yes, sir?"

Tommy puts his hand on Hunter's shoulder and gives it a squeeze. "Off the record. If you hurt this girl, you will need to find a new job. You won't want to face The Mob if you do."

This makes Hunter laugh. "Yes, sir. And I don't plan on it."

Tommy seems satisfied with that answer. "I'm leaving now. You two do whatever you were going to do when I wasn't supposed to be here. See you both in New Orleans."

Hunter and I both let out huge breaths the second Tommy leaves the room.

"I am so sorry," he says, taking my other hand in his. "I had no clue he was here."

I shrug. "I know you didn't know. It was bound to happen sooner or later."

We both lean in, our foreheads now touching. We stand like that for more than a few minutes, letting everything process.

"I think I was more scared of him than your dad," Hunter says, which makes me laugh.

"I think I was more scared for his reaction than my dad's." And that's the truth. I just didn't realize it until the second Hunter walked into the room.

"Can we trust him?" Hunter's question is legitimate. He doesn't know Tommy like I do. To him, he's just another reporter. To me? He might be one of my rivals, but he is also a good friend.

"We can. But we need to be more careful."

"No more sneaking in for a kiss goodbye," Hunter says, crossing his heart with his fingers. "I promise."

"What kiss? There hasn't been any kiss."

My words light a spark in Hunter's eyes as he closes the distance between us, bringing our lips together. Considering that we are doing it in a space that is hugely forbidden and fraught with danger, the intensity is amplified in ways I wasn't expecting.

"What time is your flight?" I ask, my finger stroking down the front of his shirt.

"I don't have to be at the airport for another two hours."

I turn away from him and quickly pack up my laptop. "Then we better get a move on so I can tell you goodbye properly."

35

HUNTER

"THIS FEELS SO... WEIRD."

I look back over my shoulder to Sadie, who is getting ready in our en suite bathroom in our hotel in New Orleans. "Weird in a good way I hope."

She shrugs, exiting the bathroom in nothing but her white lace bra and panties, her hair styled and makeup done. I swallow the lump in my throat because damn, that's a sight I could never get tired of seeing.

I don't get to see her like this often. Sadie isn't a frills kind of woman. Don't get me wrong, I love her exactly how she is. I fell in love with the girl who throws her hair on top of her head and forgets most mornings to put on makeup.

But getting to see this side of Sadie? It's like a gift. A gift I plan on cherishing, then unwrapping later.

"Yes, weird in a good way. We've barely gone on any real dates. A double date feels so scandalous," she says before slipping on a dress that takes my breath away. It's simple, and it hugs every one of her curves. The navy material in contrast to the white lingerie underneath it is doing things for me.

And for my dick.

I stand up and force myself to quit watching her get dressed. If I keep doing this, we are never leaving the room, and that bra and panty set will be wrecked.

"Brady and Kendra can't wait to meet you. Plus, we get to indulge in authentic New Orleans cuisine on his tab."

When Sadie and I decided to stay behind in New Orleans after yesterday's game—a game in which we kicked ass and took names, giving us two wins in a row—I got a hold of my old college roommate. Marcus Brady is a New Orleans boy through and through. He and his brother grew up in one of the worst parishes in the city. His family was homeless for a few months after Katrina. He and his brother were determined not to just be another statistic. So, they came up with a plan. Marcus went to Alabama on a football scholarship and got his business degree. His brother went to culinary school. Now we are about to eat at his critically reviewed restaurant right off the French Quarter.

We understood each other in college. We might have come from two completely different backgrounds and upbringings, but we knew what it was like for playing football to not be our end game. He followed his heart. He understood when I followed mine. He was my biggest supporter when I declared that I was pursuing a coaching career and not turning pro.

"I heard his restaurant is amazing," Sadie said, walking over to me so I can zip the back of her dress.

"Not as amazing as you look tonight," I say, placing a soft kiss on her shoulder after I finish helping with her dress.

"That was cheesy, even for you, McAvoy," she teases.

"I speak only truths," I say, turning her around to face me. "Now, let's get out of here before I take this dress back off and fuck you senseless."

———

"HOW IN THE hell are you dating the reporter who asked Coach the question to end all questions, and you are *just now* telling me this!"

We made it halfway through dinner before I dropped that fun fact. That story has officially won Sadie over in Brady's eyes.

Not that she needed it.

As soon as we arrived, I knew tonight was going to be amazing. She and Brady's wife, Kendra, hit it off immediately. I believe at some point during the night when we were catching up on former teammates, the two of them were sharing social media information.

The dinner was excellent. The company was better. All in all, this has been a perfect night.

A perfect, normal night.

I look over at Sadie, who is now engrossed in Kendra's photos of their dog, and all I can do is smile. I can't wait until we can tell the world about us. I can't wait until I can take her out on the town regularly, not just when we are away from the prying eyes of Nashville.

I want to give her normal. I want to give her everything. I want to give her anything she asks for.

"All right, boys, it's time for you to talk about us as we go to the ladies' room," Kendra announces.

"Who said we were going to talk about you?"

She leans over and gives Brady a kiss on the cheek. "Because I know you, Marcus. We'll be at least ten minutes. Enjoy your man time."

Sadie gives me a small wave as she and Kendra link arms and walk away from the table.

"You got it bad, bro."

I look over at Marcus, not realizing I was so transparent. "Is it that obvious?"

Marcus chuckles as he takes a sip of his drink. "I've known

you too many years, McAvoy. I've never seen you look at a woman like that. And the fact that you are willing to put your career on the line for her speaks volumes."

"She's worth it," I say matter-of-factly.

I wasn't about to lie to Marcus in regard to who Sadie is. He was shocked, to say the least. He knows from my college days that I was never a huge fan of the media. He promised that he wouldn't treat her any differently tonight, and he has kept his word.

"She seems good for you," he continues. "How does it work between you two? Do you just not talk about your jobs?"

"There is more to me than football. Give me some credit."

His eyebrow quirks up, clearly seeing through my attempt at bullshit. "Since the moment I met you freshman year, all you have wanted to do is coach. You had more notebooks for plays you drew up than for your schoolwork. You would talk for hours about plays and strategies. Even to the girls you dated for five seconds. So, you're going to sit here and tell me you and Sadie don't talk about football or work at all?"

Well, shit. He's not wrong. But I deflect.

"We have much more important things to do other than talk football."

I wag my eyebrows for emphasis. The answer is that I want to talk to Sadie about my day. She is likely the one woman on the planet who would get just as excited as I do about cracking the code to an opposition's defense.

But we can't. That's the line neither of us can cross.

"Fine. You don't want to answer that. But riddle me this, McAvoy, when Gordon retires and you become the head coach of the Fury, how will that work between you two? Are you *not* going to tell the woman you clearly love that you are up for a promotion?"

Brady's words stun me. I don't think I blink for a solid minute.

I mean, I've thought about that possibility. Gordon isn't getting any younger, and his contract is up after next season. If I have success, it could very well happen that I'm promoted to head coach.

"You haven't thought about that, have you?" Brady asks, breaking me out of my shock.

"I honestly haven't. Not in detail anyway. No one has talked about it, and I've had enough on my plate trying to fix this offense. I'll cross that bridge when it happens."

"You better figure it out soon. I saw Gordon's press conference last week. The man looks old. It could be your turn before you know it."

"Whose turn is it for what?" Kendra says as she and Sadie make their way back to the table. I didn't even see them coming.

"I was just saying that Hunter's boss looks to be only a few steps away from the grave. Our man could be the youngest head coach in football history."

I shoot Brady a glare as I slip my arm around Sadie's shoulders.

"What?" Brady asks. "I'm not exactly giving your girl top-secret information."

I turn to look at Sadie as Brady and Kendra shift away from football conversation to ordering dessert. And from what it sounds like, they are ordering the entire menu.

"You know he was just joking, right?" I ask, making sure she understands that it's not happening.

"Was he joking that Gordon is old? Because if he's actually only twenty-two, then that's the story I need to write."

I laugh, appreciating her deflective humor. "No one has talked to me about a job. Gordon isn't retiring anytime soon. He was just talking in hypotheticals."

Sadie doesn't respond right away, instead leaning a little closer, kissing my cheek. "Don't worry, Hunter. It's off the record. And not a thing. Your conversation, and Brady's imagination, are safe with me."

Everyone at the table falls into an easy conversation but me. I can't get Brady's words out of my head.

When Gordon does decide to retire, which will be after next season, at the earliest, Sadie and I would be out in the public by then. I'd be able to talk to her about the promotion then, right? I mean, this is the woman I can see myself spending the rest of my life with. I'd have to be able to talk to her about my future job.

I can't think about that now. That's a problem to think about a long time in the future.

36

HUNTER

I'M NOT one of those coaches who circles games on calendars. Every game is important. Every win is one more step to the playoffs.

However, I circled this game from the moment the schedule came out.

We hosted Cincinnati. Also known as Nick Bancroft's new team.

And we won. Correction. We kicked his fucking ass.

I've never met the man. However, that hasn't stopped him from spewing lies and bullshit to anyone who will listen about his firing from the Fury from the moment he was let go. And lies about why they hired me.

He was crying that he was unjustly fired. That he didn't get a fair shake and his firing "came out of nowhere." He even threw out that the only reason I was hired was because the owner of the Fury was an Alabama graduate, and he was doing a favor for my dad. He even insinuated that my dad financially bribed the owner to hire me.

Those words meant war. After I heard that, I grabbed the red

Sharpie out of my desk drawer and put a huge circle around this game.

I didn't have to motivate my players much for this week. The returning players hated him. They were more than happy to see him fired and wanted to stick it to him just as bad as I did.

Add all of that up, and it meant a big win for the Fury: 48-13.

More importantly? That's now five wins in a row.

That's right. After starting off the season 0-4, we are now 5-4, and all signs are pointing up. The offense has clicked. Bryce is making a case to be the Rookie of the Year. The defense is playing amazing. Everything is fucking fantastic.

"Helluva game plan, Hunter," Coach Gordon says to me, giving me a slap on the back as I make my way out of the locker room to the coaches' offices. "I still can't believe the turnaround we've made."

"You and me both, sir."

My words aren't meant to be humble. I still have no fucking clue how everything turned around. I'm not about to look a gift horse in the mouth, though.

"Are you on your way to the press conference?" I ask, knowing that the reporters' room is just a few steps away.

"Yeah." Irritation laced in his one word. "They wanted to interview Bancroft since it's the first time he's been back. They had to grab him right off the field because they thought he'd duck out if they didn't."

"I'd love to be a fly on the wall to hear what shit he's telling them."

"Let's go listen," Gordon says, nodding his head toward the interview room.

"Really?"

"Hell yeah. That man was a fucking cancer in our locker room. If he's spreading lies about me in front of The Mob, I at least want to know what he's saying so I know how to respond."

The man is devious and smart. It's probably why he's as successful as he is.

We make our way to the interview room and stand in the open doorway, which is in the back. We have a clear view of the interview room without drawing attention to ourselves. I am staring at Bancroft, who is trying to feed lines of bullshit to The Mob.

The room is smaller than the one at the practice facility. The reporters are a little more jammed together. I take a quick look around for Sadie, who, like always, is sitting up front. I can't help but smile watching her in action. Luckily, Coach Gordon doesn't notice my reaction as I watch my girlfriend raise her hand to ask the next question.

I hope she rips Bancroft a new asshole.

"Coach Bancroft, you were quoted as saying that you weren't given proper warning about being fired. Can you clarify those comments, specifically the part where an employer is supposed to give an employee they plan to terminate a warning that they are, in fact, being let go?"

That's my girl.

Sadie's question, like every one she asks, is with intent and has thought behind it. And I can see by the look in Bancroft's eyes he has not missed her line of questioning.

"Oh, Benson. It's been a while since I've been on the receiving end of one of your close-the-press-conference questions. I wish I could say I missed them."

"And I wish I could say I miss you not answering them. So, I must ask, is that your answer?"

His eyes fill with anger at Sadie's snarky response. "No, Benson. My answer is that after all the years I put into this team, all the years I spent making this franchise a name around the league, I was let go without so much of a hint of a notice. There weren't even talks of them looking to get rid of me.

That's not good business. I thought this franchise was better than that."

"Follow up, please." Sadie doesn't even wait for Paul to tell her yes. "The team had its worst offensive year in history last year. Are you saying that as the offensive coordinator, that a performance like that wasn't a fireable offense?"

Bancroft's face is now a shade of red I didn't know existed. "I'm saying that good football business gives someone the chance to turn it around."

"Are you accusing the Fury of bad or malicious business practices?"

"I'm saying that they did bad business and then brought in the owner's golden boy to replace me. That is all. Are we done yet, Benson?"

"Damn, Benson is giving Bancroft the business," Gordon whispers as we watch Sadie and Bancroft stare each other down. "That woman is a damn shark."

She is, which is what has me nervous right now. Especially when she asks her next question.

"No. I have one more question," Sadie begins. "Would you have been able to turn it around? You have said that good business would have allowed you the chance to right the ship. Hypothetically speaking, if you were to have stayed employed, would you have been able to do what the Fury has been doing the past five games?"

I see the moment that Bancroft loses it. And there is nothing anyone can do to stop it.

"Do I think I would have been able to turn it around? Could I win with an offense led by a prodigy quarterback? Anyone can. What McAvoy is doing right now is nothing special, and I'm tired of everyone thinking he's God's fucking gift to offenses. You've asked a lot of idiotic questions over the years, Benson, but this is the dumbest. Which shouldn't surprise me since everyone knows you were a token hire. You don't know shit about football, and it's clear you still don't. I can't believe you still have a job. Who are you fucking these days for your information? It's McAvoy, isn't it? Yeah, I heard you two have a thing going on. He the one you getting on your knees for these days for the scoop?"

I don't even remember bursting into the room. I don't remember grabbing Bancroft by the shirt and pulling him away from the podium to punch him. I don't remember Paul or Coach Gordon pulling me off of him. I don't remember the cameras flashing.

I do remember yelling at him to not say a fucking word about her or I'll do a lot worse than break his nose.

And I remember the second my eyes lock on to Sadie. She looks shocked. Afraid. Confused. Angry. Sad.

And then it hits me.

We are no longer a secret.

37

SADIE

I'M NEVER SUPPOSED to be the story.

Yet here I am, the talk of professional football.

You can't pick up a newspaper, turn on the television or the radio without hearing someone talk about what happened between me, Hunter, and Bancroft.

Nick Bancroft loses cool over questions from *Banner* reporter

Nick Bancroft fired after inappropriate remarks to *Banner* reporter

Hunter McAvoy comes to defense of *Banner* reporter

Love in the air? Hunter McAvoy and *Banner* reporter rumored to be in relationship

Pictures emerge of Hunter McAvoy, *Banner* reporter together on romantic getaway

Pro football's most eligible bachelor off the market?

Funny how my name is never mentioned in the headline. That doesn't mean I've been anonymous in this. My picture is everywhere. The story was all over the Internet immediately. It's not every day a coach goes on a tirade against a reporter and another coach attacks him for said tirade.

As for the pictures of me and Hunter in New Orleans? I can't prove it, but I have a feeling Nick Bancroft has everything to do with those even existing. It's no secret he has been trying to smear Hunter's name since the day he replaced him. Do I think he leaked them personally to the gossip sites? No. The timing doesn't fit. But I'll go to my grave saying he hired someone to follow Hunter to try and tarnish his image and that person knows a payday when they see one.

The fact that I was with him was icing on the cake.

Rat bastard.

Bancroft was probably holding on to those photos until the perfect time to try and get Hunter fired. Maybe he was waiting until after this game?

Even if this wasn't how he planned on it, he still might get his wish.

We're outed. Busted. And now all we can do is let the chips fall where they may.

My phone hasn't stopped ringing since everything went down yesterday. Even as I'm sitting on the well-worn couch in John's office, I can feel it vibrating with some sort of alert every five seconds.

I read some of the stories and comments. Some have been in defense of me and Hunter. Others have now speculated that the only way I've been able to do my job is because I was sleeping with a coach. I didn't point out that I was doing this job long before Hunter was hired, but the haters don't want to hear that.

And those weren't even the worst. There were ones calling me names. There were the trolls saying this is why women shouldn't be allowed in locker rooms. In one day I've created a media shit storm about reporter and coach relations and women covering male sports.

God, has it only been a day? It feels like so much longer. Probably because I didn't sleep. I couldn't. I was too shook by everything. And I haven't talked to Hunter. I think that's what's killing me the most.

Is he okay? Does he still have a job? Are they forcing him to pick between me and the Fury? All of those are possibilities.

They are the same for me.

I've been waiting, okay, fine, hiding, in John's office for the past hour. He's talking with his bosses about how to "handle" the situation.

Who knew a few hard questions would send Bancroft off like that? Who knew Hunter was listening? Who knew that in just a few seconds my life would be flipped upside down?

"I have told you for years to make sure you have a work-life balance. This was not what I meant," John's words hit hard as he walks into his office, taking a seat behind his desk.

I can't even look at him yet. My head is in my hands, staring at the floor. "This wasn't supposed to happen this way."

"How was it supposed to happen, Sadie? Tell me how in the world this was supposed to happen where everyone came out smelling like fucking roses."

I nearly flinch at John's tone. Though it's deserving, this is the first time he has ever raised his voice to me.

I finally look up at him. All I see is anger and disappointment in his eyes. "We planned on coming forward at the end of the season. We figured that if we made it through a football season without our relationship affecting our performances, then neither you nor the Fury could object. Was it optimistic and probably a little foolish? Yes. But we both agreed it was worth a shot."

"Worth a shot? Me trying a different ice cream flavor is worth a shot. You don't do something that could jeopardize everything you've worked for because it's *worth a shot.*"

"It's more than that," I say, his words making this situation seem so black-and-white when it's not.

"Please, tell me, Sadie. Please tell me how it is more than you two being reckless with both of your jobs."

"Because I love him." His eyes go wide at my declaration. "Because for the first time in my life I didn't want to work twenty hours a day. Because even if you fire me right now, I know that I'm going to be okay because I have him in my life."

John is speechless. I don't blame him. I'm speechless, and I said those words. But they are all true.

I realized them before. I knew all of that in my head, but I never admitted it out loud. Hunter showed me that I'm not just my job. I'm more than just a reporter. He showed me there was more to life than breaking news and writing about football. He showed me what it was like to have a partner who supports you and wants you to succeed, and isn't jealous of the time you don't spend with him.

He showed me what true love is.

"How long have you two been together?" John asks.

"Before the draft."

My answer makes him give me a curious look. "You're meaning to tell me that you were dating Hunter McAvoy at the same time that you wrote that he might not be cut out for the job and that he was in over his head?"

I can't help but laugh. "Yeah. He didn't take too kindly to that one."

Now it's John's turn to laugh. "I bet not."

We're back to being silent. I have no idea which way this will go. There is one huge elephant sitting in this room, and I have to address it before I explode.

"Am I fired?"

"Before I can answer that. I have to ask you a few questions."

I take a big swallow. "Anything."

"Has he given you information as an unnamed source?"

I shake my head. "No. We have a strict rule that neither of us talks about work in front of the other. My sources with the team are in the front office, not on the coaching staff."

"Would you be willing to allow another reporter to interview him on days when he gives his press conferences, to make sure that we aren't accused of unfair treatment."

I nod my head. "Yes. I would like to be in the room, though, in case I need anything for future stories."

"That's fine. As long as you promise me from here on out that you will not use any privileged information, or that if there is a conflict of interest, you come to me immediately. With that, I see no reason to fire you. However, at the end of the season we need to reevaluate things and your position."

The sigh of relief I let out could be heard throughout the city. "Thank you, John. And for what it's worth, I'm sorry I lied. I hated it. I just didn't see another way."

He gives me a sympathetic nod. "As your boss, I'm sorry you had to lie to me as well. This could have gone very different, but I appreciate that both of you were cautious and thought about this fully. Also, as your boss, I would highly consider you pursuing the US Daily job. You wouldn't be covering the Fury every day, which means that it won't be a conflict of interest for you two to stay together."

He's right. The US Daily position is a national job. I'd be writing in-depth, investigative stories around the league. I haven't heard from them in a few weeks since my phone interview.

That's not even taking into account the events of the past day. Who knows if they would even consider hiring me now? Who would want to hire the reporter who just made national headlines for having a romantic relationship with a coach?

Maybe I shot myself in the foot for a chance at US Daily. Or maybe I could write such a big story they would have no choice but to hire me. Scandal or not.

I stand up from the couch, suddenly feeling more relieved. "Thanks, John. I appreciate... well, everything."

He holds up a finger, signaling me to stop. "You didn't let me finish. That was me as your boss. Now, as your friend and a man who has known you a long time, I'm happy for you. I was really worried that you were going to become one of the statistics that this industry is known for producing."

"What kind of statistic?" I ask, genuinely curious.

"The kind that works themselves to death because they feel they have to, then before they know it, their whole life has gone by and they haven't lived it. You deserve to live your life, Sadie. And if it's with Hunter, then he is a lucky guy."

38

HUNTER

GIRLFRIEND: *I'm still employed. How about you?*

Boyfriend: Let's put it this way, it worked to my benefit that we're on a winning streak.

Girlfriend: Can I come over?

Boyfriend: Please do.

Girlfriend: Pizza and beer?

Boyfriend: Add breadsticks and whiskey.

Girlfriend: See you soon. I love you.

Boyfriend: I love you more.

I step into my condo and re-read her text messages, making sure I read what I did.

Thank God she's okay.

I grab a bottle of water before collapsing on the couch as a wave of relief rushes through me. If Sadie wasn't on her way over, I'd fall asleep right here. Instead, I force myself to keep my eyes open as the last twenty-four hours plays on repeat.

"About time you got home."

"What the fuck?" I can't help but scream as I jump off of my couch only to see my mother coming out of my bathroom. "How? What? Why are you here?"

"I saw your press conference today," she says, making her way to sit next to me. "I wanted to make sure you were all right. I also wanted to yell at you for having a girlfriend and neglecting to tell me about her."

This ought to be good.

I straighten myself while simultaneously preparing myself for what's about to come. My mom's interrogation is about to be ten-times worse than the one I got from the team.

"You didn't bring Bo along to read me the riot act?"

In a move I have never seen Francine McAvoy do in my twenty-eight years, she rolls her eyes at the mention of my father.

"Let's put it this way, your father is on my list. We were driving back to Birmingham last night after the game when we heard the story come across the radio. I did not care for what he had to say about you and Sadie, and I let him know that. I also wasn't very pleased with him after the argument I heard you two had, but I figured you two would make up in due time. But if he ever wants to be allowed to sleep in his bed again, then he better get his head out of his ass when it comes to you. I dropped him off, told him to get his mind right, and that I was going back to Nashville to see my baby and the woman he felt he needed to hide from me."

My eyes grow wide before I let out a laugh that comes straight from my gut. "You're making him sleep on the couch because of me and Sadie?"

"Darn right I am. He started spewing some nonsense about you and my future daughter-in-law, and how it wasn't right and that both of you were not thinking with the right parts of your body. I told him what I thought of that, and that until he pulled his head out of his behind, he can make himself comfy in his study."

There's a lot I want detail about, but there's one part I can't glaze over. "Did you say future daughter-in-law?"

She smiles. It's the kind of smile that only a mother can wear when she knows something her child has yet to realize. "Yes, Hunter. My future daughter-in-law. I don't know much about modern datin', but I doubt you'd punch another man if this girl was... what do the kids call it? Friends with benefits?"

I nearly spit out my water. "What do you know about friends with benefits?"

"Oh, Hunter," she says, waving off my comment like I just said something ridiculous. "I know things. I watch TikToks."

That's a conversation for another day.

"Back to you and Sadie," she says, folding her hands across her lap. "Are you two okay? What did the Fury say?"

I take the next ten minutes to fill my mother in on everything I wasn't allowed to talk about at the press conference the Fury made me do today in response to my "altercation" with Bancroft. The press conference where I had to pretend to be sorry for punching that asshole. I gave a statement, answered two questions—both from Tommy because he is the only one I trusted—and left. I know they wanted more. They wanted the sordid details of Sadie's and my relationship.

That wasn't about to happen.

After Gordon and a few of the security guards dragged me off of Bancroft, I was immediately taken back to Neil, the general manager's, office. There I was greeted by Neil, Coach Gordon, and Mr. Henderson, the owner of the Fury. Though greeted makes it sound like they were happy to see me.

They were not.

I knew at that point there was nothing to hide. I felt bad telling them everything without talking to Sadie first, but I didn't have a choice.

All three of them were angry when I told them that Sadie and I had been seeing each other for months. They were both equal parts mad that I was, because none of them trust reporters, and also that it was a secret, because they were blindsided by this. However, there is nothing in any rule book or in my contract that says Sadie and I can't have a relationship. Therefore, they can't fire me.

They also can't take away Sadie's press credentials or access, which I was relieved to hear. I assured them that I have not given Sadie insider information. Even though I didn't give them much reason to, they took me on my word that I hadn't. Coach Gordon even laughed about the fact that she wrote an article saying I was in over my head. When I left, they made me promise that I would give Sadie no inside information or tips, and that they would be monitoring her stories closely to make sure it stayed the case.

"So, everything is okay?" my mom asks, making sure she didn't miss anything.

"Except for the fact that I have a bruised hand, will likely have to pay a fine to the league for attacking Bancroft and my bosses aren't super trusting of me right now, yeah. Everything worked out."

"That makes me so happy," Mom says, standing up to take my empty bottle of water to the kitchen. "I would have hated for you two to have ended things. What about a spring wedding? That's a good time of the year for both of you. Right?"

"Slow down," I say, following her to the kitchen where she is now wiping down my counter that doesn't need cleaning. "How do you know that Sadie is the one for me? I've never talked to you about her. You met her once, and that was before we were dating. Please tell me how you have come to this conclusion based on the limited knowledge you have of my relationship."

She stops and gives me that knowing smile again. "I told you, I watched the press conference today. What aren't you getting?"

I stare at her in confusion. "I don't understand how watching a press conference equates to you knowing that Sadie and I are going to get married."

She takes a few steps toward me and puts her hand over

mine. She used to do this when I came to her after Bo and I had a fight. It always made me feel like everything would be okay. "When I watched you talk about her today, you had that look in your eye. I've only seen you have that look once in your life, and that's when you told me and your daddy that you wanted to become a coach. You were so sure of yourself. You knew it was it for you. That's what I saw today, Hunter. You know it's her. You know she's the one. And now... now that you don't have to hide anything... maybe you two can really start your lives together."

As if on cue, Sadie comes walking into my condo, pizza and booze in hand.

"Oh! Mrs. McAvoy! I-I didn't know you'd be here."

Sadie barely has a chance to put down the supplies before my mom nearly tackles her in a hug.

"My sweet girl. I knew you were special the day we met," Mom says, and if I had to guess, she's fighting back tears right now. "Be good to my boy. And when he messes up, because he's a man and he will, don't hesitate to call me. Lord knows I have years of experience with his father."

This makes us both laugh. "I will. Thank you, Mrs. McAvoy."

"Oh no. There will be none of that," Mom says, grabbing her purse off the counter. "Mrs. McAvoy was my mother-in-law. Dreadful woman. God rest her soul. You will call me Francine or Mom."

I make my way over to Sadie, bringing her into my side. "Thank you... Francine. I hope we didn't upset you by not telling you. It was... complicated."

"I understand," Mom says, giving me a kiss on the cheek before doing the same to Sadie. "It doesn't mean I like it. But I understand. That just means you two owe me a visit. I get you for a whole day. And a weekend when the season is over. And breakfast tomorrow."

My mom wraps Sadie in one more hug and gives me a kiss

on the cheek before she makes her way out of my condo and to her hotel where she'll be staying tonight.

"Sorry about that," I say, wrapping my arms around her waist. "I had no idea she was here."

"It's fine," she says, her arms looping around my neck. "I'm glad we got to see her. Now she knows. Now there's no more hiding."

She's right. Now that my family and our jobs know, we are completely free. No more hiding. No more sneaking around.

"We're free," I say, though I didn't mean for it to play out that way.

"We are."

"What do you want to do first? Date night? Movie? Want to go downtown and see some music. You name it and it's yours."

She doesn't respond. Instead, she leans up and kisses me.

"I want you to make love to me. I want you to make me forget the past few days happened. I want to get lost in you."

I don't hesitate. I sweep her up in my arms, ready to make both of us forget the past two days. "That I can do."

39

SADIE

I'VE GOTTEN USED to Hunter carrying me to his room. In fact, I now look forward to it.

Especially tonight. After the last two days, I need to feel as close to him as possible. I need to feel myself pressed against his chest. And if I'm reading his body language right, he needs this too.

Typically when he carries me to bed, he sets me down, strips himself, strips me, then we fall into each other's arms.

This is why I'm confused as to what is happening. Instead of going up the stairs, Hunter is making his way outside to his patio.

"Where are we going?"

"Trust me, gorgeous."

The weather is reasonably warm for October. That's not the problem. The problem is that Hunter lives in a condo development. With neighbors.

"Hunter..." I want to ask what he's thinking, but my brain is immediately scattered when I feel his mouth on my neck.

He doesn't respond. Instead, he lifts my shirt over my head. The October air hits my skin and sends chills up my spine. They don't last long. My body is rushed with heat when Hunter's mouth moves to kissing the tops of my breasts, his cock growing harder against my center.

"Don't worry. My neighbors are gone for the week," Hunter says before switching his mouth to the other side. "It's just you and me out here. And we don't have to hide anymore. From anyone."

Now it all makes sense. Before we had to stay inside. We were essentially trapped. Now it doesn't matter who sees us. Let them. We have nothing more to be afraid of.

We're Sadie and Hunter. And we don't give a damn who knows about us.

That thought spurs me on, and before I know it, I'm slinking down off of his lap onto my knees.

"Sadie... baby... you don't have to."

"Shh," I say, unzipping Hunter's pants. "I want to. And like you said, we aren't hiding."

I lick my lips as his cock springs free. It's already hard and it's begging for me to take it into my mouth. I give him one slow lick from base to tip before circling my tongue around his crown.

"You are killing me, gorgeous. Fucking killing me."

I slowly take every inch of him into my mouth, which makes Hunter groan so loud I'd bet the condo three units down heard him. He doesn't care. Neither do I. I begin going up and down on his shaft, my tongue circling him as I go. I'm using one hand to cover where my mouth isn't, and my other hand is quickly taken in his. His hips are moving into my mouth as if he has no control over his movements.

Every time I do this to Hunter, he has to touch me in some way. Sometimes it's my hair. He'll take it in his hand and work me up and down on him. Sometimes he'll take my fingers and slowly kiss them one by one.

This time Hunter has decided to give my chest special

attention. He has edged my cups down, letting my breasts spill out. As I work his cock in and out of my mouth, he flicks my nipples, which sends immediate shocks to my center.

"Baby, I'm not going to last long if you keep that up," he says, his breath ragged.

"Neither am I," I say, his movements in conjunction with what I'm doing to him are too much for my brain, and my body, to handle.

"Stand up, baby. Stand up right now."

I don't argue. I slowly get to my feet, and as soon as I'm upright, Hunter is peeling my pants and panties down to my ankles before shoving his jeans down just enough to allow him some movement.

He doesn't say another word. Instead, he takes my hand and pulls me toward him. Our lips find each other as if there are magnets pulling us in. My legs immediately go to either side of his, and I slowly lower myself onto him.

We both let out a loud moan of pleasure as he fills me. I will never get tired of this. This feeling of being claimed. This feeling of being wanted. This feeling of being loved.

Hunter's hips begin to move in a slow rhythm, and my hips are answering to his every thrust. This will never go down as the most comfortable place we've had sex—that award will forever belong to the hotel we stayed at in New Orleans—but this night will live in my memory forever.

We made it. Months of hiding and lying are over. We don't need to watch who we are around when we text. We don't have to use code names. We can just be us.

And right here, on Hunter's patio, is us at our best.

"You're mine, Sadie," Hunter says into my neck, his strong arms holding me tightly against him as his thrusts begin to pick up speed. "Forever."

"Forever."

My words come out in a whisper before I let out a gasp.

Hunter is hitting a spot in me I didn't know existed, and without warning, my center is clenching him as I'm ready to explode.

"Fuck, Sadie!"

I hold off just long enough so Hunter comes with me. We sit there for a long time. He's grown soft, but he's still inside me, and neither of us are in a rush to move.

We don't have to be in a rush at all now. We can go at our own pace. We can go as fast or as slow as we want.

We have all the time in the world. And to think, just a few months ago we were sitting on this same porch, deciding to give this a shot.

Now I can't imagine my life if I would have said no.

"I love you, Sadie. I love you so damn much."

I look up at Hunter and see nothing but love in his eyes. Is this always how it's going to be? God, I hope so.

Now that we're free, I can't wait to start truly living everyday with this man.

"I love you, too, Hunter. More than I can ever say."

40

HUNTER

HOLY HELL.

We're going to make the playoffs.

There is less than a month left in the regular season—four games, to be exact—and we'd have to lose all four to not be in the postseason. Considering the teams we are playing are at the bottom of the league, I like our chances.

I kick my feet up on my desk and let out the most peaceful sigh of contentment. Everything in my life is just about perfect. Sadie and I are amazing. We decided that after the season she's moving into my condo. We even talked about getting a dog.

As for things with the Fury? I couldn't be happier with how this season has gone. Yes, it started off rough. But honestly, I think it made us better. It made us work harder. If Bryce doesn't win Rookie of the Year, it will be a shock. I have no fears about being fired at the end of the season, and I'm happy to let this wave ride for as long as it will go.

Hopefully, that's to a championship game.

"Oh good, you're still here."

I turn toward my door as Coach Gordon stands in the frame. "Yup. I was getting ahead for the next few days of practice."

"You don't need to do that," he says, batting my words away with this hand. "We're playing Pittsburgh. Come on. Walk with me."

I grab my phone from my desk and join Coach Gordon. Sadie should be texting me any minute to let me know that she and Bethany are done with their girls' day, which means it's my cue to grab Davis and meet them for drinks.

Yes. We are going on a double date with Bethany and Davis. The most girly-girl I have ever met, paired with the guy who most days acts like he's still eighteen.

I don't know how I let her talk me into this. Well, I do. She was naked. I do most things she tells me to do when she's naked.

We pass by Coach Gordon's office and continue walking toward the executives' offices. You only come here if you're getting hired or fired.

"Wipe that scared look off your face," Coach Gordon says, obviously figuring out that I've turned an interesting shade of white. "You aren't in trouble. At least, not yet."

He lets out an evil laugh at his joke, which does not ease my mind whatsoever.

He stops in front of the general manager's office and signals me to take a step inside. I've been here twice. Once during my interview, and once when I had to explain to him how I was not giving my girlfriend inside information.

When I step inside, it's not just Neil. Paul is in the room, as well as Mr. Henderson, the Fury's owner. Quickly exiting the room is Neil's secretary. I think her name is Tina? Tonya?

"Hunter, glad you could join us," Mr. Henderson says. "Please, take a seat."

I look anxiously around the room as I sit at a small conference table in the corner of Neil's office. "Am I in some sort of trouble?"

Mr. Henderson shakes his head. "Not in the least. We wanted to bring you in today because what you have done with the offense this year is something to be commended. Especially with a rookie quarterback."

"Thank you," I say, feeling a little more confident in his words. "It wasn't easy at first. It took a lot of work. I'm glad it's paying off. For all of us."

"How you handled and came back from that early stuff was impressive, Hunter. As well as the media circus that came after the Bancroft situation. Not many coaches would have been able to navigate those waters. Not only did you survive them, you thrived after."

Neil's words are setting off little warning bells in my head. I've had small conversations with Coach Gordon and Neil about the turnaround. At this point, it's almost old news. And they have never brought up Bancroft. So why now?

"Put him out of his misery, Neil. Just tell him already before he throws up on your fancy carpet."

I look at Coach Gordon and then back to Neil. Then from Neil to Mr. Henderson. "Tell me what?"

"Coach Gordon is retiring at the end of this season. And we are hoping that you will want to take over and be the next head coach of the Nashville Fury."

Everything in the room stops. I play the words over and over in my head. Coach Gordon was right. I might vomit.

"I thought you had another year on your contact?" I ask Coach Gordon, because this was the last thing I was expecting.

"Technically, I do," he says, looking very nonchalant for a man who helped drop the biggest bomb on me of my life. "But there is wording in my contract that I can back out at any time with enough notice. That's the beauty of being as old as I am. My wife doesn't want to wait another year for me to be done. Something about grandkids and she's tired of spending weekends alone."

"This is why we brought you on, Hunter," Mr. Henderson adds. "We knew that you could do this, and you've proven yourself, son. None of us can think of a better man to guide the Fury into the future."

I'm stunned. I have no clue what to say.

My head is spinning.

I'm the man for the future of the Fury?

Yes, we've had success this year. I just didn't expect a head coaching offer to be on my radar for at least another two years, at the earliest. I figured teams would want to see how I developed players and offenses for at least another couple of seasons.

"What questions do you have for us," Neil asks. "And don't say none. I see the wheels in your head working overtime."

I give my head a shake, because I don't know what to ask first.

"Would I be able to still call the offensive plays?"

Neil nods. "If that's what you want to do. Yes. All play calling and coaching personnel decisions are yours. You and I will work together on player personnel."

I nod, liking that answer. "Who knows about this?"

"Just the men in this room," Coach Gordon says. "And we need it to stay that way until the season is over. Is that clear, Hunter? No one can know. Do you understand what we are saying?"

And there it is. The stern warning that I can't tell Sadie. Which I hate. Aren't you supposed to be able to tell the woman you love about an amazing job opportunity? Aren't you supposed to be able to bask in this glory with the person you love?

This is just a cruel reminder that we might be known to the public, but we still are who we are.

"I understand. I won't say a word."

"Good," Neil says. "We've emailed you preliminary contract details. Just a starting point. Send them to your agent. When the season is over, we'll circle back."

"Thank you," I say, standing up and extending my hand to shake all of theirs. "I'll definitely consider it."

"As you should," Mr. Henderson says. "It's not every day a person gets the chance to become the youngest head coach in professional football history. And an Alabama man, no less. Roll Tide!"

I hear polite laughter from the others, but I can't react. My head is spinning. This came out of nowhere, and I'm not sure how to process it.

A vibration from my pocket pulls me from my thoughts. I grab my cell phone to find a text from Sadie saying she and Bethany are ready to meet me and Davis for drinks.

Great. Just great. How am I supposed to plaster on a happy face when I'm also weighing the biggest decision of my life?

41

SADIE

I CAN'T BELIEVE the messages I'm reading right now. Luckily, I'm sitting down as Bethany is trying on yet another dress for our double date tonight.

T: Girl, Hunter just went into Neil's office with Gordon. Henderson is here too. Paul followed them in, but he looked confused AF. Per usual.

Sadie: What's going on? Was it on his schedule?

T: It wasn't. But it seems important if they are all in there. Let me go listen. BRB.

I have to wait for twenty minutes to pass before Tara responds to me. Tara, as in Neil's secretary. Tara, as in my inside source for all things Fury-related.

She knows everything. And Neil is too dumb to realize she does.

Neil is a good general manager. He's apparently a shitty boss, which is why Tara doesn't mind tipping me off when big things are coming down the pike. She's the one who told me about Hunter being hired. Every scoop I've had is because of her, and all because her boss doesn't like to close his door to meetings. I learned quickly the best people for sources in this business aren't the men who run the show, it's the women who hold everything together.

I made friends with Tara on the first day I was assigned to cover the Fury. I bought her a coffee and a donut. We've been tight ever since. And she's never once given me bad information.

T: GIRL. You aren't gonna believe this shit.

Sadie: Just tell me! You're killing me.

T: Gordon is retiring at the end of the season. They want Hunter to be the next head coach. They basically offered him the job. He didn't say yes yet. They aren't saying anything until Hunter makes a decision.

Sadie: Are you positive? You heard them offer Hunter the head coach job?

T: I swear on a dozen donuts and my nana's grave that's what I heard. Girl, your man is about to become the head coach of the Fury. Shit, I hear movement. GTG.

"How does this one look? Does it scream, 'I'll eventually put out, but not tonight'?" Bethany asks me, taking my attention away from the news that is burning a hole through my phone.

"Looks great. Totally only half slutty," I say, barely looking at her, hoping my fake enthusiasm comes through.

"Perfect." She bounces back to the dressing room, and I turn my attention back to the messages.

This news is huge. Astronomical.

Jimbo Gordon retiring is the end of an era in football. He's one of the last of his generation. If Hunter accepts the job, which I don't see why he wouldn't, he would become the youngest head coach in pro football history.

The girlfriend in me wants to scream and jump up and down in excitement.

The reporter in me wants to start making phone calls.

No one will see this coming. Gordon has another year left on his contract. How is this even happening? I highly doubt that

Tommy, or any of the other writers, are even thinking this is a possibility. I know I didn't when Brady casually brought it up at dinner in New Orleans. And it was so far out there I honestly didn't even think about it again until right now.

That was a hypothetical. This is real life.

I want to run home and start writing. I want to research Gordon's contract and start making calls.

That's what the old Sadie would do. If this were a normal date with some random guy off a dating app, I'd be texting him and canceling to write the story that will make my career.

But I can't. For one, if I canceled, it would devastate Bethany. Once I showed her a picture of Davis, she has not stopped talking about tonight.

Then, there is Hunter. I'm sure he would be suspicious if not only did I cancel, but that I also chose to stay at my apartment for no known reason. I've worked on stories at his condo, but I can't write a story about him while he's sitting twenty feet from me. Plus, I have to tell John. There is a clear conflict of interest, so he will have to put another reporter on this with me to make sure we have all of our bases covered.

None of that can happen until tomorrow. So date night lives on.

"Did you text the guys?" Bethany asks, stepping out of the dressing room donning her new dress and carrying a bag that I'm assuming has her old clothes in it. "I am ready to date."

I take my phone out and send a quick text to Hunter, letting him know we're on our way.

The story will have to wait.

———

I DON'T KNOW what the point of a double date is when the other couple doesn't acknowledge your existence.

We decided to meet at a bar downtown that has a fun patio

and Giant Jenga. What better way for two people to be set up than to have to team up in a battle of skill?

That was the plan. I didn't think they would hit it off so well that an hour into our night they would be cozied up at the bar, every signal pointing to the fact that they are going home together.

Likely soon.

So much for the "I won't put out yet" dress.

Normally, I'd be happy for Bethany. She has had her fair share of dating disappointments. Even if Davis only proves to be a good time for tonight, this girl could use a little fun.

Only problem? With the two of them looking at each other like they want to swallow each other whole, it has left me and Hunter by ourselves.

He has a secret. He doesn't know I know the secret. I can't say that I know the secret.

It's… uncomfortable. Awkward. And it's never uncomfortable with me and Hunter. Yet I'm afraid if I start talking, then somehow I'll spill that I know about his meeting today. I really needed Bethany and Davis to help ease the discomfort.

However, they are too busy eye fucking each other to help me out.

"That seems to be going well," Hunter says, nodding toward Bethany and Davis.

"Yup. We sure know how to match them. Maybe that could be our side hustle. We start a matchmaking business."

Hunter chuckles before taking a sip of his beer. "McAvoy Matchmakers. It has a ring to it."

I quirk an eyebrow. "What about McAvoy and Benson? Where's my credit?"

Hunter smiles and leans a little closer to me. "My hope is that one day your last name will be McAvoy. Problem solved."

My eyes bug out of my head. Marriage? Hunter is thinking about marriage?

"I... you... I... huh?"

This is why I write for a living and don't speak.

Hunter softly laughs, inching closer to me. Still not as close as Bethany and Davis are, who at last glance have no regard that they are in a public place.

"If you didn't know it by now, I'm kind of in love with you," he begins, taking my hand in his. "I've been thinking about the future a lot lately. And every time I do, you're there. I know we don't need to rush it. But I wanted you to know that I'm thinking about it."

I grab my beer and take a healthy drink. Not because the thought of spending the rest of my life with Hunter makes me nervous. But because knowing the information I now know, that he doesn't know I know, makes things very... unknowing.

Hunter will be in Nashville for the foreseeable future. I would also like to be in Nashville. My family is here. My friends are here. It's a no-brainer.

However, if US Daily says they want to hire me, but they need me to move to the West Coast, would I turn it down? I used to think that nothing would stop me from turning down a job with them. If they wanted me to cover hockey on the moon I would do it.

Now? Now I'm not sure.

"Sadie?" Hunter says, snapping his fingers in front of my face. "Are you there? Did I freak you out that much? I didn't think you'd be so stunned at the fact that I would one day like to marry you."

"No. Sorry," I say, giving my head a shake. "It just caught me off guard. That's all. I feel like for months everything was so slow, and now because we don't have to hide, it's going warp speed. At first I was worrying about being caught, now I get to wonder if I'll still write under Sadie Benson or Sadie McAvoy."

Wow, that word vomit wasn't a total lie.

"It's fine," he says. "I'm just going on record that one day, even if it doesn't say McAvoy in the newspaper, you'll be a McAvoy to me."

"Sounds good to me," I say, leaning in for a kiss, hoping that will take any attention away from my reaction.

The second our lips touch, Hunter's phone vibrates on our table. He opens up the message app and shows me a text from Davis.

Davis: Come to the bar. They won't let me put drinks on your tab without you.

Hunter groans and all I can do is laugh. "Do you need anything?"

"Sure. Another beer. I'll hold down the fort."

Hunter sets his phone down and makes his way over to the bar. I follow his path and Bethany gives me an enthusiastic thumbs-up. I return the gesture, sincerely happy for her that she's having a good time.

At least one of us is.

42

HUNTER

"I'LL TAKE the chicken Caesar wrap with fries and a sweet tea."

"Coming right up, Hunter."

I smile and drop my tip in the jar before making my way to the other side of the counter to wait for my food. Yes, I'm now on a first-name basis with the staff at Sandwich City.

I can't help but let out a laugh as I lean against the counter. It's been nearly a year since I first walked into this shop. Eleven months, to be exact. On that day, I was hoping that my life was about to change.

It did. In more ways than I even thought possible.

Now I smile because I know it is.

I've told the Fury that I will accept the position when Coach Gordon decides to retire. He and I had a long chat after our impromptu meeting. He plans on telling the team after the final regular-season game this week. We'll alert the media then.

That's the only part I hate. I hate that Sadie is going to find out that I'm getting the job of my dreams from a press release rather than from me.

Not telling her has been killing me. Every night I want to tell her. I want to be able to share my excitement with her.

But I can't. I know I can't.

And it fucking sucks.

I trust her. I trust her with my life. Hell, the first purchase I plan to make after getting promoted is to buy an engagement ring.

I don't want to put her in a difficult situation. If I told her, she'd feel obligated to report it. She has to. It's her job. And for her to do her job means I might not get mine.

No way they'd promote me if I leaked this information out. So here I am, beating myself up every day that I'm keeping a life-changing secret from the love of my life.

"Hunter! Your order is ready!"

I turn back to the counter and take my to-go bag, needing to head back to the Fury facility. It's Monday, which is strategy day for Coach Gordon, me, and our defensive coordinator. One more week of the regular season, and then it's playoff time.

The chill of Nashville in December hits me as soon as I step outside. It might be the South, but damn, it's cold right now. I reach into my pocket to grab my hat when I feel my phone vibrate from my back pocket. I have no clue if it's a text or a story alert, so I let it go.

The story alerts have been happening like crazy these days. Luckily, all in a good way. Even the national writers are starting to see that my offense is not only innovative, but they've dubbed my system "the offense of the future."

Suck on that, Dad.

I still haven't spoken to him since our blowup at the beginning of the season. He won't apologize first, and like hell if I will. They both come to the games. I can see their season ticket seats from the sideline, but neither stay to talk to me after. When I do talk to Mom, she tries to tell me that he wants to reach out. He also could have just told her that so she'd let him sleep upstairs again.

When I get back to the facility, I'm not prepared for the

audience in my office. But standing, and looking angry as hell, are Coach Gordon and Neil.

"Sorry, guys. If I knew you were coming by, I would have ordered for the group."

"Have you seen the latest article in *The Banner*?" Neil asks, clearly not amused by my attempt at a joke.

"I haven't. Then again, the only thing I've read in the last hour is the Sandwich City menu."

Again, my joke falls flat. "What's going on? Why does everyone look like they are ready to punch something?"

"Sadie knows."

I have to blink a few times at Coach Gordon's words.

Sadie knows?

"How? What? I'm confused."

"Check your phone," Neil says, which I do.

If I had checked the notification that I got ten minutes ago, it would have shown me a story from *The Banner*, with a headline that clearly reads:

Hunter McAvoy to be named Fury head coach when Jimbo Gordon retires

What the fuck?

How does she know?

"I'm giving you one chance to tell the truth, Hunter," Neil says, his eyes spitting fire. "Did you tell Sadie after we explicitly told you not to? If you lie to us, you're done."

I shake my head, still confused at everything. "No. I haven't said a word. Hell, I haven't even told my parents. I swear I'm telling the truth. She didn't get this from me."

"Fuck!" Neil yells, nearly pulling his hair out as he paces around my office. "How does she fucking find out these things! I swear to God when I find out who is giving her this information their ass is fired!"

Chaos ensues with everyone running around trying to figure out what fire to put out. I'm just standing there stunned.

How in the hell did she know? No one knew. Five people knew, and none of them would have leaked it. I've been careful around her. I haven't said a word. Hell, if anything, I've been overly quiet.

Where could she have found this out?

Was this from New Orleans? Could this all have stemmed from the conversation that night at dinner with Brady and Kendra? She said she knew what Brady said was off the record. Hell, at that point it was a hypothetical. That doesn't mean though that the idea couldn't have been planted in her head.

Even if that's the case, there is more. There are more pieces to this puzzle. I just don't know what they are.

My phone buzzes again, this time with an email alert. Out of habit, I swipe open the app, and then I see it. Clear as day.

The contract.

No. She wouldn't. Would she? Would Sadie go through my phone?

I want to believe she wouldn't, but right now I can't figure out a better explanation. I leave my phone out around her all the time. She knows my passcode. She would have had plenty of chances to snoop through team emails, just looking to see if she could come up with anything.

"Fucking hell!" Neil yells as he grabs his phone. "Now *US Daily* wants a comment. Fuck. Your little girlfriend has fucked everything up. We were supposed to do this on our terms. Now this is what we're going to be dealing with all week."

Neil stomps out of my office to take the phone call, and I'm left frozen in place.

US Daily. Her job. This was her ticket.

She told me she needed one more big story to lock it down. Well, you don't get much bigger than breaking the news about the hiring of the youngest coach in football history whom you just happen to be in a relationship with.

She used me. She used me for the scoop of a lifetime.

"Your girl really did a number on us, McAvoy. A real fucking number."

He turns and leaves my office. I'm left standing behind my desk, ready to punch something.

Sadie fooled me once, thinking she was different. She might not have used me to get to Bo, but she sure as hell used me for herself.

And that's much worse.

43

SADIE

HUNTER HASN'T CALLED.

He hasn't messaged.

He hasn't said a thing.

And I have a feeling I know what's coming.

I hope I'm wrong, but I don't think I am.

I'm about to lose the only man I've ever loved because of a story I wrote.

I knew the consequences when I told John I had this information. I volunteered to pass it to another reporter. While he was happy that I offered that, he made the decision that he and I would work on the story together. I had the sources, and he could be on the calls with me to make sure that everything was on the up-and-up.

I also had thoughts about keeping my mouth shut. I could have pretended Tara never told me that information, and I could have found out when everyone else did. Or worse, after another reporter would have broke it. But if it ever came to light that I knew this information and didn't write about it, I could kiss my career goodbye.

I look at the clock in Hunter's kitchen, and it's nearly eight o'clock. My story has been online for four hours now, and he still isn't home. I grab one of his sweatshirts and head out to his patio. As soon as I step outside, my teeth start chattering. Yet this is exactly what I need.

I need to be wrapped in Hunter's scent, in the spot where we decided to give this a try. I need to be in the spot where we knew we were worth the risk and pray that everything is going to be okay.

I picked my job over Hunter. I know this. But the more I thought about it, the more I knew I had to report it. Plus, it's a positive. Hunter is getting his dream job. He's getting to stay in Nashville. One might think this would be cause for celebration. But I threw the Fury for a loop. Tara told me that Neil's head was about to explode when he saw the headline. The one thing about professional sports teams is that they like to control the narrative. They want to tell the story in their words, to their fans, on their time frame.

I fucked that all up.

And now, I fucked up everything with Hunter in the process.

I knew he would be upset. But I didn't think it would be *this* bad. I figured we would have a fight about me writing stories about him and not telling him. A little argument which would lead to some makeup sex.

Which is why the longer he stays away, the more worried I am that we won't survive this.

I don't know how long I sit outside, but I know the instant that Hunter comes through the door. Even out here on the patio, the air shifts. And not in a good way.

I take a deep breath before I stand up and make my way back inside. Part of me hoped that Hunter would be standing in the kitchen, pizza and beer in his hands, ready to talk this out rationally. Like we did before when I was expecting a fight.

Now? All I see on his face is hurt and anger.

"I understand you're probably mad, but I can explain—"

The laugh he lets out is downright bone-chilling. It's colder than the air I just walked in from. It sounds nothing like the Hunter I've come to know and love.

"Explain? What would *you* like to start with, Sadie? Because I have no fucking clue where to even begin."

I take a breath. "I'm sorry I didn't tell you that I was writing the sto—"

"That's what you think your biggest fault is?" he begins, furiously pacing back and forth. "Out of everything that you set in motion from the second you decided to report this story, you not telling me about it is your biggest regret? I always thought you were smart, but right now, I'm not impressed."

"What are you talking about?" I shake my head, because he's not making sense. "I wrote a story that shocked you. Yes, I know that it's not ideal. I know I said I'd give you a heads-up when I wrote stories about you, but I couldn't on this one. What I don't understand is why you are this upset about it? You got the job of your dreams! You should be elated!"

"Because you fucking used me for the story!" He stops in front of me and I can see nothing but rage in his eyes. I stare at him in shock. That's what he thinks? "You used your access to me for your own personal benefit! That is the one thing we promised each other we would never do! When did you do it? When I was asleep? When I was in the shower?"

"Hunter, I would never do that. I don't even know what you think I did! How did I use you?"

"My emails! My emails, Sadie. I know you went through them. That's the only way you could have found out about the promotion is if you saw the contract that was emailed to me. Five people knew about it and guess what, you were not one of them. I thought you were better than that, but apparently not. This is what I get for letting the enemy into my bed."

"Fuck you, Hunter," I say, my anger now coming to a boiling point. I could understand him being upset that I reported the story. But accusing me of going through his personal property for a scoop? It's like he doesn't even know me. "Did you ever think for one minute that maybe I did my job and used my sources when I was tipped off about the story? That I reported it without having to use my boyfriend?"

"Who are your sources then? Tell me. Clear everything up right now. Because the five people who knew sure as hell weren't the ones."

"I can't."

"You can't?"

I straighten my stance. "I don't care how much you are pissed at me. I don't care that you think I'm a shitty human right now. I will never name sources. Not for you. Not for anyone."

Hunter looks at me in shock. "You're telling me that you would rather protect your source than save our relationship?"

What? Are we...? Is he...?

"Hunter. It's not like that. It doesn't have to be like that."

"No Sadie. It is. It's exactly like that. Either you're picking me or you're picking your job. That's what this comes down to. But hey, at least now we are both going to get the jobs we wanted. I'm sure *US Daily* will be calling you soon. Glad I could help with that. Next time, though, you don't need to fuck me for a story."

He didn't...

No...

He wouldn't have...

I can't believe those words just came out of his mouth.

"That is the lowest fucking thing you could have ever said to me, Hunter McAvoy. I know you're pissed. I get it. But if you think for one second that I used you for a chance at that job, then you don't know me at all."

All the bastard does is shrug. "Everyone uses me, Sadie. Reporters have used me for years. You're just joining the club."

"I'm not justifying that statement with a response." My voice is starting to falter as the tears well in my eyes. But I'll be damned if I start crying in front of this man. "I was doing my job. I was tipped off about a story. I reported it. My boss had to watch over my shoulder every step of the way to make sure I *wasn't* using you. That's my job, Hunter. You knew what you were getting into with me when we got together."

"You're right, I did." His voice is somewhere between sarcastic and resigned. "You told me up front that you were a reporter first. I did this to myself. And I knew you were good. Hell, that first day you wrote about me right in front of my face and I didn't even know! What kind of idiot am I? How did I not think it would come to this?"

I want to scream. I want to hit something.

More than anything, I want to cry.

I can't be here anymore. I can't be in the same room with him.

I rip his sweatshirt off, thankful I kept a T-shirt on underneath. I don't want anything of his touching me right now. I grab my keys and purse and march toward his door.

"You thought I was different?" I say as I open his door. "I thought you were different too. I thought you were the one man who wouldn't think that I had to fuck my way to a story. Turns out we were both wrong."

I slam the door shut behind me and all but sprint to my car. I can't hold back my tears another second.

I cry the whole way home.

I cry all night.

I cry the next day.

And it turns out Hunter was right. *US Daily* offered me the job.

Then, I cried some more.

44

SADIE

FOR THE FIRST time in my entire career, I called out sick on a game day.

I couldn't do it. I couldn't be in the same space as Hunter. Yes, he would be coaching and I'd be working and I don't even see him on most game days. But just the thought of knowing that he was there was too much for me to handle.

So I did what any girl going through a breakup does. I ordered pizza and breadsticks, called Bethany to bring over ice cream and booze, and I put on my rattiest pair of sweatpants.

At least, I think this is what people going through breakups do. All of my relationships never made it past two weeks. They never required this kind of therapy.

The worst part? I don't know if we broke up. The words were never said.

It sure as hell felt like it, though.

Neither of us has reached out. No texts or phone calls. I did all of my work from home this week. John sent another reporter to the press conference the Fury had to have because of me breaking the news about Hunter taking over for Gordon.

Today when I started to get ready, I just started crying. I thought all the tears were gone. I've been crying for six days.

I texted John to tell him to send someone else. Then, I texted Bethany asking her to come over.

I hate myself right now. I really do. I'm not this girl. I don't cry over men. I don't cry because I put my job first.

Yet, here I am, curled up in a blanket on my couch, not remembering the last time I showered.

I thought I was stronger than this. I've survived haters telling me I couldn't do my job. I've stood up to Internet bullies who thought they could hide behind a username and tell me that I'm shit at my job and to get my fat ass back in the kitchen.

What I couldn't survive was Hunter looking at me like I was a stranger. Or that I used him to get ahead.

That's what broke me.

"Oh God. This is worse than I thought."

I don't acknowledge Bethany as she walks into my apartment. I'm really glad I gave her my building code so I didn't have to get up to let her in.

That would have required effort. I don't have that in me today.

"Sadie… Oh, sis," she says, moving my legs onto her lap as she sits down on my couch. "Why didn't you call me sooner? I would have come over. At least… maybe I could have done some dishes."

I peek over my blanket to see what she's talking about. I don't know whether or not she means the stack of cups on my coffee table, or the pile of dishes in my sink.

"You know before I met Hunter I didn't have any real dishes?"

"What did you use to eat?"

"Paper plates. Plastic cups. I didn't see the point in having nice things for just me. Now it's just me again, and now I have to do the fucking dishes."

I know I'm rambling and making zero sense. But these are the thoughts that go through my brain these days.

"Is that why you have a pile of pillows in the corner?" Bethany asks, as I assume she now sees the pile of throw pillows, curtains, and every other knickknack that I bought the day Hunter and I went apartment shopping.

"They reminded me of him," I say, not able to hold the sadness back. "Why does it still hurt, Bethany? Why does it hurt? I want it to stop hurting."

She pulls me up and immediately brings me into her arms. And I just cry. And not a pretty cry. I'm straight ugly crying on my stepsister's shoulder.

If there is one good thing that has come from all of this, it's that Bethany and I are now close. I used to laugh when she called me sis. I don't anymore. We might not be related by blood. We might not have one single thing in common. But she's my sister.

And I couldn't do this without her right now.

"What can I do?" she asks, stroking my hair. "We have food. We have booze. I've never committed a crime before, but if that's what's needed, we can do that."

I let out a laugh, which comes out as a hiccup between my tears. "I really should shower. I'm a mess."

"Oh, thank you, Jesus. I didn't want to be the one to say it."

Bethany gives me a squeeze before she lets go of me. She stands up and holds out her hands to help me off the couch.

"You shower. I'll start cleaning up the kitchen. Then we get sloppy drunk on a Sunday and complain about men."

————

"SINCE WHEN DO YOU WATCH FOOTBALL?"

Bethany turns to me like a deer in headlights. "I don't know what you mean. I watch the Fury every Sunday. It's great to have on when I'm cleaning."

I eye her suspiciously as she turns her attention back to a dish that doesn't look like it needs washing.

"Okay, Miss Fury fan. Name a player. Any player. Doesn't even have to still be on the team. If you can do that, then I'll drop this conversation."

Bethany doesn't say anything for a minute. "Oh! There's that guy. He throws the football. He plays for the Fury."

"Does this player have a name?" I ask as I reach for a slice of pizza.

She bites her lip as I can visibly see the level of concentration on her face. "Starts with... a *B*? Bobby? Brian? Bryce! His name is Bryce! I win!"

This makes me laugh, which feels nice. It's been a long time since I did that.

"Fine. You win," I say, grabbing a glass to start making myself a drink. "I won't ask if you are watching the Fury game to maybe get a glance at a certain coach."

Bethany's face begins to blush at the mention of Davis. "I don't know what you're talking about. Plus, I'm not here to talk about me and my Fury coach. Today is about yours."

"A-ha! So you're saying there is a Fury coach who is yours?"

She swats a dish towel at me and we can't keep our laughter in. This feels nice. Normal. The shower did wonders for me. I only feel like I want to kind of cry.

That is what I call an improvement.

We gather our food and beverages of choice and make our way back out to the living room. The Fury game is still on the television, and the sight that I see as soon as I sit down threatens to tear my heart in two.

The camera pans to Hunter on the sidelines, and it takes everything in me not to start crying again.

I've never really got to watch him coach. From my angle in the press box, I can only see his back, and he's too far away.

Right now, I can take him all in. He's bent over, his hands on his knees, and he's watching as Bryce calls the play. The television goes back to the action of the game, and I want to scream to put the camera back on him. I wasn't done looking at him.

I wasn't done loving him yet either.

"I heard you got the job at *US Daily?*" Bethany asks, breaking our silence.

"Yeah. I got it." My words are the opposite of how they should sound when someone gets the job of their dreams.

"You have to be so excited. Your dad was gushing at dinner the other night. He told me and Mom about all the mornings y'all would read the paper together. Which is adorable. I'm so happy for you."

All I can do is shrug. "Thanks. But I haven't accepted it yet."

"What!" Bethany shrieks, nearly dropping her pizza. "What do you mean, you haven't accepted it."

"It means what it means. They called me. I said thanks, but that I needed a few days to think it over. They told me to call them Monday."

I look over to Bethany who is staring at me like I'm growing horns out of my head. "I'll admit that I've never been super smart, but you're going to have to help me out with this. You're telling me that you were offered your dream job. The job that you earned by giving up all forms of a social or personal life. You worked your butt off for years, got that job, and you didn't accept it on the spot?"

Well, when she puts it like that.

"It didn't feel right," I say. It's now my turn to not make eye contact.

"It didn't feel right because the job isn't what you thought it would be? Or it didn't feel right because of Hunter?"

For being the girl who says all the time that she isn't the smart one, she sure does get it right when it comes to my life crises.

"The job is perfect," I admit. "They said I could stay in Nashville. Or if I wanted to move, I could do that as well. I would be writing more in-depth and investigative pieces and not covering just one team. They also know about Hunter and that our relationship wouldn't be a problem. Not that it will be a problem anymore."

"So what *is* the problem?"

"The problem is that I'll always know that my dream job came at the price of my chance at love. And I don't know if I can live with that for the rest of my life."

Surprisingly, I don't cry after saying that out loud. I want to. I feel the heat burn behind my eyes.

But I don't. Instead, I stare at the television with my head on Bethany's shoulder and wonder what the hell I'm going to do with my life.

Likely without Hunter in it.

45

HUNTER

"WELL, McAvoy. We did it. We fucking did it."

Coach Gordon tosses me a beer as we each take a seat in his office. Him behind his desk. Me on the couch next to it.

Soon this office will be mine. At this time next year I'll be the one seated behind the desk passing out beers to my coaches. Hopefully, as we are making our way to the playoffs.

"We did, sir. I can't believe we did it. Thank you for everything this season. It was a true team effort." Even though we made the playoffs a few weeks ago, it still hasn't hit me that we went from the worst team in the league, to a favorite to win the championship.

"You know, son, it was at this time last year that I was sitting with Bancroft, wondering whether or not to boot his ass."

I nod but don't speak. I've always wondered how that conversation went down, especially now knowing what kind of hot head Bancroft is like.

"I was going to keep him," Coach Gordon begins, telling the story like he's remembering stories back from the war. "Part of me said that it was one bad season and the man deserved another chance. He was right in that aspect. He had done a lot for us on the field. Off the field, he was a mean motherfucker with a horrible temper. How no one ever wrote about that before his blowup is beyond me."

I shake my head but edge myself a little closer. It's like I'm listening to a ghost story around a campfire.

"I suggested that maybe he bring in some help to run the offense. I brought up your name. I knew you had a bright future ahead of you and selfishly I wanted you on my staff."

Wow. I didn't know this.

"I'm assuming he didn't take too well to that?"

Coach Gordon shakes his head. "Not at all. The man lost it. He went into a rage. You think he was bad a few weeks ago? You should have seen him then. He trashed my office. Started yelling profanities. Was blaming everyone but himself on why the offense was so bad. Told me that the media, specifically Sadie, got in my head. We had to call security on him and have him escorted from the facilities."

Holy shit. "How did none of this ever leak out?"

"The media were taking part in their end of the season beers that we give them. The timing was lucky."

Wow. I never knew any of this. Everything makes much more sense now though. Why he was so hellbent about bashing me in the media. About why Sadie's questions set him off.

Sadie.

I haven't thought about her much today. And like always, at first I miss her. Then I remember what she did, and the anger boils back up in me.

After Sadie's initial story went viral, instead of prepping for this week's game, almost all of my time was spent fielding phone calls or doing interviews about becoming the youngest head coach in league history. Luckily, Davis was able to handle all the game prep for me. The man is really making a case to replace me as offensive coordinator.

Coach Gordon has been ribbing me all week, telling me I

better get used to doing all of those interviews. "That's half the damn job. At least you have a pretty face for the camera," he joked after a day when I did four different television spots back-to-back.

He has now found humor in the situation. Neil and Mr. Henderson are both still upset that Sadie found out and have made it their mission to find the mole, though no one is talking.

Probably because a mole doesn't exist.

She didn't have a source. She used me. Plain and simple.

"Your girl wasn't here today," Coach Gordon says. "It was weird not seeing her when I looked into the front row. It was some pimply face kid."

This takes me by surprise. "She wasn't?" That's odd. Sadie one time told me how she prided herself on never taking a sick day. She boasted that her personal record was working forty-three consecutive days without a day off.

"Nope, an intern filled in for her," Paul says, entering the office. "Got a call from her boss before the game to make sure we had a credential for him."

My first thought is to wonder if she's all right. The second thought is to kick my own ass for having that thought.

"That girl, she might have been a pain in our ass this week, but she wipes the floor with those guys," Coach Gordon says. I have to do a double-take because I'd bet this is the most positive thing he's ever said about someone in The Mob. "Don't you ever tell her this, but I look forward to her questions. The ones the guys ask me my granddaughter could answer, and she can't talk yet."

I don't say that I won't tell her that, because I'll likely never talk to her again. I don't say that he's right.

I just don't say anything.

"I know I can't ask her, but I would love to know who her source is here," Paul says, inviting himself to take a seat next to me. "The scoops and tips she gets are almost impressive, if it didn't make my life hell."

I quirk an eyebrow. Source my ass. "How do you know she has a source? No one knows who it is. Maybe she doesn't have one."

"Oh, she has one. We just can't figure out who," Paul says. "Reporters will never give up their sources. But it's the only plausible explanation. Either she has a mole or she somehow figured out how to plant listening devices around the facility. Two years ago, she had just taken the job, and she called me to confirm that a player was getting traded. I hadn't even heard about the trade yet. I had to go ask Neil. The only people who knew at that time were Neil and Gordon. She's doing this shit all the time. One day, I'll figure out how she's getting her info."

Fuck.

"Hunter? Why does it look like you saw a ghost, all the while wanting to vomit?"

I ignore Coach's comment. "Paul, can you tell me exactly what Sadie asked from you before she wrote the story?"

"She called me the day after we offered you the job requesting Coach Gordon's contract, which she has every right to do. I thought something might be up then because of the timing, but then I didn't hear from her after. So I chalked it up to coincidence. Then, at the beginning of this week, she came back asking if it was true that you were taking over next season as head coach. She asked about the clause in Coach Gordon's contract letting him retire early and that if I could confirm you were his replacement. I had to confirm it because though I hate that she got it first, it would have been worse for us if I lied to her."

"Did she say anything about my contract?"

Paul shakes his head. "No. It's funny you mention that. She asked if I could give her contract specifics, but I declined, saying that it was still being negotiated. I was actually surprised that there were no suspected contract numbers in her initial story. That means her source isn't anyone in legal. Or that she saw a copy of your contract. Hell, I even thought for a minute she saw the contract we emailed you, but clearly that wasn't it. Which is why I say she has to have a spy."

Fuck. Fuck. Fuck.

I was so angry at Sadie the other night; I didn't even listen to her. She tried to tell me all of this. She tried to tell me she reported the story straight-up. That she didn't go through my phone or email. I just didn't want to listen.

"Paul, is The Mob still here?" I say, shooting up from Coach Gordon's couch.

"Yeah. Why?"

"Tell them there is a press conference tomorrow morning. Tell them all if they help me, they can each get a one-on-one with me after the season. And call Sadie. Make sure she's here. I have an apology I need to make."

46

SADIE

I HAVE ABSOLUTELY no clue what I'm doing here. Or what any of us are doing here.

I also have no clue as to why there is a single red rose on my normal chair in the Fury's press conference room.

Mondays are usually off for the team and media. Unless there is a big announcement. I honestly can't figure out why Paul called me last night to make sure that I was here this morning for a press conference. Especially since I let the cat out of the bag in terms of the big announcement last week.

Everything looks normal. The reporters are milling around waiting for the press conference to start. The videographers from the television stations are setting up their cameras.

The only difference? No one is looking at me.

In fact, if I had to guess, everyone is blatantly ignoring me.

Case in point? Tommy just walked right by me and didn't say a word.

"Tommy!" I say, walking a little faster to catch up with him. "What's going on?"

"I don't know," he says, though he's doing everything he can not to look me in the eye. "I know just as much as you do."

While I find that hard to believe, I don't press him. Paul walks into the room, signaling for all of us to take our seats.

I do, moving the rose to the seat next to me.

I begin to take out my laptop and recorder when I feel him in the room. I don't even have to look up to know he's there. I dig in my purse for as long as possible for nothing particular. Anything to distract me from having to come back to the present where Hunter is a mere ten feet away from me.

When I do muster the courage to look up, my breath hitches. My cheeks are turning about six shades of pink. I'm glad I don't have to talk right now because I don't know what I would say.

Hunter is more handsome than I remember.

He is dressed in a full suit. Jacket, tie, and if I had to guess, a vest underneath. He wore a suit like this in New Orleans. We missed our dinner reservation that night.

Bad breath.

The smell of cat pee.

Liver.

God, it hurts to see him. I thought I hurt last week, but that's nothing compared to being in the same room with him. It's probably a good thing that I'll be working for *US Daily* next season. I'm not sure I could endure this kind of suffering every week.

Our eyes make contact, and for the millionth time in the past week, I have to fight back tears. I'm sure he can see the sadness in my eyes. The only thing consoling me right now is that there is sadness in his, too.

"Thank you all for coming," Hunter begins. "I'm sure you are all wondering why we dragged you out of bed this morning. To show my appreciation, I made sure Paul brought donuts."

The guys laugh but I don't.

Why is Hunter talking? He's not the coach yet. Unless Gordon died and no one told me, there is no reason for Hunter to be speaking to the media right now.

"The reason I gathered everyone here today is because I have something I need to say. And it needs to be on the record. What better way to do that than in front of a room full of reporters?"

He pauses and looks directly at me. Those six shades of pink earlier? They are now ten shades of red.

"When I was first hired by the Fury, a smart person once told me that the choice of words was key to figuring out what people really meant. Last week, after the news broke about me becoming the next head coach of the Fury, I said things to a very important person to me that spoke quite loudly. They were mean, hateful, and born out of rage. And for that, I will be forever sorry."

I'm not typing a single word. I don't think I've blinked or even taken a breath.

Did Hunter really call a press conference to apologize to me?

No. That's ridiculous. I'm reading too much into this.

But then he pins his eyes back on me, and I don't know how to react.

"No matter what I've done in my life, I wanted to be the best. I wanted to be the best son. I wanted to be the best football player. I wanted to be the best coach. Over the past nine months, I wanted to be the best partner to a woman I didn't deserve. Most of those have happened. As we know, I was never going to be the best football player."

He pauses for effect, which works because these guys are eating out of the palm of his hand. Me? I'm waiting for a shoe to drop.

"I've tried to be a good son. Sometimes I do better than others. After a rough start to the season, I think I became a good coach. My efforts were rewarded with a promotion. It's a job I will not take lightly. I will always strive to be the best coach I can be. And every one of you can hold me to that every time I step up to this podium."

He pauses again, but this time, his eyes train on me. "What I have failed at is being the best partner. I think I had my moments. But when the going got tough, I failed. I assumed things without trying to validate facts. I let past experiences dictate my reactions. And the worst part? I lost my best friend in the process. Because, Sadie Benson, you are not just the woman I'm madly in love with, but you are the best person in my life."

And there they go. The tears. They are falling. I can't stop them.

And the butterflies. Fuck, those damn butterflies are back.

Hunter steps away from the podium and makes his way over so he is standing right in front of me. He picks up the rose and extends his hand for mine. I give it to him without question as he pulls me up to stand in front of him.

I'm too close to him now. I can smell his cologne. It's the same cologne that drew me to him all those months ago. His blue eyes are trying to see through my soul like they did in Memphis. I want to look away, but I can't.

I don't think I ever could.

"Sadie, there aren't enough words or enough press conferences to tell you how sorry I am. I was an idiot. The things I said to you… I am ashamed that they left my mouth. Please, don't ever tell my mother that I said those things."

I laugh at his joke, which helps the tears for all of two seconds. "You are a damn good reporter. The best one in this room. Sorry, guys, but you know it's true. You scooped me on my own story not once, but twice. I should have never doubted you as a reporter. And I should have never doubted you as my partner. My best friend. The love of my life. Please, Sadie. Forgive me?"

The room goes silent. This is as quiet as it's ever been in here. I'm sure if I took a second to look around, I'd see a bunch of middle-aged men leaning forward on their seat in response. I know I'd be.

Instead, I'm standing in front of Hunter and I can't form words. I want to forgive him. I want to jump in his arms right now and kiss the hell out of him.

Can I do it that easily? Can I forgive the pain and hurt he caused me just because of one grand gesture?

"Sadie, what's your answer?" someone asks.

"Sadie, what did he say that was so horrifying?" another person, I believe Joe, asks.

"Sadie, have you already moved on and that's why you are keeping Hunter here waiting?" Tommy asks.

This makes me laugh. "No comment to the last two questions."

"What about the first?"

I give a small smile to the men who have become my peers before looking back up at Hunter. "I forgive you. And that's on the record."

Hunter doesn't waste a second before bringing me in for a kiss that I'd guarantee will be on every sports page and gossip column tomorrow.

I hate being the story.

Right now, I don't mind it.

47

HUNTER

"WHY DID he hand it off? He's an idiot for not running a pass play."

"Did he think he had them fooled! Princess over here knew he was doing that! And she's only watching the game for the commercials."

"Excuse me. I take offense to that. But you're right. I totally did. And I totally am."

All I can do is smile and laugh as Sadie, Davis, and Bethany each give their commentary about the championship game that's currently playing on the flat-screen television in my living room. Somehow, I drew the short straw to go get another round of drinks.

I don't mind. I don't even mind that I'm not coaching in the game that every football coach wants to be in.

No. Tonight it feels right watching the game in sweatpants in Nashville.

The Fury's playoff run lasted two games. The next day, Coach Gordon officially stepped down as the Fury's head coach and I was promoted. I moved into his office, put together my coaching staff, which included promoting Davis to offensive coordinator and hiring Tara, Neil's former secretary to come work for me. Neil is still the general manager, but Sadie suggested that I see if Tara wanted a change of professional scenery. She also said it would be a good idea that if I didn't want things to get out to the press, to treat Tara right. And to buy her donuts.

That is how Sadie revealed her source to me without ever saying the words.

More importantly, Sadie and I are better than ever. After the makeshift press conference, which made national headlines and even got me an interview with *Cosmo* about grand gestures, we had a long talk. A few parts got tense. A few parts were sad. In the end, we're stronger than ever.

We're now officially living together. She has been slowly moving her things over to my condo, including her decorative pillows and coasters, which she now says she can't imagine ever parting with.

With the league season over after tonight, we'll both have some downtime, so we decided to take a trip to Memphis at the end of the month to celebrate our sort of one-year anniversary.

I hope I come back being able to call her my fiancée.

"What did I miss?" I ask, handing drinks off and taking my place back on my sectional next to Sadie. I also can't help but notice how far apart Davis and Bethany are sitting tonight.

Definitely not as cozy as they were at the bar a few months ago.

"You missed the worst play call in championship game history," Davis says, his eyes never leaving the television.

"That true?" I whisper to Sadie, who has snuggled her way into my side.

"Yup. Shit play call. They had to punt after it. Made no sense."

I still get hard when Sadie talks about football. I don't know if that will ever change. But getting to watch it with her while we debate strategy and comment on plays? I sport a hard-on the entire game.

"Halftime!" Davis yells, standing up. "Time to refill the plate."

"I'll come with you," Bethany says a little too eagerly. Which Sadie doesn't let slide.

"I thought you wanted to watch the halftime show?"

"I'll watch it on Facebook later."

The two of them make their way back to the kitchen, and all we can do is laugh. They are not sly. At all.

"Why are they sitting on opposite ends of the room when it's clear they are still sleeping together?"

Sadie stands up to stretch, and the sweatshirt she's wearing comes up just enough to give me a peek of some skin. Which gives me all sorts of ideas.

"Because they are ridiculous and swear it was just a one-time thing."

That sounds like Davis. "I'm glad we were never a one-time thing," I say, standing up and taking Sadie's hand in mine as I make my way to the patio.

"Where are we going," she asks.

I pull the patio door open and signal for her to go outside. "Consider it our own halftime show."

I sit down and bring her to my lap. It's chilly for February, but neither of us care. She naturally puts her legs over mine and snuggles in close to me. Whenever we need to reconnect, or if things are feeling off, or if we just want a minute to breathe, this is where we come. It's like our reset button.

Tonight, I don't need a reset. I just need her alone for a few minutes. And I know if I take her to bed, we won't be watching the rest of the game.

"Are you ready to start your job tomorrow?" I ask, running the tip of my nose up and down her neck.

"Is it weird I'm nervous?"

I place a kiss right under her ear, which causes her to shiver against me. "I don't think so. This is a big deal, and you want to do well. I know I was nervous as hell at the first press conference."

Sadie shoots me a look that screams "I don't believe you."

"What? It's true!"

"Hunter Michael McAvoy, you're going to sit here and tell me that you, the man who can wrap a room full of reporters around his pinky by just smiling, the man who used the press to win me back, were nervous when you were officially introduced by the Fury?"

Sadie found out my middle name the last time we went to Birmingham. She now uses it every chance she gets.

Yes. We've been to Birmingham. Yes, I've spoken to my father.

And in a shocking turn of events, he congratulated me on being named the Fury's head coach. He and Mom even came to my press conference after Gordon officially retired.

Are we best friends yet? Not by a long shot. Maybe one day we'll get there.

"I was. I must have smoothed down my tie ten times before I walked out there. I think the intern thought I was going to pass out."

She studies me for a second, probably deciding whether or not to try to catch me in a line of bullshit. "Fine. I'll bite. Why were you nervous?"

"Because," I say, giving her a quick kiss before I continue, "I knew you'd be there."

I've come to expect a playful slap when I dish out my overly cheesy comments to her, even though they are all the truth. This time, though, Sadie surprises me.

She twists herself so she's now straddling me and brings my mouth to hers for a kiss that could heat all of Nashville.

My hands slide around her back and down to her ass. I

remember when I first saw her, and this was the first thing I noticed. Such a guy move.

It didn't take long for me to notice the rest of her. And not just her physical features, which are stunning, and I'm in love with every inch of her.

I love her for her heart. I love her for her humor. I love her for the fact that she never lets me settle for less. I love her for her determination.

I just love her.

"Gorgeous," I reluctantly say as I pull away from her lips. "As much as I would love to keep doing this. And you know I have no problem with patio sex. We probably should get back inside. We do have guests."

She turns back to look through the patio door.

"They left."

I crane my neck to look over her shoulder. "How do you know?"

"Davis's keys were on the coffee table. They aren't now."

Without another word, I stand up and carry Sadie back inside. Her laugh follows us in as I shut the door and make our way straight to my bedroom.

The game can wait.

Sadie can't.

EPILOGUE

SADIE

FIVE YEARS LATER

I SWEAR I didn't used to be a crier.

Before Hunter and I started dating, I barely shed a tear.

These days I cry at everything.

That is also Hunter's fault.

I cry at dog food commercials. One time I cried when the new cashier at Sandwich City told me to have a nice day.

That's what happens when you're six-months' pregnant.

Tonight, though, I'd like to think that I'd be crying whether or not I was preggo.

I don't even try to contain the tears as I stand off to the side of the stage next to my dad, Helen, Bethany and her daughter, and my in-laws as we watch the league commissioner hand the championship trophy to Hunter, who led the Nashville Fury to its first championship in team history.

My man, my husband, the father of my children, got to hoist his trophy.

And I couldn't be prouder.

"Look at him up there," Francine says, giving my hand a squeeze. "I'm just... I'm just so proud of him."

"We all are," Bo says as he holds Camden, our two-year-old son. "Do you see your daddy up there? Wave to Daddy!"

If you would have told me five years ago that Bo McAvoy would be having a proud father moment as his son, a coach, held up the league championship trophy, I'd tell you that you were crazy. I'd then ask you what you were smoking if you added that he was doing it as a proud grandpa.

I'm sorry. Pappy. He prefers Pappy.

A lot has changed with Bo over the years. After Hunter was named head coach, the two of them finally sat down and let out years of pent-up emotions. Granted, Francine and I might have tricked them into having this discussion by locking them in a room, but nonetheless, it happened. And we are all better for it. Hunter has slowly learned that some things Bo says are indeed helpful, and Bo has become better at expressing his advice to not sounding like a criticism.

That is when he's not too busy being Pappy. That man loves his grandson more than anything in this world. He tells me on a weekly basis that Camden will one day play for Alabama and continue the McAvoy lineage. I tell him that Camden will do what he wants and carve his own path.

It's now the only thing we disagree about.

I laugh as I watch Camden try to wave to Hunter, who is handing the trophy to the game's MVP, which of course was Bryce. It's funny that all those years ago we wondered if he was going to be a bust. Five years later, under the guidance of Hunter and Davis, he is the best quarterback in the league.

I look back at my son, who is still trying to get his father's attention. He is one hundred percent McAvoy in every way. He was literally born with a football in his hand, Francine made sure of that. She also made sure to buy him his first Alabama onesie.

He only wore it when she came over. I'm still a Vol for Life, after all.

Camden is also very excited to be a big brother and tries to talk to his baby sister every day through my belly.

That makes me cry because it's damn adorable.

I wipe a tear away as I see Hunter and Davis walking toward our crew. They shake hands and give each other one of those back-slapping hugs before parting ways, Davis to go see his family, and Hunter to see his.

The pride and happiness on Hunter's face are unmistakable. He deserves to bask in every inch of joy he is feeling right now. The last five years haven't been easy.

Nothing worth fighting for ever is.

As soon as he can reach me, he scoops me in his arms and swings me around. Yes, I might be six-months' pregnant, but that doesn't stop Hunter from lifting, or carrying me, whenever he sees fit.

I don't mind it one bit.

"Holy!" *Kiss.* "Hell." *Kiss.* "We." *Kiss.* "Won!"

"Yes, you did. I'm so proud of you."

He sets me down and reaches over to his dad to take Camden, who immediately latches his little arms around Hunter's neck. But before he can step away, Bo extends his hand, which Hunter returns. The look the two share has so many unspoken words in it. Only now they are all of happiness and love.

And there I go, crying again.

"Won!" Camden shouts. "Daddy won!"

"Yeah, I did, buddy!" Hunter says, giving him a kiss on the cheek.

My heart melts every time I see them together. Which is a lot. I still work for *US Daily*, but I have transitioned my role to editor. I still get to work from home, only with a little more stable hours.

And I do it under the name Sadie Benson-McAvoy.

It was perfect when we found out I was having Camden. It will be even better when Carli joins us in a few months.

Hunter reaches for me with his free hand and kisses the top of my head.

"How does it feel?" I ask, looking up at him with all the love I can muster. "How does it feel to be the champ?"

He kisses Camden before leaning down and kissing me one more time.

"It now feels like I have everything I have ever wanted."

THE END

BOOKS BY CHELLE SLOAN

Want to read more by Chelle?

Reformation: A Salvation Society Novel

ACKNOWLEDGMENTS

As I'm writing these acknowledgments, it's September of 2020. A year ago at this time I had not written a book. This year might have been insane and crazy on so many levels, but it will always be the year that my life changed for the better. I became a published author. And there isn't a day that I'm not thankful for that.

First and foremost, thank you to my parents. I've lost count of how many times I've come to you guys with a change in life plans, and never once have you tried to steer me toward a safe course. You've allowed me to follow my dreams and my path, and for that I am forever grateful. And like always, the free rent is appreciated.

To my family and friends: Your support has been amazing. Many of you have no clue how I ended up here, but that doesn't mean the support hasn't been there. I love you all.

To Kelly. You've been with me on this book journey since day one. Not only are you an amazing beta reader, but you are an amazing friend. Maybe one day we can go on a book trip again.

Elaine, thank you for once again dotting the Is and crossing the Ts I forgot to. Marla, thank you for your detailed eye. One day I'll stop overusing common phrases. Michele, thank you for your keen eye and being an amazing cheerleader. Jill, thank you for not telling me no when I emailed for help at the eleventh hour. Kari, you brought my cover idea to life in ways that I didn't think imaginable. You are a true talent and I'm hiring you forever. Angela, you're hired.

Corinne, I'm here because of you. If you wouldn't have given me a chance I wouldn't have started writing. You forever changed my life.

Adriana, thank you for making me "feel." This book is better because of you.

Evie, Georgia, Gail and Tori. You ladies are my people. My tribe. Thank you for welcoming me into the book world with open arms. And answering my 10,000 questions.

To my Book Squad and my Thirst Squad on TikTok, thank you all for coming on this journey with me. Let's keep it going!

ABOUT THE AUTHOR

Chelle is a contemporary romance author who writes happily ever afters with a lot of love with a little bit of humor mixed in.

A native of Ohio, she decided that after a decades-long career in sports journalism, it was time to take a step back. She is currently working on her Master's degree in journalism and is set to graduate from her program in 2021. She is a diehard Cleveland sports fan, is the owner of way too many, yet not enough, tumblers and will be a New Kids on the Block fan until the day she dies. She also does her best writing at Starbucks, where you can usually find a Venti Caramel Frappuccino on her table.

And yes, you saw her on TikTok.

Follow her on social media!
Facebook: Chelle Sloan
Reader Group: Chelle Sloan's Book Squad
Instagram: Chelle_Sloan
TikTok: @chellewritesromance
Twitter: @Chelle_Sloan
Website: www.chellesloan.com
Sign up for her monthly newsletter!